LONG CHAIN OF DEATH

LONG CHAIN OF DEATH

Sarah Wolf

WALKER AND COMPANY
New York

M
Wolf
sar
c.1

First published in the United States of America in 1987 by the
Walker Publishing Company, Inc.

Published simultaneously in Canada by John Wiley & Sons
Canada, Limited, Rexdale, Ontario.

Library of Congress Cataloging-in-Publication Data

Wolf, Sarah.
    Long Chain of Death

    I. Title.
PS3573.0489M9   1987   813'.54   86-26565
ISBN 0-8027-5671-9

Printed in the United States of America

10 9 8 7 6 5 4 3 2 1

For Kent,
of course

Prologue

NOVEMBER 1944

ALLEN LUNDY, EIGHTEEN years old and five months in the army, lay in the wet grass of a Belgian field and watched a broken stone wall fifty yards away. Nothing moved.

"Any minute," someone whispered.

Al nodded curtly without taking his eyes from the stones. Three days of making their way through woods and fields in a steady drizzle had brought them at last to the outskirts of this town whose name he didn't even know. They'd been here since before midnight, lying silent in the wet, waiting for dawn, waiting for enough light to see. It was no longer raining. The clouds had drifted off to the north, but in the air the moisture was still palpable. Fog lay thick in the woods behind them, and it drifted in patches in the field around them, but in the town ahead there was none. One stroke of luck, he thought; at least we'll be able to see.

He glanced to his right and saw Deac pull back his helmet, listening intently. Now Al could hear it, too, a faint throb in the air. He grinned at Deac and put his thumb up. Right on time. The roar was unmistakable now; he looked again at the wall ahead of him and the town beyond. They won't even know what hit them, he thought; first the planes and then us. He could see them now in the west, flying low, bombers in tight formation— one squadron—the most beautiful sight in the world.

1

Moisture condensed on the rim of his helmet, and drops fell in front of his eyes. He gripped the sodden grass with his left hand. One pass, he thought, and they're all ours. Something touched his foot, and he jerked his head around, staring into a pale, frightened face. "It's OK," he whispered, "keep with me and it'll be OK."

The planes came in low from the west, hammering the air, and then the bombs began to fall, coming out of the gray sky, falling on the gray town. The air was bursting around them, from the planes, from the bombs, and they were up and running before the last of the bombs had even hit, running the last hundred yards, the bombs falling ahead of them, the air screaming around them. He had his eyes on the nearest building, or what had been a building before the bombs hit—a shell now, smoke pouring from where the roof had been, the cement of the walls cracked and crumbling. His only thought was to make it there, across the open field—vulnerable—to the safety of the wall, running, his chest sore, his right hand gripping his gun, running through the muck of a soggy field. And just as he reached the safety of its shelter a blast blew behind him, and he turned in time to see the rain of mud and stones falling back to earth—a bomb? a mine?—and then he screamed, *"Shitless! Goddammit, Shitless, where the hell are you?"*

2

1

OCTOBER 1986

ON THE LAST morning of her life, Elizabeth Brett made blueberry pancakes. She kissed David good-bye when he left, lingered over coffee and the newspaper, gathered the breakfast things and put them into the dishwasher, brushed her teeth, ran a comb through her hair, picked up her purse, and went out to the car. She put the key in the ignition and turned it. The blast blew out one whole side of the garage.

Rebecca Myers, in the house across the street, was washing dishes. The blast so startled her that she banged a glass against the sink and broke it, cutting her finger. "My God," she said, staring out the window, not even noticing the blood that was coloring her dishwater.

Elvin Haney, retired, had been putting out tulip bulbs when he heard the explosion. He ran around his own garage, saw the hole in the side of the one next door, and stopped dead in his tracks. "Elizabeth?" he said, taking a cautious step forward. "Elizabeth, are you in there?"

Sandra Augustina, out jogging, heard the noise and thought it had come from her own house. She cut through the neighbors' yards until she came to Elizabeth's garage and saw the damage and a torn purse lying on the grass. Then she screamed.

Rebecca Myers, her cut finger in her mouth to staunch the blood, dialed the police.

"You'd better sit down," Gale said, "this isn't going to be easy."

"What on earth is it? You pull me out of the classroom, it'd better be—"

"Dave," Gale interrupted him. "Sit down." He sat.

Gale came around from behind his desk, sat down on the edge and leaned forward. "There's been an accident at your house, Dave. . . ."

"Elizabeth?"

"They want you over at the hospital."

"How bad is it?" He was out of the chair, heading for the door.

Gale grabbed a coat. "I'll come along."

"No, it's OK. Just tell me how bad."

"I'm coming along."

Dave turned to face him. "What happened?"

Gale put an arm across his shoulders. "Dave, she's dead."

"Oh, God, no."

Cummins nudged a piece of torn chrome with his foot. "Wired to go off when she turned the key. Simple as that. Just as we thought."

Phillip Decker shook his head. "Elizabeth Daly. Who would've wanted to kill her?"

"Elizabeth Brett."

"Elizabeth Daly . . . Brett." He looked up at the cloudless sky. "Twenty-eight years old. Getting into her car on a sunny October morning. Who the hell would've done it?"

"No kids?"

Decker walked over to the hole torn in the side of the garage. "No kids . . . no kids. Just one . . . husband."

Cummins looked at him for a moment. "Is that supposed to mean something?"

4

Decker looked back, his face blank. "What in the world would you think it might mean?" he asked ingenuously.

"Why would anyone have wanted to kill your wife?" Decker stared across the room at Brett, and Brett gazed abstractly back.

"I can't imagine. It's got to have been a mistake."

"She wasn't working?"

"She quit last year."

"She was depressed, perhaps?"

"You're saying she . . . no, no way."

"She was sorry she quit? She was tired of playing house?"

"We were going to start a family. She liked taking care of the house—look, the paintings are all hers, she made the drapes, the wall hanging, everything."

Decker stared at the wall hanging—woven of handspun wool in reds and oranges. He wondered if she had her own loom, if she'd spun and dyed the wool herself. Elizabeth would have. "She couldn't get pregnant? She was depressed about it?"

"For God's sake! She was the least depressed person I know! She *was* pregnant. She was going to the doctor, she had a doctor's appointment. That's where she was going."

He was right, of course. It was a house filled with love and fresh flowers. Elizabeth had not been the kind of woman who kills herself. And no woman kills herself by blowing her car up. Nobody commits suicide like that. "I can tell you something, Brett. Blowing up a car is a very deliberate act. You don't do it by mistake. Someone had to come into the garage last night, wire it up, and get away without being caught. Whoever did it was not making a mistake."

"Who would have done such a thing? *Why?*"

Decker gazed at him for a moment. The shock still showed in Brett's eyes. On the other hand, Decker thought, some people are very good actors. "Why?" Decker repeated. "You're going to help me find out why. Two of my men will be coming here, and you're going to let them have the run of the house. They're going to look at everything they can lay their hands on, from the book she was reading to the old love letters she might have kept in the attic, to her appointment calendar, to the phone numbers she wrote down. Everything, *everything* is going to be made available to them."

"OK."

"And then," Decker said, rising and moving toward the door, "if you and I are lucky, we'll know what was going on around here."

David Brett watched Decker go down the front steps, out the walk, and open the door of the waiting squad car. His eye caught on the yellow chrysanthemums that bloomed in profusion along the curve of the walk. "But it won't bring her back," he said softly.

"Well?" Cummins asked as Decker let himself into the car. "Did he do it?"

"I don't know. Give me another day and I'll tell you."

2

WHAT HELD HIM were the eyes. Green one moment, gray the next, they looked deep into him; through him, it seemed. They were crinkled now with laughter, and her honey laugh warmed him. He'd said something funny, or she had. "I can't stop looking at you," he said. She made a crazy face to mock him, meaning to look ugly. He pulled her down on him—he was lying by the hearth, watching her hair catch the glow of the fire. He held her close and her lips found him, kissing his face, his ear, his neck, and he spoke her name again and again into the curve of her neck.

And he lay in the bed in the dark knowing it would never happen again. Beside him the sheet was cold. He touched the place where she should be and there was nothing. She's gone, he told himself, and it didn't seem real. This was the dream—wasn't it? He swung his legs over the side of the bed, walked in his bare feet through the house, and opened the garage door. The hole was there, gaping into the night, ragged edges cutting the moonlight. He stared at the edges for a long time, as if they made a shape, as if they had something to say. "Why?" he said into the night. And then he began to cry.

"Yeah," Decker said into the speaker on his desk. "It's OK, let him come in." He stood when the door opened, and Brett paused in the doorway, looking uncertain. "Come in," Decker said, smiling now. "Sit down."

Brett looked terrible. He's been up all night, Decker thought. Figures.

Decker sat down again, leaning back in the swivel chair. "They still at it over there?"

"They came just after eight this morning. That surprised me; I didn't think they'd get there so early."

"Get you out of bed?"

"No. No, I didn't sleep much."

Decker nodded. "It'll be rough for a while."

Brett didn't say anything.

"Can't say we found anything yet."

"I've been thinking. Sometimes you read, you know, about . . . people who've gone off the deep end. People who go around killing for no reason, at least no rational reason. Mad bombers. That kind of thing."

Decker leaned back and the swivel chair creaked. "That might happen in the city," he said, "but it almost never does in a small town. And even then, there's a reason, even for the crazies. Random killings are very rare. And I don't know anybody in town who's that crazy."

"You never know."

"You want to know an interesting fact?" Decker was playing with his pencil, not quite looking at him. "Three out of four people who are murdered are killed by someone they know, someone they know well, as a matter of fact. Most people are killed by their own relatives."

Brett stared at him but said nothing.

"Best bet in the world, when you can't find the motive, it's the spouse who did it."

Brett watched him play with the pencil. Good God, he thought, what does he expect me to do? "I loved my wife," he said finally. Even to his own ears it sounded stuffy.

"I'm sure you did."

"You're trying to say I might have killed her."

"I'm saying that, yes," Decker still stared absently at the pencil.

"I'm sitting here, and I'm still numb because my wife was just . . . just killed. Yesterday. It hasn't even completely sunk in yet, and now you're telling me you think I did it. I should be punching you out, and instead I'm sitting here talking to you as if you were a civil human being. Do you have any idea what it's like? Do you have the least conception what this feels like? Why the hell aren't you out there doing whatever it is you do? Why on earth aren't you out there finding out who did it?"

"Mr. Brett, I've known your wife all her life. That's a hell of a lot longer than you have. When I went into the service, she was a pretty kid, a nice kid, OK? When I came back, she was a senior in high school, the prettiest girl in town. Half the available men from fifteen to ninety-five were lined up at her door. She could have had anybody. OK, so she goes off to college, and I guess we all thought she'd find some guy there, someone who'd be good enough for her—some jock, some rich guy, someone like that. Any nobody would've begrudged her. She deserved the best, she was that kind of person. But no, she finishes college and she goes off to Europe or someplace, and eventually she comes back home and ends up teaching school right here, right in the same school she graduated from. Not married. And again the guys are beating a path to her door. And then you come along— new in town, another teacher, I don't even know what the hell you teach—and she falls for you. And marries you. And all the guys in town that wanted her, but also thought she deserved the best and to be perfectly honest weren't so sure they were it, they look at you and they don't see how you deserve her, either." The chair creaked again as Decker leaned forward, his eyes fastened on Brett's. "And now let me tell you what we're thinking, all us guys: that if Elizabeth hadn't married you, she'd be alive right now."

Brett was leaning over the desk, rage flushing his face. "God damn you! Elizabeth is dead! No one's hurting as much as I am! If I could go back and change one thing to bring her back, I would! If my not marrying her would make her alive today, I'd go back and change that. In the meantime—God! Have compassion! I don't need you harassing me!"

Decker leaned back in his chair. "It's not my job to treat you with kid gloves. I'm not a goddamned psychiatrist."

"You're not a very good police officer either!"

"Why don't you go on home and get some rest. You could use it, I'd venture to say."

Decker swiveled his chair around to face the window, not even waiting for Brett to leave. He was still sitting that way when Cummins came to the door. "Anything new?"

Decker slowly swiveled back. "If I were a betting man," he said, absently picking up a piece of paper from the floor, glancing at it and slowly crumpling it into ball, "I think I'd bet that he didn't." He threw the balled paper in a high arc toward the wastebasket, and missed. Grinning, he turned back toward Cummins. "But then, I do make my mistakes."

It was a boy, David Lane Brett III. He would never have named him that, but she insisted. By the time he was two, he was the picture of her—same green-gray eyes, same thick chestnut hair, same throaty laugh. There were photographs of them all over the house: stop-time moments in his life, kept forever. Her holding him when he was a baby, pleased, happy, glowing. Him gazing intently at a colored fall leaf. Him laughing: his first balloon. Him perched high atop his father's shoulders, strolling through the woods, both laughing. She had taken that one.

He looked through the car window, out across the lake. He leaned his forehead against the steering wheel and wept for David Lane Brett III, who would never be. And for himself.

"You should move out of the house," Sandy Augustina said. They were still at the dinner table, though dessert had been finished an hour ago and the children had gone off somewhere. "It's not healthy to stay there. All it can do is bring back memories. You should get an apartment, or something. Get yourself away from there."

"Sandy," Frank said reprovingly, "let it be. He's got plenty of time."

Sandy stood, fingered the sugarbowl tentatively, then left it and went out to the kitchen.

"They've gotten a sub for you at the school?" Frank asked.

He nodded.

"You might think about going away for a while. Take Sandy's car—we don't need it. Go to Florida and sit in the sun. Go up north and hunt. Keep the car as long as you want."

"What was she like before, Frank? When she was younger?"

"Elizabeth Daly, prettiest girl in town. No, that doesn't really do it. She was younger than me by two or three years—we used to play baseball over in Harry Jamison's backyard, and as I remember she was the only girl who played. Not that she was so good or that she was so much of a tomboy. It was just that she liked to, and it was OK with us. A girl? If it had been someone else, it might have been another story, but Elizabeth was different. She was fun to be with, you enjoyed her. Even then. Some people have everything going for them. Elizabeth was one of those. Everybody liked her."

Brett was tracing circles with the handle of his spoon on the tablecloth.

"We had a saying back in high school, when we were all dating. If there was something a guy really wanted bad, he'd say to his buddies, 'I'd give a night with Elizabeth Daly for that.' Nobody I knew ever *spent* a night with her, but that's how we felt, that it would be the ultimate. I suppose half the guys in town fantasized about her."

Brett stared at the tablecloth.

"I guess nobody's perfect," Frank went on awkwardly, "and she probably wasn't, either. But she was one hell of a person."

"Yeah."

Frank put his hand on Brett's arm. "I'm sorry, buddy, but you asked."

"Frank? Who would have killed her?"

"Nobody."

"Somebody did. How the hell am I going to find out who?"

"Let it alone, Dave. You'll tear yourself up if you try going after it yourself. Let the police take care of it; that's their job."

"Yes, sure. Let the police do it."

"Dave, I'm serious."

"So am I."

At one-thirty every Saturday and Sunday morning Harvey Rogers did the same thing. He drove to the parking lot by the lake, made a wide circle with the patrol car, and drove back out. He'd been doing it for four years, ever since he joined the force. At first he'd done it for his own amusement, to watch the high-school couples uncouple in the glow of his headlights. Now he did it as a matter of duty, because anybody still there at one-thirty ought to be thinking about getting home. Or so Harvey Rogers thought. Nearly always he recognized the cars; sometimes he caught a fleeting glimpse of a face, but he never told. What went on in the parking lot before one-thirty was not anybody's business, he figured, except for the people involved.

There was one car this night, Lane Carpenter's. Harvey grinned. It's time you get home, Lane, he thought, or you won't be in any shape to get up in the morning to bag groceries at Leonard's. His lights swept the lot, but there was no movement in the car, and that was a little unusual. Harvey stepped on the brake, paused, backed up until his lights swept across the car again. Still no movement. Harvey frowned. "Lane, are you fucking with that cheerleader?" he said softly to himself. He thought about driving on, but something made him stay. He played the lights on the car for a good three minutes before he decided what to do. Then he got out of the patrol car and walked over to peer into the driver's side of the parked car.

What he saw made him want to throw up.

There were two more patrol cars there by the time Decker arrived. "The whole damned force," he muttered to himself as he drove into the parking lot.

Harvey ran over to him before he even had a chance to get out of the car. "I didn't touch anything! I called in right away! It's just the way I found it!"

"Parking duty again this week?" Decker asked. Harvey didn't say anything.

The three patrol cars had the other car surrounded, all shining their lights on it as if it were a fugitive. Decker walked into the light and bent down to look inside. "Oh, good God," he breathed. Jenny Wilson leaned against the passenger door, and Lane Carpenter had fallen against her; they looked like a pair of discarded store mannequins. Both were fully clothed, Jenny with her cheerleading outfit still on. Each had a neat bullet hole in the forehead. Decker's eyes took everything in. There were no bullet holes in the car—not the windshield, not the side windows. This was not the job of some passing sniper.

Decker stared at the two for a long time. He'd been at the football game earlier in the evening. Fairfield had won, 7–0. Lane had kicked the extra point.

When he straightened up, he felt himself going dizzy. He blinked his eyes and the feeling went away. Goddamn blood pressure, he thought. "Do everything by the book," he ordered, "everything. No mistakes, no stone left unturned. Call the coroner. Get an autopsy. I want to know everything about those two from what they had to eat for supper to when they last had the flu. If anyone can tell me." He signed and turned away, then turned back. "I'll take care of telling the parents." He walked toward his car, already wondering what he was going to say to Shirley Carpenter.

Jack Turner breezed into the office and flicked on the light, then stopped in surprise. "Sorry, Lieutenant, I didn't know you were here."

"It's all right," Decker said, still squinting at the sudden light.

"I thought you would've gone home."

"How the hell could I go home? Three murders. Three murders, Jack, in one week. What the hell's going on?"

Turner laid a half-sheet of paper on Decker's desk. "Preliminary report," he said. "Doc thought you'd want to know."

Decker looked at it. "Holy shit," he said, not even looking up. "How sure is he?"

"Pretty sure, I think. You can see how far along he thought it was, but he couldn't save it."

Decker looked up. "Does this make sense to you?"

Turner shook his head.

"Would the killer have known?"

"Not unless they told him."

"They?"

"She?"

"And it's not suicide," Decker said to himself, glancing down at the paper again. "Then what the hell is the pattern?"

"Pattern?"

"When was the last murder committed in Fairfield, Jack?"

"I don't know. I don't remember any."

"Me neither, and that's why there's got to be a pattern."

"You think they're connected."

Without answering, Decker swiveled his chair around and stared out into the dark. For some reason he thought of Shirley Carpenter. Another loss for her, he thought. And that's one gutsy lady. Behind him, Turner didn't move. After a while Decker looked at his watch. Six-twelve. In an hour it would be getting light. He didn't even feel tired. He turned back toward Turner. "I want David Brett in my office by nine o'clock."

"You think he did it?"

"I think he's involved somehow."

Turner leaned over the desk. "You really think he killed his wife?"

"I don't believe I said that."

"You said—"

"I said they're connected. I said I think he's involved. There's a thread there; I wish to hell I knew what it was."

"So why do you want him in here? You're not going to arrest him?"

"No, I'm not going to arrest him. I'm going to throw him a hot potato and see which way he jumps. In fact, Jack, maybe it would be a good idea if *you* see which way he jumps. Why don't you go home and get a couple hours' shut-eye and be back here by ten. I'll get someone else to pick him up."

Turner started out of the room, but paused when Decker spoke again. "Better bring a duffel bag, Jack. Maybe he'll jump farther than we think."

"What if he doesn't jump at all?"

Decker grinned. "Then that'll tell us something, too, won't it?"

3

HE WAS DOWNTOWN, shopping. He wasn't sure exactly what it was he needed—something that would make the car run right, some kind of tool. No one was speaking to him. Even when he asked for the tool he needed, no one answered. Everyone just stared at him while he went from store to store, but no one spoke. Then he was in the middle of the street, and the sidewalks were filled with people staring. "What's going on?" he yelled. "Is everybody going crazy?" And an answering voice came from behind him: "If Elizabeth hadn't married you, she'd be alive."

He woke sweating, the accusation still in his ears. He got out of bed and walked through the house. He opened the door to the garage and saw that the hole was still there. He stared at it for a long time and then he knew. He knew that what they'd said was true.

"Sorry to keep you waiting," Decker said as he breezed into the office, taking his jacket off, hanging it on a hook at the back of the door. "Hope you haven't been waiting too long."

"More than an hour. Am I supposed to be under arrest?"

Decker sat down at his desk, shuffled through some papers, and looked up. "Brett, when you're under arrest, believe me, you'll know it."

"I tried to leave a while ago and they wouldn't let me."

"I wanted to talk with you, that's all. I'm sorry I kept

you waiting so long; I've already apologized. This has been," he said pointedly, "one hell of a morning."

"I would say," Brett countered just as pointedly, "that this has been the worst week of my life."

"Yeah."

"I hope you haven't brought me back in here just to harass me some more."

"Tell me, Brett, what do you know about Jenny Wilson?"

"I have her in class."

"And?"

"She's a cheerleader, cute girl—live-wire kind. Above-average student, senior, goes with Lane Carpenter. They're pretty thick."

"Are they?"

"Why do you ask?"

"You wouldn't by any chance know where Jenny is right now, would you? Or Lane?"

"What are you driving at?"

"Sometime around midnight, out by the lake, somebody put a bullet into Jenny's head, and another one into Lane's. I don't suppose you can tell me what you were doing around midnight?"

"That's it! I've had it! I'm not going to stay. When you—"

"Sit down," Decker said quietly.

"—have something reasonable to say, then I might, I just *might*—"

"Sit down," Decker said again. "I can keep you here legally, if it comes to that. It's called 'keep for questioning.' Is that the way you want it?"

Brett sat back down, on the edge of the chair. "You're a son of a bitch."

"That's not the way to win friends and influence people."

"What do you—"

"Let me ask the questions for a minute, OK?" Decker leaned back in his chair and stared intently at Brett. "Fairfield's a small town. Everybody knows everybody. Occasionally somebody new moves in. Those people we don't know. Five years ago you moved in, right? Right?"

"Yes."

"We don't know you, Brett. We don't know anything about you."

"My father was born and raised here."

"Yes, your father. He left . . . how many years ago? We still don't know anything about you except for the last five years."

"Do you have to have a letter of recommendation to move into Fairfield?"

"Don't get sarcastic on me. Why did you come?"

"I grew up near Chicago, in the suburbs. My dad never liked it there, but it was where his work was. He used to talk about Fairfield, how good it was to grow up in a small town, how sorry he was that his sons didn't have that. Fairfield became a kind of symbol of the way life was supposed to be. So when I saw that they had a math opening here, I applied. They hired me. That's all there is to it."

"OK. Now let me tell you something. I've lived in this town all my life—except for when I was in the service. In all those years there's never been a murder in Fairfield. Not one. In fact, I'd venture to say that hardly anybody can remember when there was a murder here. Maybe never. And now, within a few days' time, three people are dead. And all in what the city newspapers would call 'execution style.' I mean, those people weren't just killed. They were killed with a vengeance. We have to think they're connected. I mean, I believe in coincidence as much as the next guy, but this is too much. So I ask myself, what's the connection? What did Elizabeth . . . Brett . . . have in common with Jenny Wilson? What one person had a close enough connection with them both that he might have killed them? And guess where the finger points? The husband and the teacher. Now that's a very close connection, I'd say."

"You're out of your mind! What possible reason . . . how in the world can you think—"

"Let me finish before you blow your top. Why? That's what I asked myself. Not why would you kill Elizabeth, because there's a million reasons why a husband might kill his wife, or vice versa, and nobody's ever going to know what they are. But what I find more intriguing is why would you kill Jenny, if we assume that you did. I asked for a full autopsy on those two kids. I've gotten a preliminary report and they've found something very interesting. Would it surprise you to learn that Jenny was pregnant?"

Brett slid back in the chair. "Yes, that would surprise me."

"So here's what you might call the scenario. The teacher has an affair with the student—heaven knows why, but he does. She's a cute girl, after all—you said that, didn't you?"

"What the—"

Decker waved a hand. "Let me finish. And sit down, you're not going anywhere. Let's say she gets knocked up, and she comes and tells him. And that puts him in a bind, because, while she's a cute enough girl, she's still just a girl, and he's got a wife at home who's a knockout, and he doesn't want her to find out. And she's also pregnant. Pretty virile guy, by the way. Maybe he tries to get the girl to have an abortion—I don't know, but anyway, the problem doesn't go away, and he has to do something about it. But let's say the wife finds out and wants a divorce. Now that's going to look pretty bad, him a teacher and all. I mean, what school's going to want him after something like that? So, to save his own

20

skin, he's got to get rid of them, of them both. And that, in a nutshell, is just what he does. Reasonable? Make sense?"

"You forgot about Lane."

"Oh, sure, Lane. Well, he thought Jenny was *his* girl. Somehow he finds out the truth—maybe she even told him. Or at least, maybe the teacher was afraid she had told him. So Lane has to go, too."

Brett sat down. His legs no longer seemed strong enough to hold him, and suddenly he felt very dizzy. "I can't believe you're saying this. I loved Elizabeth. You can't know how much I loved her. And Jenny was just a kid, just someone I had in class, a nice enough girl, but just a child. And she and Lane were . . . everybody knows. You're out of your mind if you think I did it."

"There's only one problem, Brett. I've got it all figured out, but right now I can't prove it." His eyes narrowed. "But I'm going to build a case on you. I'm going to get that proof, and when I do I'm going to go into court with the kind of case that can't be beat, no matter what. I can't arrest you now, Brett, but be warned: I'm going to be coming for you one of these days."

Brett leaned over the desk, face to face with Decker, and spoke with controlled fury. "You're worse than a son of a bitch, Decker. You're an incompetent ass. My wife was the dearest thing in the world to me. I would never have killed her, not to save my skin, not for anything. While you're out looking for proof against me, the man who really did it is getting away—with murder. First it was Elizabeth. And now it's poor Jenny and Lane! If there's a connection, maybe it's just that they were pregnant!" He waved his hand wildly. "Maybe there's some kind of crazy person—"

"Then why did they kill Lane? No, there's a connection, but it's not that they were pregnant. My next-door neighbor is eight and a half months pregnant, for Christ's sake, and she's not dead. Besides, who knew Jenny was that way? Her own parents didn't even know."

"What if you're wrong? How many more are there going to be before you admit you're wrong, Decker?"

"I'm not wrong about that. Neither your wife nor Jenny was obviously pregnant. Whatever the connection was, it wasn't that."

"You're incompetent, Decker, you're goddamned incompetent! If you're the best that Fairfield can do, then God help this town."

"You tell me," Decker said evenly, "If you're so damned smart, then you tell me what the connection is."

Brett straightened up, still looking down at Decker. When he spoke again, his voice was low, barely under control. "God help whoever else he's going to kill," he said. Then he stalked out the door.

Decker got up and walked into the squad room and stood at the window where he could see the front entrance of the building. He followed Brett with his eyes as he left, crossed the street without bothering to look, went to the parking lot, and got into a car. He's borrowed Sandy Augustina's car, Decker thought. He watched as Brett sat for a while in the driver's seat, then started the engine and tore angrily out of the lot. "OK, Brett, do it," he whispered. Behind Brett, another car pulled out of the parking lot, and Decker grinned.

He turned around and looked at Cummins, who was watching from behind his desk. "I am a son of a bitch," Decker said.

"Have you thought what it means if they really are connected?" Cummins asked.

Decker nodded slowly.

"And you're still doing it?"

"When I was a kid, I used to read missionary pamphlets. Do you know what they do in India when a tiger is around? They tie out a goat as bait and then they wait for the tiger to get its scent and come so they can kill it."

Cummins stared at him without saying anything.

Decker threw up his hands. "Those villagers can't afford to lose a goat, you know. That's why they have guys in the bushes waiting for the tiger."

"Decker, maybe you really are a son of a bitch."

Decker looked back seriously. "We can't arrest him on nothing. We have to let him go, anyway. Think about it, Cummins; have we got any other choice?"

"We could have warned him."

"Yeah." Decker nodded. "But the way I see it, he's going to figure it out soon enough anyway."

"Morning, Elvin."

Elvin Haney looked up from his work. He was painting the trim on his shed. "Why, Dave! How're you doing?"

"I'm managing."

"Takes time, son. Takes time. What do you think? This color look OK to you?"

"Looks fine to me."

"Not to the wife. Sheds should match the house, that's what she thinks."

"Well, a change is nice now and again. Say, I came by to ask . . . I need to get the garage fixed. Who's a good carpenter?"

"Can't do better than Joe Watkins. If you catch him sober anyways. He does a bang-up job." He smiled slyly. "That's a pun." Haney pulled a painting rag from his back pocket, searched for a clean spot, and blew his nose into it.

"I was down at the police station this morning, heard some bad news down there. Jenny Wilson and Lane Carpenter, you know who they are? Cops found them dead down by the lake. Shot, I guess."

"You don't mean it!"

"Unfortunately."

"Them two, close as peas in a pod! Suicide, do they think?"

"No, I don't think so."

"I could believe suicide. The wife was just saying the other day how those two were going to get into trouble if they didn't watch out. Too much togetherness ain't good, given the way young people are these days. But it ain't that? What in hell's happening, then?"

"There's something I've always wondered about Lane."

"Now there was a kid. The picture of his father, the very picture! God knows how his mother's taking this. You know her?"

"I know who she is, that's all."

"Now there's a woman who's seen trouble. My Lord, what she's been through. And now Lane!"

"How long has she been a widow?"

"Oh my, the wife'd have to tell you that. Seems to me it's been . . . fifteen years? Maybe more. Yep, it is more, now that I remember. Lane was just a baby, year old maybe. And now he's—how old would he have been?"

"Seventeen, eighteen."

"Well, that's how long."

"It's always seemed a little curious to me. He and I shared a name—Lane's my middle name. It's not common as a name, so it's always struck me as odd."

"Nothing odd about that. Lane was named after your dad."

"I didn't know that."

"Oh, sure. Your dad and Mike Carpenter, now they were just about inseparable. You never saw one without seeing the other. From the time they were old enough to cross the street, off they'd go together. They were some pair!"

"I had a brother named Mike. I wonder if he might have been named after Mike Carpenter."

"No doubt about it. Lane Carpenter after your dad. Why not Mike Brett after Lane's dad?"

"But what's odd is I never knew it; I'm sure my

brother never knew it, either. My father never even mentioned Mike Carpenter, as far as I can remember. If they were such good friends, why didn't he?"

"I don't know, Dave. Something happened there. Something went on between those guys. Your father never came back to Fairfield once he went away to college."

"He always wanted to come back. He was just too busy."

"Was he? For the whole rest of his life?"

Brett leaned over, picked up a stick, snapped it in two, and studied the jagged edge. "How did Mike Carpenter die?" he asked.

"Fishing accident. You know, them doctors and dentists think they have to take off all the time, go fishing. Well, anyways, he was out there in the lake. Something happened to his boat, and he never made it back to shore. They never found the boat. I suppose it's at the bottom of the lake somewhere, but the body floated to shore eventually. He'd been pretty athletic as a kid, but then later he grew something of a stomach on him. Too many beers. Too much good life. Couldn't make it to shore. He drowned. That Shirley Carpenter. Husband dead. Two sons now. That's pretty rough."

"Was he out there alone?"

"He always fished alone. I think he probably got so tired of seeing patients parading through his office that he just liked to go off by himself. Guess I can't blame him for that."

"You said two sons?"

"The first one was Kevin. He was the oldest. Last year, year before, he died. They lived somewhere in Iowa—taught at a college. Wife, three kids—stairsteps, just little tykes. Kevin wasn't even thirty, probably. The furnace blew up one night, killed 'em all. Hell, never even had a chance. Them little kids. I'd just bought each one an ice-cream cone last time they was in town to see

Shirley. Kevin used to always stop by to see me whenever he was in town. Worked for me when he was in high school. Good worker, that kid. And had brains. Won every scholarship in sight. Now Lane, he liked partying more. He was a good-time boy, that Lane."

"I wonder what happened between Mike Carpenter and my dad."

"Hard telling."

"I wonder if Shirley Carpenter knows."

"She might. What difference could it make now? They're both dead."

"Doesn't it strike you as odd, Elvin? Everybody's dead."

"People die, Dave."

"How much would you bet against all the males in a family dying before the age of . . . forty, forty-five? And not just dying, but dying of accidents. Isn't that odd?"

"You said Lane was shot. A bullet's not an accident."

"No, it's not."

Haney took off his cap and scratched his head. "I suppose those things happen."

"What about all the males in two families?"

"You said you have a brother—"

"I said I *had* a brother. He died four years ago in a motorcycle accident."

"You look very much alive to me."

"I took the car every day. Elizabeth only kept it on Fridays, to shop. The only reason she had it that day was because she had a doctor's appointment."

"You're saying you're the one who should have been killed in that explosion."

"When Decker told me that if Elizabeth hadn't been married to me, she'd be alive right now, he wasn't kidding. She would be."

"There's no way you can know that."

"Oh, yes, I know it. I just don't know why."

4

SHE OPENED THE door hesitantly, and it was obvious she'd been crying. Her face was haggard, her eyes red-rimmed. She's been up all night, he thought. "Mrs. Carpenter? I don't think we've ever met, but I'm—"

"Oh, yes." The smile was quick and genuine. "I know who you are. David Brett. Did . . .did you hear about Lane?"

"I was at the police station this morning. I'm very sorry. I wanted to tell you—"

"Come in, come in. I feel guilty now. When Elizabeth . . . I wanted to come over and tell you how much I thought of her, how sorry I was. I hadn't gotten around to it, and now—now it's Lane and you're here. She was one of my favorite people. Won't you come in and have a cup of coffee?"

He stepped inside and closed the door. "Is someone else here?"

"My sister's in the kitchen."

"I wonder if I could talk with you alone."

She looked at him curiously. "Sure. Just a minute." She walked down the hallway and disappeared into the kitchen. A minute later she returned with a tray of coffee and cups. "Come into the den, it's cozier there. It's a barn of a house," she added, "much too big." She led him into a small book-lined room furnished with three comfortable chairs and a low round table. "This was my husband's favorite place, his getting-away-from-it room."

"He must have been a reader."

"The books were my idea. Cream?" He shook his head. "I'm the reader. He read some." She sat down and motioned him to a chair. The coffee tray was on the table between them. "I'm glad you came by. It's good to have someone here who understands what it's like. I tried calling the Wilsons, but they were pretty cold. Well, it's been difficult for them too. They weren't too crazy about Jenny going with Lane. I think they thought he was too wild. I guess I spoiled him." She picked nervously at a piece of lint on her skirt. "I'm not sure why I'm telling you all this. You came to sympathize and it's very nice of you."

"Unfortunately, it's not the only reason I came." He watched her reaction, but she only frowned slightly. "I was told today that Lane was named after my father."

"Yes, he was."

"That my father and your husband had been very good friends."

"Inseparable is the word. Mike and I were what you'd call high-school sweethearts. But sometimes I didn't know if I was going with Mike or Deac."

"Deac?"

She tilted her head and gazed at him. She's very attractive, he thought; she must have been a knockout in those days.

"Everybody called him Deac, didn't you know? There's a story behind it, of course. There was always a story where those two were concerned. . . ."

"What happened between my father and your husband?"

"I don't know," she said. "Yes, I do. It was the war. We were all innocents before, but afterwards—it's as if they saw too much. I suppose it's trite to say that they went away boys and came back men, but that's what happened. The innocence was gone. Mike was . . .

different. They all were." She shook her head. "They were too young for that, too naive. Maybe the war made it impossible for them to be boys anymore. Maybe there were things that happened that they didn't want to remember. When Mike came home, the first thing he wanted to do was get married. It was like he wanted to rub away everything that happened over there. He and Deac both went to the university, but we were married, living in the trailer courts—that's where married students lived in those days. And Deac rented a room someplace. We never saw much of him. They drifted apart. They didn't seem comfortable with each other anymore. It was almost as if they shared some terrible secret. I guess in a way that's what war is. If the rest of us knew how terrible it was, we wouldn't keep getting involved in wars, would we?"

"Your husband died in a boating accident."

"Yes."

"Did he know how to swim?"

She cleared her throat nervously. "I don't know what kind of shape he was in. He drank too much. They did an autopsy and he'd been drinking."

"Was there ever a question . . . that it might not have been an accident?"

"Why should there have been?"

"A man fishing in his own boat. Did he really get so drunk that he would have fallen out of the boat and drowned?"

"You're saying that someone killed him? But who would have wanted to do that?"

"Who would have wanted to kill Lane? And Jenny? And Elizabeth?"

"It must have been a psychopath who killed Lane and Jenny, who else would? Surely that's not related to what happened to Elizabeth. And even if it were, how would that have anything to do with Mike?"

"You had another son, didn't you? Kevin. What happened to him?"

She took a deep breath. He could tell her mind was racing now, thinking of other things even as she was speaking. "He died—with his family—two years ago. Their furnace exploded and the whole house burst into flames. They were trapped inside; there was no chance for them. It was an old house—a farmhouse they were redoing—and it went up like a tinder box."

"And no one questioned that it was an accident."

"I had three grandchildren. Who would have done such a thing on purpose?"

"And did you have any other children?"

"I have a daughter, Joan, who's very much alive. She's coming this evening, by the way. She lives in New York City."

"Mrs. Carpenter, my father died fourteen years ago. He was driving home from work. Something went wrong with the car, and he left it at the side of the road and was walking—probably to a gas station for help. He never got there, because he was struck by a hit-and-run driver. He was killed and no one questioned that it was an accident. They never found who did it. My brother died four years ago in a motorcycle accident. No one questioned that it was an accident either, although I should have because I knew Mike—yes, he was named after your husband, I think—Mike was careful about his bike and about the way he rode. But in both cases, murder was so out of the question that no one even considered it for a minute. Your husband died in an accident. Kevin died in an accident. Lane died, obviously not in an accident. And if I had been driving the car on Monday, as I always did on Mondays, I would have died."

She was shaking her head even before he finished. "No, it's not possible."

"Why not?"

"Because to believe that, we'd have to believe that

30

someone—the same someone you seem to think—wanted all those people dead. There's no one, there's no *reason*."

"That's why I came. There's someone all right, and there is a reason. Your husband and my father were the best of friends. Now they and all their progeny are dead. Except me, of course, because I should have been killed Monday instead of Elizabeth. And except your daughter Joan."

"Why Jenny? Why would they have killed her?"

"I might say that she happened to be in the wrong place at the wrong time, as did Elizabeth, and that would be believable, wouldn't it? Except that I learned something at the police station this morning that perhaps you didn't know. Jenny was pregnant. I would presume Lane was the father. To kill Lane's child it was necessary to kill Jenny." He could tell from her eyes that she hadn't known.

"I don't understand why the police told you that, even if it is true. It's really none of your business."

"They've made it my business. They think I did it."

Her hand went to her mouth in surprise. Then, self-consciously, she laid it back on the arm of the chair. "Why do they think that?"

"The theory is that the baby was mine, that Lane and Elizabeth both found out and so I had to kill them."

"No one who saw Jenny and Lane together would believe that."

"They do."

She got up and went to the one window in the room and looked out. A maple tree was just outside, its leaves dropping color on the lawn. "So you're here to get me to help you clear your name."

"That could be a reason. Another could be that I want to get whoever killed Elizabeth. Another could be that if what I think is true, I'm due to die one of these days."

"And so is Joan," she said softly.

"Will you help me?"

She turned to face him again. "I don't know how I can."

"You said there was no contact between by father and your husband since my dad left here."

"Not that I know of."

"Then it has to be someone from those days."

"Or someone who knew them in the army."

"Were they together?"

"Yes, they enlisted together and everything. They went through the whole thing together. Wait a minute, let me show you something." From a lower shelf of the bookcase she pulled a large blue book; imprinted in white along its spine was the word PIONEER. "You recognize the name, of course, you being a teacher. This was our high-school yearbook. Let me show you how your father looked." She leafed through the pages until she found the one and held it out for Brett to see.

He caught his breath in surprise, then looked more closely. "It could be my brother Mike." It was the same brown curly hair, the same wide strong face, the same warm smile, the same firm chin. Only the nose was different from Mike's. "I never realized before how much alike they looked." The caption underneath read: *Deac . . . wears bow-legged pants . . . fancy footwork on the football field and on the dance floor.* His eyes strayed to the next picture. Beneath unruly blond hair was a broad triangular face, long in the chin, MICHAEL WILLIAM CARPENTER. His mouth almost looked pursed, as if he were trying to suppress laughter; his eyes were obviously pale blue, even in this black-and-white picture. Like his son, Mike Carpenter must have been built like a truck. *Mike . . . "but I'm not awake yet!" . . . bound for gridiron glory.* "My brother's name was Michael William," David said.

"It doesn't surprise me," she said thoughtfully. Her hair, cut just above shoulder-length and flecked with gray, partly hid her face as she leaned over the book. "They cared a great deal about each other."

"Then why did they stop seeing each other?"

"Because they were different when they came back. They were not the same people. Mike used to be carefree, joking, loved people—the kind of guy who does practical jokes. When he came back he wasn't much like that anymore. He needed to get away, to be alone. That's why he had this room, why he went fishing when he could, even why he drank too much, I think. Somehow, he wanted to keep the world at bay."

"Something happened over there."

"A lot happened over there. People were shooting at them and they were shooting back. They were kids, just out of high school, a few months older than Lane. What did they know about killing people?"

"My father never talked about the war. I used to try to get him to, but he never would."

"Let me show you some more." She turned a few pages. "Buddy Kramer." She pointed to a picture; the caption said RICHARD JAMES KRAMER. Her hand moved across the page. "And Al Lundy." ALLEN KENNETH LUNDY. "They were a gang. Good friends. Mike and Deac were the closest, but they all were pals. Buddy always had a car—some rattletrap that was about to break down, but he'd put it back together with shoestring and baling wire and it'd be good for a few more miles. I had my first real date in one of Buddy's cars. Anyway, during that winter, all they did was talk about the war. And then D-Day happened. There was such patriotism, you wouldn't believe it nowadays. Everything for the war effort. Mike used to moan and groan, 'Everybody's over there fighting and what am I doing? *Going to school!*' He wanted to enlist the minute he turned eighteen, but his father talked him into finishing out the year. The day they finished, they drove over to Indianapolis in Buddy's car and enlisted. All of them together. Somehow they managed to stay together through training and got sent off together. I didn't believe they could really work it, but they did."

"And did they all stay together during the war? Did they come back together?"

"As far as I know, they were together through the whole thing—Mike and Deac and Al and Buddy. Al came back, married a hometown gal like Mike did. I think he had several different kinds of jobs, nothing ever seemed to work out. When Mike finished dental school and we came back here, he and Al used to see each other now and then. I could never figure it out—it was like . . . like they knew each other better than they wished. Like they remained friends because they sort of had to. After a while Al just—sort of wasn't around anymore. He must have moved away. His wife—ex-wife—stayed here. Eventually she married someone else, so I guess there must have been a divorce. She still lives here—Evelyn McAndrews, do you know her?"

"No. Would she know where he is now?"

"I have no idea."

"What about the other one"—he looked at the page in front of him—"Richard Kramer?"

"Buddy. Well, cars were his life, so it isn't surprising that he ended up in Detroit. Works for one of the auto companies. We exchanged Christmas cards for a number of years, then somehow we lost touch. You know how those things happen. His family—his parents, I mean—moved to Florida, and there was no family left for him to visit here anymore. His sister moved away long ago. I know what you're thinking."

"Isn't there anyone in town who would know what happened to either one of those men?"

"My sister would know about Buddy, or she'd be able to find out. She was good friends with Buddy's sister; I think they still keep in touch. I could ask her."

"What about Lundy?"

"I don't know where any Lundys are now. The only one who could help you would be Evelyn. Do you want me to call her?"

"No. You've got enough on your mind. But if you could ask your sister . . ."

"Sure. She'll have to call Buddy's sister. I'll let you know what she finds out."

"I just need an address. I'd like to talk to him myself, face to face."

"I'll get it for you."

Bell doesn't work. Please knock. The small neat sign was taped beside the door, at eye level. The ink was faded, the tape yellowed and peeling. David Brett stood on the gray-painted porch and knocked again. Through the glass of the door and the curtain beyond it, he could see a figure coming toward him, and he felt the vibrations of her footsteps on the porch floor. "Mrs. McAndrews?" he asked as she opened the door.

She couldn't have been more than five feet in height, but she must have weighed three hundred pounds. Her faded print dress was covered by a flour-dusted apron. She had pink fluffy slippers and bleached blond hair and a genuine smile. "That's me. What can I do for you?"

"I'm David Brett. I teach at the high school. Maybe you knew my wife—I married Elizabeth Daly."

"Oh, sure. Come on in." She opened the door wider for him. "Let me tell you—you could have knocked me over with a feather when I heard about Elizabeth. Such a pity! And what can I do for you? Won't you come into the kitchen? I'm just making some pies, just finishing up. It wouldn't be Saturday afternoon if I weren't making pies! I was so sorry to hear about Elizabeth, poor thing. Have you any idea how it might have happened?"

He followed her into the kitchen, a tiny bright yellow

room cluttered with pots and pans piled carelessly atop one another, mixing bowls filled with water in the sink, and bags of flour and sugar sitting open on the counter. Three pies were cooling on the counter and two more were nearly ready for the oven, sitting on the table waiting for their top crusts. "Here," she said, pushing a chair toward him, brushing it off with a floury hand. "Sit down and tell me what brings you here. How about a piece of apple pie?"

"No thanks."

"You sure? Best pies in town, everybody says so." She patted her stomach good-naturedly. "I'm a pretty good cook, if I do say so myself. Here, I'll just give you a little piece." She cut him a wide wedge and set it before him. "Coffee?"

"OK," he said, grinning. She'd begun to pour it from a battered pot before he even answered.

"Now," she said, setting the coffee mug beside his pie, "I'll just keep on working, and you tell me what brings you here."

"You were married to Al Lundy?"

"Sure was." She rolled out a ball of pastry and slid it atop one pie. "What's your interest in Allen?"

"Do you know where he is now?"

She shook her head. "Haven't the foggiest." She crimped the edges of the crust, then drew something with a knife on the top crust. "Why should you be looking for Allen? Your dad and he knew each other, I suppose you knew that. Were classmates, hung around together. Poor Allen."

"Why do you say that?"

She rolled out another piece of dough. "Because that's the way I feel about him. He never could quite manage to get his life together. The others all did, but not Allen. Everyone else came back from the war and knew what they wanted to do and did it, but Allen just went from one thing to the next, never quite knowing what it was he was supposed to be doing." She finished the second pie, dusted her hands off over the table, and lowered herself onto a chair. "I'll just have to wait until the others come out of the oven before I can put these in. How's the pie? Good?"

"Delicious. You're right; I think you do make the best pies in town."

She smiled knowingly. "People keep telling me I ought to go into the business. I suppose I should, but I think that'd take all the fun out of it. More coffee?"

He shook his head. "Did he ever talk to you about the war?"

She laughed. "Allen never talked about anything. *I'm* the talker, if you haven't noticed. No, he never said much. Men are in two camps when it comes to war, it seems to me. Those who like to talk about it are the ones who were never much involved. Those who were on the front lines don't usually like to talk about it. That's the way it seems to me, anyway." She paused, staring into space, thinking back. "They joined right after they grad-uated—your father, Mike Carpenter, Buddy Kramer, and Allen. All the others made something of themselves afterwards, but not Allen. It about broke my heart to watch him. It's what did the marriage in, I think, him not being able to get his life together. Never bothered me much, but he couldn't handle things. Never wanted kids, for example—was terrified we might have one, in fact." She laughed openly. "That doesn't make for the best kind of sex life, I'll tell you. Still," she said wistfully, "he was the kindest guy I ever knew. I can't imagine how it was for him in the war, shooting people. It must have torn him up."

"How did he feel about my dad and the others after the war? Did he ever see any of them?"

"Your dad went away to school—went to Bloomington, didn't he?—and I don't think Allen ever saw him again. I don't remember him ever mentioning your dad's name. Buddy went off to Detroit, I believe. Now I do think that there might have been some contact there, but I'm not sure. Seems to me there was. Of course, Mike Carpenter was right here in town. But Allen and Mike didn't run in the same circles. Why do you ask?"

"Something happened between those men. I think it might have happened during the war."

"What makes you think that?" There was an edge in her voice that hadn't been there before.

"Things that happened after. If you know what it was, I'd appreciate your telling me."

She looked at him for a long while before she spoke. "I don't know what happened."

"It's important."

"I don't know what it was." She got up, opened the oven door to check the pies, then closed it and faced him again. "He was not the same person when he came back. He could hardly stand to be around people. He'd wake up in the night screaming. He had a haunted look, like something was on his mind that he couldn't get rid of. Nothing I did could make that look go away. In the end, that's what broke us up. I'm a happy-type person, and there was no happiness in him anymore. Nothing I could do would make the look go away."

"Do you have any idea if he's alive or dead?"

"Oh, he's alive."

"You seem pretty sure, for someone who doesn't know where he is and hasn't had any contact with him."

"Yes, I'm sure. I'm what you'd call psychic. I always know when bad news is coming, when someone dies or something like that. If Allen were dead, I'd know it."

He finished off his coffee and stood. "Thanks for the pie and coffee. Next time I want a good piece of pie, I'll know where to come."

"You don't believe me, do you?" She looked up at him defiantly. "Do you?"

38

"I'm not sure. I'd believe it more if you could tell me where he is."

"He's alive, I'm certain of that; and he's living by himself, away from people. But if you're looking for him, I don't know how you're going to find him."

"You thought he might have kept in contact with Buddy Kramer. Any chance Buddy would know?"

"I doubt it."

"Why?"

"Look, it wasn't an angry divorce. I know you take it with a grain of salt when you hear people say that, but in our case it was true. It's just that Allen had no business being married, you know what I mean? He couldn't take that kind of closeness anymore. He stuck around here for a while, and after he left, he dropped me a card from time to time. If anyone knows where he is, it would be me, and I don't know, so I doubt that Buddy does, either."

"Thanks anyway. And thanks again for the pie."

She walked behind him to the front door. Just as he put his hand on the knob, she spoke. "I had a baby, but it was still-born. Even though he didn't want kids, it just about killed him. He didn't say a word to anybody for two weeks. That's what brought him finally to divorce me. No matter what else I said, I know that's the real reason. That's why he left town, too, I think. After all that killing in the war, he thought he was being punished."

"I appreciate your telling me."

"Why are you looking for Allen?"

"I just wanted to ask him some questions—about my father."

"Is your father living?"

"No." He opened the door, then thought of something and turned back to her. "Do you happen to have any pictures of him?"

"They'd all be old."

"That's better than nothing."

39

"Wait a minute." She shuffled away in her pink slippers. He watched her absently. *He was the kindest guy I ever knew,* she'd said. David wondered, Does a wife ever know what secrets her husband might be carrying around? Did Shirley Carpenter know why her husband needed to get away, why he drank too much? And was there something about his own father that no one ever knew?

"It's the best I have," she said, coming back. "It's old—more than twenty years old—but it shows him the best of any I have."

"May I keep it for a while?"

"I'd like it back."

"OK. I'll get it back to you."

"Are you going to find him?"

"I'm going to try. Have any ideas?"

"No."

"There was never any place he talked about, any place he thought he might like to live?"

She shook her head. "But I know one thing, you won't find him in a city. He'll be where he can be by himself."

"You can be pretty much alone in a city, if you want."

"He's not a city kind of person. He won't want being around the people."

"I'll take care of the picture."

"If you find Allen, tell him . . . hello from me, will you?"

"I sure will."

The phone was ringing when he came into the house. "It's Shirley Carpenter," she said when he answered it. "I've been trying to reach you."

"I was at Evelyn McAndrews's place, and then I went out for a drive—to do some thinking. Sorry."

"Did Evelyn help?"

"She doesn't know where he is. Is there a Mr. McAndrews?"

"Yes. He's a trucker, I think. He's not home much. I found out about Buddy."

"Oh?"

"He went to Detroit, worked for a while with one of the big auto companies, but Buddy was a tinkerer, and there wasn't enough of that to suit him. So he opened up his own place—where they rebuild cars, modify them and customize them, you know the kind of place? Fourteen years ago he was working late, all by himself, and there was an explosion. He was killed. They thought it was gasoline fumes or something—and a spark or a cigarette. No one suspected anything other than that it was an accident."

He didn't say anything.

"David, are you there?"

"Yes. I'm just putting some things together."

"It looks bad, doesn't it? Do you think it might be Al? Or maybe he's dead, too?"

"Evelyn McAndrews thinks he's alive."

"Does she have any reason?"

"Not really, she just thinks he is."

"If he is, then it must be Al?"

"When did your husband die?"

"Sixteen years ago."

"My father died fifteen years ago. Buddy Kramer died fourteen years ago."

"There's something else. Buddy and Phyllis—that's his wife's name—had five kids. Three are dead."

He felt suddenly cold, the receiver too hard and brittle against his ear. "Run that by me again."

"I have it written down here. Jimmy—he was ten—was killed five years ago by a hit-and-run. That's what happened to your father, didn't it? Fred died in a boating

41

accident three years ago—he was on his honeymoon at the time. Georgine died last year while she was at college. They thought it was an intruder—a robber or a rapist or something—and that he panicked and ended up killing her."

"Good God."

"Dave? My Joan came tonight. She flew in from New York and we picked her up in Indianapolis. She's here now."

"I don't know what to tell you. Who knows she's here?"

"Anyone can figure it out—her brother dead and all."

"You know this town better than I do. Find someone or someplace safe. Maybe you know someone who lives in another town—somewhere close-by that you both can go?"

"It's Al, isn't it?"

"We don't even know if he's alive."

"Who else could it be? Dave, I'm scared."

Allen Lundy, he thought, where the hell are you? What's going on?

"Dave? Where are you going? You can't stay there. He's after you too."

"I'm getting out, don't worry. Did you get the Kramers' address?"

"Yes, and I'll give you my sister's phone number, in case you want to get in touch." She gave him the information. "Be careful, David," she warned.

"Take care of Joan." He hung up and turned away from the phone. "OK, Brett," he said aloud, "what the hell do you do now?"

5

HE SAT IN the upstairs den, in the dark, scenes playing again and again in his mind, and he couldn't stop them. He thought of Elizabeth going to the garage, getting into the car, turning on the ignition, and that would have been the last thing she would have known. He thought of Lane and Jenny, sitting in the car in the dark by the lake—were they just talking, making love, worrying about how they were going to tell her family and his? Did they know? Did Lane know? And someone must have come to the car and opened the door—or did they open it for him?— because whoever it was hadn't shot through the glass, had shot through the door or the open window . . . and then rolled up the window? With the door open (he guessed), for however long it was before they'd been shot, they'd surely seen him; they knew what was going to happen and who was going to do it. And had he told them why? Of all the victims, Lane and Jenny had seen him, perhaps knew why he was killing them.

Or maybe they weren't the only ones to know. Buddy Kramer, working alone at night in his shop, perhaps had seen him too. Someone coming out of the shadows— someone he knew? Allen Lundy? Someone explaining, perhaps, saying, "You know why I'm doing this. You know why it is you all have to die." And Mike Carpenter, sitting in his boat, fishing, a little drunk, and another boat coming along, and Mike recognizing the man, saying, "What the hell—?" and the man shoving him overboard, maybe knocking him out or holding him under? And David Brett, his father—the name Deac still sounded strange, the name of a stranger—had he seen? In that last moment before the car hit him, did he see the driver? Did he know why?

Allen Lundy. Was he alive? Was he the one? Did he know why?

He got up and walked barefoot to the desk, feeling his way in the dark. His hand touched it, reached for the reading lamp and turned it on. From a drawer he pulled a sheet of paper and a pencil and he began to write. On the left side of the paper he wrote:

Richard Kramer (Buddy)—killed in a shop explosion
Jimmy—killed by a hit and run
Fred—killed in a boating accident
Georgine—killed by an intruder

In the middle of the paper, he wrote:
Mike Carpenter—killed in a boating accident
Kevin—killed with his family in a furnace explosion
Lane—shot
After a pause, below Lane's name, he wrote:
Jenny Wilson—shot

On the right side of the paper:
David Brett—killed by a hit-and-run
Mike—motorcycle accident
Beneath Mike's name, very slowly
and deliberately, he wrote:
Elizabeth—car explosion

He looked at the paper and the names on it for a while. Then, at the bottom of the column for Buddy Kramer, he drew two lines; at the bottom of the column for Mike Carpenter he wrote Joan's name; and at the bottom of his father's column he wrote his own name. Then he went back across the columns again, this time writing:

5 children—3 dead
  3 children—2 dead & Jenny; 3 grandchildren—
  all dead
    2 children—1 dead & Elizabeth

"And two who were never born," he whispered to himself.

He looked for a long time at Elizabeth's name, knowing that the line at the bottom of his father's column should read: *2 children—2 dead.* And Elizabeth would have been alive. As Jenny should have been left alive. "And I should be dead," he said aloud.

He folded the paper in half, then in half again, creasing the folds angrily between his fingers. Then he snapped off the lamp and walked over to the window. In the light of a quarter moon, the fir trees in the Myerses' yard threw long shadows halfway across the street. Nothing stirred. "I should be dead," he said again, "and Elizabeth should be alive." He leaned his head against the cool glass of the window and absently watched the play of moonlight and shadow on the lawn. He wondered where Shirley Carpenter and Joan had gone. He thought of the stupidity of staying in this house, where Elizabeth had already been killed and where, for all he knew, he might be the next one. Then he thought about the two Kramer children who were still alive, and didn't know.

The road curved around a little lake. Bright sunlight glittered on the water's surface. At the far end, a lone sailboat leaned with the wind. It was unseasonably warm for October and he rode with the car windows open. He was driving slowly now, looking for the number—or the name—on each mailbox that stood sentinel along the roadside. When he came to the mailbox, there was no name, only the number he'd been looking for—30592. He paused, then turned down the asphalt drive that led to the house.

A woman opened the door. She looked younger than he had expected Buddy's wife to be, but too old to be one of his children. She was dark haired, tanned, painfully slim, in white silk pants and pale yellow shirt. "Mrs. Kramer?" he asked hesitantly.

She stared at him in uncertain surprise. "I'm sorry," she said distantly, "I don't believe I know who you are, but I'm not Mrs. Kramer."

"Excuse me, then. It's the address I was given—30592 Island Lake Road, West Bloomfield?"

"Mr. Kramer died a number of years ago."

"I know that. I'm looking for his widow."

"Why?"

"It's a long story, a private long story. Does she live here?"

"Mrs. Kramer does not live here. I'm Mrs. Jacobs and I live here."

"Oh. Then, can you tell me where she lives?"

She looked at him warily. "I'm not in the habit of giving out personal information unless I know to whom I'm giving it."

"I'm sorry. My name is David Brett. My father—whose name was also David Brett—and Mr. Kramer grew up together. The rest of what I have to say I'd rather tell Mrs. Kramer in person."

A girl appeared behind the woman. She was stunningly pretty, with long black hair held back from her face with barrettes on each side. She was in jeans and a red T-shirt, and she was barefoot.

The woman saw him looking beyond her and must have sensed the girl's presence. "I'm the one you're looking for," Mrs. Jacobs said guardedly. "I used to be Mrs. Kramer, but I've been remarried for some time."

"I'm sorry to disturb you, but I have some important information that you ought to know, and your children should know, too."

She turned to the girl. "Nickie, how about getting us some coffee?"

When the girl had gone, she let him in the house, leading the way down a flagstone hall. The living room was all glass on the lake side and filled with plants. "I only have a few minutes," she said, gesturing toward an easy chair. "I hope you can be brief with your long story."

"I understand that your husband—your first husband, I mean—died in an explosion at his place of work."

"Yes."

"Was there ever any question that it might not have been an accident?"

"Certainly not. Why on earth would there have been?"

"And that happened fourteen years ago, am I correct?"

She nodded. "But I don't really see—"

"Fifteen years ago my father was killed on a highway—by a hit-and-run driver. Sixteen years ago Mike Carpenter drowned while fishing. Three deaths, each a year apart, each of a man who was normally careful about things, who did not lead a particularly dangerous life as far as I know. All accidental deaths, or so it would seem. And these three men were good friends through childhood, in high school, in the war together. It seems a little strange—"

"Accidents happen," she said, clearly impatient with him. "That was a long time ago. Why bother to dig around about it now? Even if it weren't an accident, what could you possibly gain from knowing it now? I certainly wouldn't want to know."

"If it had stopped there, I might agree with you. But unfortunately, Mrs. . . . "

"Jacobs," she said impatiently.

"Unfortunately, it hasn't. Those three men between them had ten children. Six of those children are dead, too, all by accidents. Except one who died last Friday night with his girlfriend—both shot. That was obviously no accident. And I forgot to mention that there were three grandchildren who are also dead. Three of those six children were yours, Mrs. Jacobs, isn't that right?"

She got up from her chair. "Are you trying to blackmail me? Are you trying to make something out of the fact that I've lost three children?" she demanded angrily.

"What I'm trying to do is warn you."

"What happened to Bud happened a long time ago. I'm not interested in digging that up anymore. If it wasn't an accident, then I'm sorry for Bud, but there's nothing I can do. Or even want to do at this point. Maybe you don't know this, but I was left a widow fourteen years ago with five children—yes, five children, and they were all under the age of ten. My youngest wasn't even one year old when that happened. And Bud, who might have had the goingest business in town, left virtually nothing in capital. I had five children and nothing else. I was a great deal younger than Bud, and I had no work experience outside the home and five children to take care of. I went to work as a secretary, entry level, and I was paid next to nothing. Thank God, Sid came along, a man with enough love in his heart and enough money to take care of us. I've had a good life with Sid. I'm not interested in digging up any old skeletons about Bud anymore."

The girl came into the room carrying a tray with coffee cups, and stopped abruptly. Brett stared at her in open

48

curiosity. She looked seventeen or eighteen; she had to be Buddy's daughter.

"Thanks, darling," the woman said, her voice suddenly changed. "Just leave it on the table there for us, will you please?"

It was obvious the girl had heard part of what had been said. She looked in confusion from Brett to her mother and back to Brett. "Is this your daughter?" he asked.

"Yes," the woman answered curtly.

He took his wallet from his pocket and pulled the photograph from it. "Have you ever seen this man?" he asked, showing it to the woman.

"No," she said, barely glancing at it.

"Please, look at it. All I'm asking is if you've ever seen him before."

Reluctantly, she looked again, and he was watching the expression on her face. She had not expected to recognize the man in the picture, but her face told him that she did. "Yes," she said finally.

"He's been here, then?"

"I've already answered your one question. Please leave now."

He stayed seated, sensing that the two women were alone in the house, guessing she did not want him alone with the girl and would stay there—and talk—as long as he did. "Please, for my sake, if not anyone else's, tell me what you know about him."

"He was a friend of Bud's, from before we were married, that's all I know. He came to our house, they had a lot of private talks. I don't know what it was about. He stayed for a while. I didn't want him to, but Bud insisted. There was a room above the garage where he stayed. He was after something from Bud, but I never knew what it was. He was a strange person, never said two words to me, didn't even look me in the face. It was scary, and I was glad when he left. One day he was gone, that's all. He appeared, he disappeared."

"What was his name?"

"I don't remember."

"How long did he stay?"

"A couple of weeks. Maybe it only seemed that long."

"Did your husband ever have any contact with him again?"

"Not that I know of."

"What was your husband's reaction to him? Was he glad when he left?"

"I don't know. It was like he owed him something, like he would have gotten rid of him but he didn't know how. It wasn't much like Bud, because he could be a very blunt person. It seemed to me he was relieved when the man left, but maybe it was only that I was."

"Did he leave an address, anyplace that he'd come from or was going to?"

"No."

"Might your husband have had it?"

"For all I know, he might have, but after fourteen years I can guarantee you it's not around anymore. It would have been thrown out long ago."

"Would you look?"

"I don't know how I can be more clear. I don't have anything of Bud's anymore."

"Mrs. Jacobs, someone is killing off members of your family, and of mine, and of another family. Three of your children are already dead. The others should know."

"They were not related. They were accidents."

"How can you be sure of that?"

"Jimmy was killed five years ago, for God's sake, and it was an accident. What happened to Fred was an accident, it couldn't have been anything else. Neither one has any relationship to what happened to Georgie. They were all unrelated things, and I resent your trying

50

to make something more of them. Now, I'm asking you to leave one more time before I phone my husband or the police."

"This daughter of yours—her name's Nickie?—are you willing to bet her life on that?" He looked at the girl instead of the mother. The girl stared back, solemn black eyes in a still-tanned face.

"Perhaps you'd better leave," the girl said. "You've done your duty; I've been warned." She turned and left the room.

"You have another child."

"She doesn't live here."

"Tell her."

"Even if I believed it, what good would it do? Accidents happen to people, there's no way you can stop them. They aren't going to cloister themselves for the rest of their lives just because somebody appears at our doorstep with wild stories."

"Tell her anyway; she has a right to know."

"It's time for you to leave."

"Why don't you call your husband? Maybe he'd take me a little more seriously than you do."

"My husband would not appreciate your having come, I'll guarantee you that. And he would not think much of your theories. People just don't wipe out whole families. There's no reason in the world for it, and I haven't yet heard you give a reason even for one person to have been killed, to say nothing of whole families."

"There may not be a reason that you and I would consider rational. This is not a rational thing that's happening."

"I'll correct you: This is not a rational thing you're telling me. Now, do you go, or do I call the police?"

He rose and walked to the door; she followed behind. At the door he turned and faced her again. "Wherever your other daughter is, she's not safe. Tell her."

"Good-bye, Mr. Brett." She watched him walk to his car and get in.

She's not taking any chances about my staying around, he thought as he drove back out toward the road. And she's not going to tell the other girl.

He paused at the main road, then turned right. He braked immediately when a red-shirted figure emerged from the shrubbery that lined the road. The girl ran around to the driver's side and handed him a slip of paper. "It's my sister's address. Go see her," she said, out of breath from running.

"I thought you didn't believe me."

"I don't know whether to believe you or not. Andy will."

"Andy?"

"Andrea. My sister."

"Your mother's not going to tell her, is she?"

"You have to understand about my mother. She's had a lot of bad things happen in her life, losing a husband and three kids. Jimmy was only ten when he was killed; he was the youngest of us."

He took the picture out of his pocket. "Do you remember this man, when he was staying with your family?"

"Are you kidding? I was four when my father died, I can barely remember him." She tapped the paper he still held. "Go see my sister."

"Do you understand what this means if what I'm saying is true?"

"Yes," she said, serious-eyed.

"A couple of days ago a girl was shot in the forehead. The only reason she's dead is that her boyfriend happened to be in one of the families. She was just about your age, and now she's dead. Her name was Jenny."

The girl blinked slowly. "I'm sorry."

"Be more than sorry. Get yourself away from here. Go

visit a relative in another state, in another town at least. Go someplace where he won't be able to find you."

"Is that man in the picture the one who did it?"

"I don't know. Promise me you'll go away."

"I don't know if I can."

"You have to."

"My mother won't believe it."

"Go anyway. Even if you have to go without telling her. Go."

"For how long? Won't he just come later, when I'm back home? I can't disappear for the rest of my life."

"At least go until I've tried to find out who's doing this."

"How will I know?"

"Stay in touch with your sister. Let her know where you are."

"I'll try."

"You have to. If you think your mother's had a hard time so far, how will it be when you or your sister dies, and she knows that she might have been able to stop it?"

"You'd better go now." She stepped back from the car, then leaned toward it again. "I'm sorry about that girl."

"So am I," he said. He put the car in gear and drove slowly away. And about Elizabeth. And about all of them. Especially about Elizabeth.

6

"LIEUTENANT!" CUMMINS POKED his head around the corner of the office door and pointed at the phone on Decker's desk. "It's for you."

Decker lifted the receiver. "Decker," he said absently.

"Lieutenant, it's me."

"Jack?"

"I lost him."

Decker bolted out of his chair. "Say that again."

"I lost him. He went into Detroit and I lost him there."

"What the hell did you do that for?"

"I'm sorry. I was trying not to, but he was going to some real weird places—I think he was trying to buy a gun. They could've smelled me a mile away, so I had to stay way back. I lost him finally."

"How the hell could you have done that?" Decker shouted.

"I'm sorry."

"Where was he? Why didn't you get to his car?"

"He was in his car. They were making the deal in his car. They were driving around. He looked so straight I had to keep back, or else they would have thought he was one of us. And it didn't work. Do you know how they drive in Detroit? They're all crazy. There's no way I could tail him when I couldn't stay close."

Decker breathed out heavily. "Where are you now?"

"At a motel. The Kingsford. On Michigan Avenue."

"Sit there until I call you back." Decker hung up the

phone and looked at Cummins, who still stood in the doorway. "Shit," he said, his voice cold. "He's on his own now."

"I don't understand," Cummins said.

Decker looked through Cummins as if he weren't there. "The goat's broken the tether," he said softly.

She sat cross-legged on the couch in an oversize sweatshirt and faded jeans. She was studying the piece of paper he had given her, frowning. Her black curly hair was cut very short, and she was tan enough that at this distance he couldn't see her freckles. He'd noticed them before, when she'd opened the door. Her eyes were dark blue, the darkest blue he'd ever seen.

"The blanks stand for Nickie and me," she said without looking up.

"I didn't know your names when I wrote it." He glanced around the room. Books were piled everywhere—on the floor, on a straight-backed chair, two piles on the table.

"What does my mother say?"

"She thinks I'm crazy."

She looked up at him, the frown still creasing her forehead. "She would think that. She wouldn't want to think that there was a reason for it. It would blow her mind to have to think that. The only way she's been able to handle it is to think that it's been a horrible series of accidents. Each time something happened, to think that it's another in a series of . . . of bad luck or something. To think of each as an isolated incident. If she thought that it was going to keep on, that it wouldn't end until we were all dead, she wouldn't be able to take it."

"I told Nickie to get away, but I don't know if she will."

"I'll call her, but it's going to be very hard, getting Nickie out of there without destroying my mother."

"If she stays there and something happens to her, won't it be worse?"

She sighed and nodded. "Yes, it would."

"Both of you have to go. Why don't you go together?"

"It sounds good to say that, but how can a person just do it? I mean, for how long? Won't he just wait until we pop up again? We can't hide out for the rest of our lives. We're not going to go into a monastery."

"You're beginning to sound like your mother."

"No, really. For how long do we do it? Forever?"

"What's the alternative? To go through life day to day knowing that sometime, probably when you least suspect it, he's going to get you. Would you rather do that?"

She looked intently at him. "What are you going to do?"

"I don't know."

"Can't we stop him?"

"We don't even know for sure who he is."

"For sure? Do you have an idea?"

He handed the photograph across the coffee table to her. "Have you ever seen this man before?"

She took the picture and looked at it. "Did you show this to my mother?"

"Yes."

"What did she say?"

"That he'd spent a couple of weeks at your house when your father was still alive. That she didn't like him very much. She didn't seem to know why he was there. Do you remember him?"

"He was the strangest person I ever met. I must have been eight or nine—nine, I think. He was almost like a child, like an angry child. He was full of anger, hurt . . . pain. It's true my mother couldn't bear him. She didn't make any secret of it either. I never knew why he was there, but he did talk to me some."

"What about?"

"I'm trying to think of his name."

"Allen Lundy."

"Yes. My dad called him Al."

"What did he talk to you about?"

"I had a horse then. It had come up lame—a break, a pretty bad break. Everyone thought it should be shot, but I wouldn't let them. The vet came, and even he thought it should be done away with, but I was crying and carrying on. Finally my dad asked if there was any way it could be saved. The vet told him it was possible, but it would cost a lot and take a great deal of care. Dad put it in my hands. He'd pay the money, but I'd have to provide the care. It would be up to me. All that fall and winter I took care of that horse. On the worst nights I'd take two electric blankets out to the barn, one for Misty and one for me. I almost came down with pneumonia, but I pulled her through. My father used to tease me about that afterwards, but I knew he was really proud of me, that I'd had the guts to stick to it, that I'd defied them all and brought her through on my own. It was shortly after that happened that Al Lundy came. He heard the teasing; he heard the story. I was always bringing home sick birds, or rabbits that the cat or dog had gotten and half-killed, stray animals nobody else wanted. My mother almost killed me when I did. My father thought it was a big joke. But Al Lundy seemed to think it was OK, that I was doing the right thing. He thought a lot more highly of animals, it seemed to me, than he thought of people."

"Do you know why he left?"

"No. There was a big fight; he had an argument with my dad and then he left. There *was* something odd between them. Even I felt it. My dad wasn't the same person when he came, and for a while after he left. He was moody; he'd get angry over nothing. It was as if whatever was making Al Lundy angry had spilled over and was making my dad angry, too. In a way, even though he was nice to me, I was glad to see him go because of it. For a while after he was gone, my dad was still the same way, but then he got over it and everything seemed all right again. You don't think he's the one who's been . . . doing this?"

"If he isn't, he knows why. And if he knows why, he most certainly knows who."

She looked off into space, narrowing her eyes, thinking. He said nothing, waiting for her to speak. "You know," she said finally, her voice carrying a new tightness, "as nearly as I can figure it, it must have been about four months after he left that my father died."

In the silence that ensued, a car outside revved its motor and tore away down the street. "I don't think he would have done it," she said.

"But they did have an argument just before he left."

"Yes."

"Would your mother have heard the argument? Would she know what it was about?"

"She wasn't around right then. I was the only one who was home."

"Did you hear it?"

She shook her head. "I don't think he killed my father."

"But you did hear it."

"I heard part of it."

"Tell me what you heard. If he didn't do it, he can help us. If he did, then we have to know."

"What I'm going to tell you is going to make him look bad. You didn't know him; I did. He wouldn't have done anything like that."

"Children can be fooled."

"He couldn't have. I know it."

"Tell me what you heard."

"They were shouting at each other. I was in my room,

58

and they were in the living room, right below. They probably didn't know I was there, or they didn't realize how loud they were shouting, that I could hear them. First they were talking more quietly, and I didn't hear them, didn't even pay attention. I was reading, I think. Then it got louder and louder, and pretty soon I couldn't help but hear. It was all about people dying, about people being killed and people being dead. My father was saying that it wasn't his fault, and Al Lundy was saying that it was, that he was guilty as sin—I know that's the expression he used because it was the first time I'd heard it: *guilty as sin*. He kept yelling that whether my father wanted to admit it or not, he was guilty. That people who were guilty probably deserved to die, that they didn't deserve to have happy families and children to come after them. Then my father got really mad and told him to get out—to pack up his things and clear out as fast as he could, that he had no right to be staying under his roof if he were going to talk like that. And Al Lundy said it wasn't going to make any difference, that my father was going to die anyway, that it was going to happen to him just like it happened to the others and he might as well face it, and my father was yelling at him to get out and he was yelling back, 'You're a dead man, Buddy! You're as good as dead right now!' And I was terrified, and I tried to stop up my ears, but I could still hear them. So I climbed out on the roof of the porch, which was right out my window—you know, it was one of those flat-roofed places over a sun porch. I climbed over the railing at the edge and jumped down to the ground and ran away from the house. I ran as far as I could, and then, when I was too tired to run, I stopped running and I walked, and I was still going away from there, walking down the road, when Al Lundy came by in his car. He'd packed up his things, just like my dad had told him, and he was going away.''

"And that was the last you saw of him."

"Yes."

"He was really talking like that? Saying your father deserved to die, that he would die just like the others had?"

"When he passed me in his car, I pretended not to notice, because I didn't know what else to do, whether to wave or not. But he saw me, and he stopped and rolled down the window and called me over to the car. I was a little scared because of everything I'd heard, but I went. He said he was leaving, that he might not ever see me again, but he wanted me to know that he thought I was a good person. That bad things might happen to me someday, but I shouldn't be afraid. Then he took my hand in his and said that if I ever needed him, he'd be right at the tip of my little finger, that every time I looked at my hand I should look at my little finger and remember him, that he would be that close. Then he said good-bye to me and drove away."

"At your fingertip? He must not have gone away then. He must have stayed close-by."

"I guess he must have, but I never saw him again."

"Where did you live then?"

"In Farmington. That's not far from where my mother and sister live now."

He leaned forward in the chair. "How big is Farmington? Could he have stayed right in town?"

"Someone in the family would have seen him, I'd think. It isn't that big a town—or at least it wasn't then. On the other hand, my dad died shortly after, and then my mother went to work. I was the oldest—we were all just kids. We really didn't get around town that much."

"Al Lundy stayed around, and your father died four months later."

"I don't think he did it."

"Your father might have seen him in town, might have

60

gotten angry again. It could have happened. And then Al Lundy might have killed him."

"How are you going to find him?"

"How do you find people? I guess you start with the telephone book."

"Are you going back there tonight?"

"I might as well." He stood as if to go.

"Why don't you spend the night here? I've got room for you, and you look like you could use a good night's sleep. A good supper too, I'd guess. And then in the morning we'll go."

"You're not going."

"I want to. It's important to me."

"No." He shook his head. "You're not going."

"My father was killed, and both my brothers and one of my sisters. I have as much stake in this as you do. I'm going." She got up from the couch and headed toward the tiny kitchen. "We'll fix something for dinner and get a good night's sleep, and in the morning we'll go."

"What are you talking about—we'll do this and we'll do that. I'm doing it, not you."

"You think you're the only one."

He looked at her and frowned.

"Yes, you do, David. You think no one else can hurt as much as you do. You think that gives you more right to go after him."

"Elizabeth was my wife. She shouldn't even have been killed at all. . . ."

"What do I have to match that? That's what you mean, isn't it? You don't want anyone to hurt as much as you do. You want to hoard that precious pain and you don't give a damn about anybody else. You want to think that losing Elizabeth was worse than anything that could have happened to the rest of us."

"You're not going!" he shouted at her. "You didn't even know her! You don't even know me!"

61

She stared at him from the doorway, her eyes wide, her mouth open in surprise, and he was stunned by his own sudden anger.

"How long has your wife been dead?" The dark blue eyes held him across the room.

"A week . . . today."

She walked back and touched him gently on the arm. "In a week's time Elizabeth was killed, those kids were killed, and you learned about all the rest of this. David, you're going to have to stop for a while. You're going to have to let your emotions catch up to the rest of you."

"I can't. Don't you see, I can't! People are dying."

"Joan is safe with her mother, isn't she?"

He nodded.

"Then there's only Nickie and you and me. I'll phone and make sure Nickie goes somewhere safe. I'll talk with my stepfather. Mother's probably already told him about your visit, but if I tell him I think Nickie had better go away, he'll make sure she does. And then you and I are going to stay here, or go someplace safer, and you are going to take it easy for a while, until you've worked out some of your feelings. Right now you're as tight as you can be. If you try going after him when you're like this, you'll only end up killing yourself."

"I can't do that. I can't wait around. And you have no business—"

"David, listen, I'm only trying to be a friend."

"But in the meantime, God knows what he's doing."

"In the meantime he's doing whatever it is he does when he isn't killing people. You say this has been going on for sixteen years. It can wait another day or two."

He sat down again, suddenly very tired, and put his head in his hands. "I can't stop now. I have to keep going."

She knealt beside him. "Is this what you think your

wife would want you to do? Drive yourself to distraction? Push yourself over the edge?"

He looked up at her, close enough now to see the freckles. "That's unfair."

"Yes." She grinned at him. "I'm playing dirty, aren't I, and that's not what you expect in the way of a friend, is it? But I'm the best you can do right now, so you're stuck with it. What are we going to do for supper?"

He kissed her hard on the mouth, wanting to pull her into him, wanting to make her part of him, to pull her inside him, so that they could be one, so they could feel together and touch together and rise and fall together and be one, together. They rolled over on the white sheets, her long body against his, and he went into her and she closed around him and they came together. She was groaning softly and they were together, exactly together, and it was like they were sailing. There was nothing beneath them and nothing above them and they were sailing, and the sky was blue and warm like water and they sailed and sailed and sailed.

When he awoke, he was still moving, but he was on the couch and there was no one with him and it was still dark and the blanket had fallen off. He closed his eyes to find her again, but he couldn't get back into the dream, no matter how hard he tried, and he began to cry.

When he awoke again, Andrea was sitting in the chair across from him, a mug of coffee cradled in her hand, and she was watching him. "Good morning," she said, smiling. Full daylight poured into the window-wall beyond her. It must be late already, he thought. He considered her and the morning and the coffee for a minute. "What time is it?"

She looked at her watch. "Nine-fifteen."

He sat up with a jerk. "I've got to get going."

"You want some coffee? Bacon and eggs? Omelet, maybe?"

"Whatever you've got is OK."

Walking into the kitchen, she called back to him. "It's all arranged. I've got a place for us to go. We can stay there as long as we want. It's only about a half hour from here—one of the professors has a cottage on a lake. It's usually empty this time of year. No problem."

"I can't. I have to get going."

"You can. You have to. One day, two days, a week. However long it takes."

He leaned back against the couch. "One day," he said.

They pulled the canoe out into the lake, she sitting in front, paddling lazily, he in back, steering. He was afraid she'd talk, but she didn't. The lake was still; theirs was the only boat. He heard the slosh of her paddle and the water's drip across the surface as she reached for another stroke. The trees that crowded the shore reflected color into the water—crimson and yellow and purple among the green of pines. Elizabeth would have loved this place, he thought. Ahead of him the black curly head leaned forward with each stroke. And she would have liked Andrea.

They walked in the woods, quiet save for the wind rustling the pines. "When this is all over, you should go up north," she said. "You think the fall color is beautiful here; you should see it—" She stopped, stood still, thinking. She bent to pick up an acorn and rolled it absently between thumb and forefinger. She grinned at him. "You think I talk too much?"

"No."

"Yes. Well. Sometimes I run on." They walked along in silence, leaves rustling beneath their feet. "My family laughs at me. They think I'm going to go to school forever, a perennial student. They think Ann Arbor's a hothouse—not the real world. It's not that I don't want to face life; it's just that I have this curiosity. I have to know about everything. Do you know how long it takes to get through school when you have to know about everything? Anyway, I ought to have my master's by spring. What in the world one does with a degree in anthropology is going to be the next question."

He built a fire in the fireplace at the cottage and they sat on the floor, leaning against pillows, staring into the fire and eating chili and crackers. "Tell me about Elizabeth," she said.

"She was beautiful—tall, auburn hair, green eyes. But it wasn't just the way she looked. Warm is the word for Elizabeth. Warm in every way. She made you feel good about yourself. Everyone liked her. Everyone. Half the men in town would have married her, if they'd had the chance. I found that out . . . after."

"David," she said, looking at him curiously, "might her death have had nothing to do with your father and mine and all the others? Might it have been someone who was jealous?"

"Elizabeth was not the kind of person to inspire murder. No. It was part of the rest."

"You must have loved her very much."

"I did. I still do."

The fire slowly died to embers, and they were still sitting in front of it. "I'm going in the morning," he said.

"We're both going."

"No, this is something I have to do by myself."

"Why?"

"Because I do. Because I'm the one who worked it out and I'm the one who has to do it."

"You have to take me with you," she said confidently.

"No."

"Yes, you do. Because I know where he is. I realized this afternoon when we were walking in the woods. I know where he is, and it's not in Farmington."

"Where?"

"If I tell you, you have to take me."

"Don't play games with me, Andrea. This isn't for fun; this is for real."

"I know that."

"Can you shoot a gun? Would you shoot a man?"

"Is that what you're planning to do? Are you going to kill him?"

"One step at a time." His voice was deliberate. "First I find him; then I find out if he's the one."

"He isn't! I already know that!"

"I'm the one who's going to have to know that."

"You didn't answer me. Are you taking a gun? Would you shoot him?"

"I'm taking a gun. I don't know if I'm going to have to use it or not, but there's no point in your going along. It only takes one to pull a trigger."

"He didn't do it! I'd bet my life on it."

"Would you bet Nickie's?"

"You know I can't do that."

He smiled smugly. "I thought so."

"I'll help you find him. Then we'll decide what to do about it."

"Where is he?"

"I'm going with you, right?"

"If that's the only way you're going to tell me."

"You know it is."

"Okay, then. Tell me."

"I'm going?"

He nodded reluctantly. "Tell me."

She held her left hand up in front of him, palm outward. "What are you looking at?"

"Your hand."

"What else?"

He laughed. "I don't know."

"You know that Michigan looks like a mitten. But I'll bet you don't know that when those of us who live here want to tell where a place is, we talk of the state in terms of a hand—the thumb, for example. Or we'll hold up a hand, like this, and point to the corresponding spot on it. 'At the tip of your little finger,' he said. The little finger in Michigan is the Leelanau Peninsula. He's at the end of the Leelanau Peninsula."

"You're sure he said the little finger?"

"Positive."

"Well," he said, leaning back into a cushion, "and how long is it going to take to get there?"

"Five hours, give or take some. We can leave first thing in the morning."

7

SHE STRETCHED LAZILY in bed. Everything was quiet except for the call of a duck on the lake. By the light she guessed it must be almost eight o'clock; her watch lay on the dresser. She swung her legs over the side of the bed, stood, and pulled on her clothes, thinking of Allen Lundy. Did you kill my father? she wondered. Whenever she thought of her father, she remembered him laughing. Bud Kramer always laughed; everything was a joke for Bud Kramer; the world was sunny, everything went well. And she, Bud Kramer's eldest child, was just like him. But her father had changed when Allen Lundy came into their lives. "You're a dead man," Allen Lundy had said to him, and four months later he had, indeed, been a dead man. And now people were dying again, and Allen Lundy was mixed up in it somehow.

She walked past David's closed door; let him sleep, she thought, what's the hurry? She stepped outside and breathed deeply, smelling wood smoke, wondering who would be having a fire at this time of day. She heard the duck again and looked for him, but couldn't find him. She walked around to the other side of the house, and stopped dead in her tracks. David's car was gone.

She ran into the house, through the living room, and pulled open the door to David's room. Everything was just the way it had been when they came. The bed was neatly made. He was gone.

On the counter in the kitchen she found the note he left for her: *Thanks for everything. I've thought it over and I have to go by myself; hope you aren't too angry. I'll let you know what happens.*

She crumpled the note into a ball in her fist. "Damn you, David," she said, and her voice sounded hollow in the empty house. "After all this, you still want to be the only one."

She picked up the phone and dialed. It was Sid who answered. "Andy! Where on earth have you been?"

"I told you I'd be OK. David and I came out to this cottage—"

"Is Nickie with you?"

"Nickie? No, I'm here alone. Isn't Nickie there?"

"Oh, God."

"Isn't Nickie there?"

"We've been calling you all night, your apartment, hoping she was with you."

"Where's Nickie?"

"She was supposed to be staying at Janice's, but she never got there. We've been trying to call you. I thought you said you were with this Brett character."

"He left this morning. *What's happened to Nickie?"*

"You'd better get home. All hell's going to break loose."

She hung up the phone. David, she thought, find him.

The sun had been in and out of clouds all morning; it was raining now, just a light passing shower. He turned on the windshield wipers and glanced down at the map that lay open on the seat beside him. He had passed Traverse City and was on Highway 22, heading north. The map showed a state park at the tip of the peninsula; the last town before the park was Northport. It couldn't be a very large town, according to the map. If Allen Lundy had lived in the area since Buddy Kramer was killed, then someone in town ought to know him.

The rain stopped and the sun straggled out. In a few

miles the pavement was dry again. The houses that had lined the road since Traverse City began to thin out. The road still followed the lake shore, and the lake glittered now in the sun. He ought to be in Northport before one.

Once again he thought of Andy, of her finding the note. In his mind's eye he saw her reading it, the anger rising in her dark blue eyes. He chuckled when he imagined her cursing him; then he grew serious again. He wished he'd thought to tell her to stay where she was. There was nowhere safer for her than that cottage. Or, he thought, she should find out where Nickie was and go stay with her.

The road pulled away from the lake, ran through alternating open countryside and sparse woods. The trees this far north were beyond the height of their color; they looked drab now, the red turned to brown, the yellow faded, most of the leaves on the ground. The road came back to the lake at Sutton's Bay. It looked like a tourist town, as he guessed Northport would be. All he had of Allen Lundy were a name and a battered fifteen-year-old picture. In a tourist town, protective of its privacy, how hard would it be to find him?

The road came into Northport from the south, lined with big trees and large houses, then jogged closer to the lake and became a street of small businesses before it turned once again and ran down to the harbor. The highway turned left again just before the harbor, running north to the end of the peninsula. David stopped at a gas station, checked the telephone directory, and found no listing for Allen Lundy. Then he asked the attendant for directions to the post office.

"Is there an Allen Lundy who lives around here?" he asked the clerk at the post office. She'd been counting sheets of stamps, and she looked up at him guardedly.

"Excuse me?"

"I'm looking for Allen Lundy."

"Sorry. No one by that name gets mail here."

"I need to find him. Who would know where he might be?"

"Beats me. Do you have a letter to mail?"

"No."

"Sorry, then, but I can't help you."

He walked out and stood on the sidewalk. The clouds were back again and it looked like rain. He walked down to the harbor and stood for a while, his hands in his pockets, gazing at the few boats still docked there. They rocked gently at their moorings; no one was in sight. At this time of year, he supposed, they would be used mostly on weekends. Even so, it must be almost time to put them up for the season. It began to sprinkle, and he walked back toward town.

By the time he passed the grocery store, it was raining harder, and he ducked inside. There were few customers in the store, and no one was at the check-out. He took the picture from his pocket and showed it to the cashier. "I'm looking for this man," he told her. "His name is Allen Lundy. Does he ever come in here?"

She looked at the picture, then at Brett, then back at the picture, shaking her head. "Does he have a place around here?" she asked.

"I think he does," he said, "or at least he used to."

She handed the picture back, smiling. "We get an awful lot of people coming in, tourists and everything. It would be impossible to remember every face that I see even in one summer."

"But he's not a tourist. He would live here."

"Even so," she said, still smiling, "when you see so many different faces all the time, it's really hard to remember one in particular."

"He'd have moved here about fifteen years ago."

"Really?"

"That's my understanding."

"I'm sorry. I can't help you. You'll have to excuse me now." She turned away from him to wait on a customer.

He went back outside. It was pouring and he stood in the shelter of the doorway, waiting for the rain to let up. The door behind him opened. "Hey, man." He looked to be in his early twenties, dressed in jeans and a faded red flannel shirt. "Hey, man, I heard you back there. No way she's going to help you, man." He was carrying a small bag, holding it by the neck of the bottle inside.

"You're telling me she knows who he is."

"I'm telling you that if she knows who he is, she's not going to tell you. *If*. That's a big if, but if she does, she's not going to tell. You've got to understand this place, man."

"I take it they don't like strangers."

"No, that's not it; that's not it at all. This place is like two towns, like two towns laid atop each other. The natives and the tourists. You think this is just a tourist town? Hell, no, there's other ways to make a living besides that. It's not that people don't like strangers— they just don't want you in their back pockets all the time. Just because we share our town with you doesn't mean we've let you into our lives. If you move here, like I did, maybe eventually you'll become part of the real town. But if you're a tourist, no matter how nice to you people are, you'll never be more than that."

"How long have you been here?"

"Three, four years now. I've got me a little leather place across the street and around the corner there. I'll make anything you want—hat, wallet, belt—mostly belts are what I make."

"If you've been here that long, maybe you know the man I'm looking for. Allen Lundy—have you ever heard of him?"

"Name doesn't ring a bell. Why do you need to find him, anyway?"

"I think he might be able to save someone's life, if I can find him."

"How could he do that?"

"It's a long story; you don't want to hear it."

"Hey, man, I've got all kinds of time. Look, it's quit raining. Why don't you come over to my place and tell me about it? Who knows, maybe you'll find something you'd want to buy, and maybe I'll figure out a way to help you."

"I'm not really in the market for—"

"Hey, be easy. The name is Trim. That's not my real name, of course, but it's what everybody calls me. Come on, it's just across the street."

He ran across the street, and Brett, with no better options at the moment, followed. They went into a dingy one-room shop lighted by a bare bulb hanging from the ceiling. Two dilapidated tables stretched along each side of the room. One was piled with an array of leather goods—wallets, belts, vests, hats, and caps. The other held pieces of tanned leather, still bearing the rough shape of the animals they had once been, and a ragged assortment of knives, hammers, awls, and leather punches. Trim turned and grinned, the edges of his smile lost in the drooping fringes of his mustache. "This is it; it's not so much, but it's all mine. Have a seat." He pulled up a folding chair for himself and motioned toward a cane rocker whose seat sagged ominously. "Now tell me who's the guy you're looking for and how come you're looking for him."

"His name is Allen Lundy. Have you ever heard of him?"

"Can't say that I have. Did I see you showing her a picture? I'm a lot better with faces than I am with names."

David held the picture out to him, and he took it, looking at it intently. "How recent is it?"

"Not very. Twenty years, probably."

"He could be gray by now."

"Or bald."

"Yeah, or bald. He could wear glasses," Trim mused.

"Do you recognize him?"

"I don't think so. What did you say the name is?"

"Allen Lundy."

"What's this about saving a life?"

"I guess I was exaggerating some," Brett backped-aled, wondering how much he ought to tell this young man who might, in the end, prove more trouble than he was worth. "He . . . ah . . . might have some information about . . . about a . . . disease my father died of. They went to school together and were in the war together, and I'm trying to track down just what happened to my father. He, ah, died of something that might have been related to the war."

"How's that going to save a life if your father's already dead?"

"What I'm wondering is . . . if it might be something I could eventually get—if I might die in the same way. You see, at the time that my father died, we thought it was an isolated thing, but then my brother died, too, so now I can't help but wonder if it might be something that's in the family. And if it is, then maybe I could do something to prevent it. But, you know, I need to find out about certain things that my father was exposed to during the war so I'll have a better idea what we might be dealing with." How easy it is, he thought, to get into the story once you've committed yourself to it.

Trim nodded. "And what makes you think this guy—Lundy—might be around here?"

"Years ago he told a friend of mine, who was just a child at the time, that he lived here."

"In Northport?"

"Around here someplace. He said he lived at the end of the little finger."

"Well, that could be anywhere all the way out to the lighthouse. You might try driving out there, see if anybody out that way ever heard of him. In the meantime, I'll ask around to some of my friends and see if anybody's ever heard of him. Of course you've got to understand, that many years ago—hell, that's a long time. The guy could have died in that time."

"I realize that."

"Or moved away. I haven't been here that long myself. This is going on my fifth year. It'd be really easy for me not to know him. But, hey, listen, you go on out there; then stop by on your way back and let me know how you're doing, OK? In the meantime, I'll nose around and see what I come up with. Sort of double the troops, ok?"

The sun was back out, filtering through the trees. Trim stood in the doorway and watched as Brett crossed the street, walked up to the corner, and turned out of sight. Trim stood for a little while longer; then he snapped off the overhead light and stepped outside, closing the door behind him. "OK," he said to himself, as if he had just made up his mind.

More than two hours later, David Brett was driving back into town. He'd followed the blacktop to the end of the peninsula, to the lighthouse, without finding a sign of Lundy. On the way back, he'd stopped at several houses along the road. He'd found an elderly couple who had welcomed the diversion of his visit, had invited him in and given him coffee and cookies and had listened to the story he told them—an expanded and refined version of the one he'd told Trim—but in the end they had looked at each other and shaken their heads. They'd never heard of Allen Lundy; they didn't recognize the picture. At each of the other places the story was just the same. No one knew Al Lundy; no one could recall having seen him.

He considered driving past Trim's shop and not bothering to stop, but there seemed no other recourse, and Trim had appeared genuinely interested. Maybe, just maybe, he'd been able to discover something. But the reality was that David had given up on finding Lundy in Northport. It was just too long ago; too many things could have happened in the meantime. Or, just possibly, Andy had been wrong about what he had told her. He might, after all, have meant Farmington when he said *at your fingertip*. Still, it wouldn't hurt to stop and check it out.

He pulled the car to the curb in front of the shop. Leather Trim, the sign said, red paint on a board weathered to gray. The light was on; now, in late afternoon, it would be almost dark inside the shop, huddled as it was between two much larger buildings, and set back from the street.

Trim looked up from the belt he was working on and smiled. "Any luck?"

"Nothing."

"Sit down. Coffee?" Trim was out of his chair, heading for the back room before David even answered.

"I think I'm pretty coffeed out. I spent an hour or more having coffee with Harold and Geneva Evans. By now we're old friends. Unfortunately, they never heard of Allen Lundy."

"It looks like he must have done a fairly good job of disappearing."

"It looks like it. So it's back to square one for me. Short of going door to door in this town, I'm just about out of ideas."

"But not a perfect one."

"I don't follow you."

"I said, it looks like he must have done a fairly good job of disappearing, but not a perfect one."

David leaned forward in the chair. "You found him?"

"Don't get all excited. Maybe. Maybe I've found him."

"He *is* here, then!"

"Maybe he is. It's worth your going out to check. I would have, but I was afraid I'd miss you if I went out there."

"Where? Where is he?"

"*If* it's him, and that's still an if, he's the caretaker of an old hunting lodge, out on the road you were on, as a matter of fact. You know where the blacktop turns off to the right to go to the Point, where the big summer places are, the place where there's a guard and you can't get in?"

"Is that where he is?"

"No, lucky for you. Just beyond there, on the left, is an old gravel road; well, it's hardly even a road now. You can't see the place from the main road, only this gravel drive, but if you turn off there you can drive part of the way. I think there's a gate across the road after a while, so you won't be able to drive all the way—the gate's locked. You'll have to get out and walk. You'll come to this old lodge—it used to be a skeet-shooting club or something like that. The place hasn't been used for years. It's for sale, I think. There's a guy who's the caretaker, just makes sure no vandals come around, that sort of thing. I got this friend who says he looks sort of the way I described that guy in the picture, and he says the guy's name is Al. That's all he knows. It's worth a try."

"It sure is."

"Want me to go with you?"

"No, it would be better if I go alone."

"That's just as well. I've got some orders I've got to fill. Summer people, you know—fudgies, we call them. All of a sudden they decide they want something, so they write me for it. And I was just about ready to close up shop. Pain in the neck."

"Don't complain. It's business."

"Yeah. Hey, let me know how you come out. I'd be interested." He didn't get up from behind his table when Brett left, but he followed him with his eyes until he'd gotten into the car. Then he rose and went into the back room and picked up the phone. He dialed a number, waited for a moment before it was answered, then spoke just one sentence: "He's on his way."

8

HE TURNED OFF the blacktop onto what had once been a gravel drive. Now the weeds had nearly taken over and only traces of the road remained. The track began climbing almost immediately, ascending toward a bluff that would overlook the bay. Within moments he came to the gate Trim had mentioned—a steel gate—and it was locked. He braked in front of it; the lodge was still out of sight, though he could see now the sloping grounds of what had once been the skeet range. He turned off the motor and reached over to open the glove compartment. From it he pulled a .38, bought yesterday on his way to Ann Arbor to see Andrea.

He got out of the car, gun in hand, walked the few steps to the fence, climbed over it, and started up the steep hill. Partway up he could begin to see the lodge, set well back at the edge of the range. He paused. There was no point in advertising the gun. He slipped it behind his belt, where his jacket would conceal it. The place was for sale, Trim had told him. As far as Allen Lundy was concerned, he could be a man looking to buy a piece of property, nothing more.

He climbed farther and the whole lodge came into view, an old two-story building, painted green. A roofed porch ran around the two sides of the building that he could see. Small windows in the upper floor indicated bedrooms or perhaps dormitory-style bunk rooms. A good possibility for a summer camp, he thought, turning around now that he had crested the hill. As he had guessed, Grand Traverse Bay lay spread out before him. An investor, checking out the site for a possible summer camp. The lodge already built, the obviously extensive grounds, the proximity of the bay just down the hill and across the road. Having heard the place was for sale, he had decided to check it out before getting involved with a realtor. Simple.

There was no one in sight. A caretaker would be . . . where? In the main building? Living in a cottage nearby on the grounds? In the big metal storage shed at the back of the lodge? He walked casually toward the lodge, just a curious passerby, thinking of buying the property. A row of windows downstairs and another upstairs faced him. He could be watching me, he thought. He doesn't know who I am, though. He certainly won't guess that I've traced him here. And then he stopped dead in his tracks with a chilling thought: If he killed Elizabeth, then he's been to Fairfield; he knows where I live, has been in my garage, surely he saw me before he did it. If he takes the time to set up a murder, to know when the victim will be where he can get him, then surely he has seen that victim. *He knows me better than I know him!* All I have is a faded photograph. By now he could be gray, as Trim had said, or bald, or wearing glasses. In a crowd, he could pick me out, but I might not be able to recognize him!

He looked intently at the windows, but the sun, falling now toward the horizon, was coming from his left, shining obliquely on the windows ahead, and they reflected the light. He could see nothing in them. He thought about the gun at his belt, but to take it out would only be a warning. He was a dozen yards or so from the building. Better to keep coming as he had been doing, and hope that Lundy, not expecting him, would be taken by surprise.

He tried the front door of the lodge. It held at first,

then gave way; it had not been locked, only stuck. Playing his role as a prospective buyer, he held the door open only a few inches. "Hello!" he called inside. "Anybody here?" His voice echoed around what must have been an empty room. No one answered. "Hello?" he called, louder this time.

He opened the door wider and stood for a moment in the doorway. "Anybody here?" It was the lodge recreation room, now bare save for a few battered wooden chairs scattered around the room and a billiard table at one end. At the far end of the room a huge stone fireplace reached nearly all the way across the wall and up to the ceiling. At the opposite end, beyond the billiard table, were the stairs to the second floor, and beneath the stairs two doors, both closed.

He stepped inside, leaving the door open behind him. "Anybody here?" he called again. The place remained silent around him. He took a few steps forward, the two closed doors and the stairway ahead of him. He'll know who I am, David kept thinking; he won't be fooled about my being a buyer. He's been to Fairfield, he's seen my house, been in my garage, surely he's seen me.

He took the gun out of his belt and walked cautiously toward the stairs, his eyes on the door ahead.

"Put the gun on the table and turn around slow." The voice came from behind him. He paused, trying to think. *"DO IT!"*

He lay the gun down on the green baize, now dusty with disuse, and turned slowly around. The man was standing in the open doorway, a double-barreled shotgun pointing at Brett's chest, his finger already on the trigger. The man looked weary. He was not gray, nor was he bald, and he did not wear glasses. Even in the fading light David Brett recognized Allen Lundy.

"Before I kill you, I want to know one thing," Lundy said. "How did you know I was here?"

David Brett took a deep breath. Was there anything he could say that would stop Lundy from shooting him now? He thought of Elizabeth dead in the twisted metal that had once been a car, and he knew there was not. "I've been looking for you."

"You could not have found me!"

"I'm here."

"How did you know I was here? Who told you?"

He thought of Andy, of the child that Andy must have been. If he told, would Andy die the sooner? "No one."

"He said someone told you, someone who knew me when they were a kid. It was the curly-headed girl, wasn't it? That oldest girl in the family where even the girls had boys' names. Buddy's daughter."

"He told you? Trim told you? He told you I was coming here?"

"I've got some friends in this town. They look out for me. There's no way you're going to sneak up on Al Lundy. She told you, didn't she?"

"Why are you doing this? Why are you killing all these people? *What happened?"*

"Me? I'm not killing people. But if I have to, I'll kill you, because somebody has to stop it."

"Stop what? What are you talking about?"

"You know damn well what I'm talking about, because you're part of it!"

"Part of what? I'm not part of anything. I only came to find you, to find out why everybody's dying and if you were doing it. Before you shoot me, you ought to have the guts to tell me *why!"*

"What are you talking about? Who's dying?"

"My wife, for one. Blown up when she tried to start our car."

"I don't even know your wife."

"Elizabeth Brett. The least you can do is know her name. You meant to get me, but you got her instead."

"Elizabeth . . ." He frowned. "Who are you?"

"I'm David Brett."

"David Brett is dead."

"No, it was Elizabeth who died."

"David Brett has been dead for years, and his wife was not named Elizabeth."

"You're thinking of my father."

"Who the hell are you?"

"I told you. I'm David Brett. My father went to school with you, was in the army with you."

"You can't be."

"I'll prove it." He made a move with his hand but stopped in midair at Lundy's scream.

"Don't move!" The man had thrust the shotgun forward, had been ready to shoot.

"I was going to get out my wallet. I was going to show you who I am. If you're going to kill me, you ought to have the name straight."

"Slowly. With your left hand. Take it out slowly. Slide it across the floor."

David did as he directed. Without taking his eyes from Brett or his finger from the trigger, the man bent down and picked up the wallet. He flipped it open with his free hand, then quickly glanced down and back up. He looked at David for a long time, searching his face for a resemblance to his father. "If you're really David Brett, why are you here?"

"Because of Elizabeth."

"Whatever happened to your wife, I had nothing to do with it."

"Either you did, or you know who did."

"I don't believe you're him, I don't think you're this David Brett. If you were, you wouldn't have any reason to come here. You wouldn't need me to find out who killed your wife, or whoever she was. You could have stolen this wallet. How do I even know it's yours?"

"Why would I steal it? Why else would I come?"

"You know why."

"*I don't!* That's what I came to find out. Why did my father die? Why did Mike Carpenter and Buddy Kramer die? Why have most of their children died?"

"Children?"

David Brett took a deep breath and tried to calm himself. "My father and the other two had ten children between them. Six of those children are dead, plus assorted others who happened to be in the way."

"You're not dead."

"I would have been. Elizabeth died in my place. You know why. You warned Buddy Kramer four months beforehand that he was going to die. How did you know if you didn't do it yourself?"

"Who told you that?"

"Never mind who told me; it's true, isn't it?"

"Why don't you go back and ask the man who sent you?"

"*No one sent me! What is going on?*"

The man glanced down at the open wallet in his hands again. "Anyone can steal a wallet. Just because you carry it doesn't mean it's yours."

"Look at the picture on the driver's license! It's me, for God's sake, it's me!"

"It's half dark in here. It could be you, but maybe it isn't. Anyway, you could have gotten a license in someone else's name. There's only one reason I've lived as long as I have, and that's because I don't trust nobody. I'm not trusting you on the basis of this one picture."

"There's another picture there, in the folder with the credit cards—two guys on a sailboat. Look at it."

Al Lundy flipped through the credit cards, barely glancing away from Brett, until he came to the picture.

"One of the men is me. It's a good picture; you should be able to recognize me."

"Good Lord." Lundy stared at the picture.

"The other one is my brother. His name was Mike. He's dead—killed in an accident. You ought to recognize him; he looked just like my father did when he was Mike's age."

The older man looked at him with a new curiosity in his eyes. "Why would David Brett's son be looking for me?"

"Because you know and you're the only one left alive. You warned Buddy, or you threatened him, but either way, you knew he was going to die. Whoever killed my father and my brother, killed my wife, and I want to know who it was and why."

Allen Lundy lowered the shotgun just slightly. "Then you didn't come from Victor?"

David Brett stared back in stunned silence. "Who's Victor?"

Allen Lundy held the gun low now, still pointing it at David, as if he weren't quite sure whether to trust him. "Victor Schott, Lester's brother."

"I never heard of either one."

"I don't suppose you did, did you? We didn't exactly sit around talking about Lester after the war. It wasn't exactly something we were proud about. It wasn't something we wanted to remember."

"What do Victor and Lester Schott have to do with this?"

"Let me ask you a question. What did your father tell you about the war?"

"Nothing. He never said anything about it at all. I never heard of you or any of the others either, until my wife was killed. And then Lane Carpenter and Jenny Wilson were shot, and I began to realize that something was going on. It was Shirley Carpenter who told me about you and Buddy."

He lowered the gun, letting it hang from his hand,

pointing toward the floor. "Your father never told you about the war. So you don't know that we all went off together the day after graduation and signed up."

"Shirley Carpenter told me that. The four of you going off in Buddy's car to Indianapolis to join the army."

"Not the four of us. The five of us. Lester Schott went, too, and to understand about what happened after, you're going to have to understand about Lester." For the first time, Al Lundy looked away from David. He gazed out a window, then walked over toward it, still carrying the gun. A fly, trying to get out, buzzed against the glass, and Al Lundy stared at it, or beyond it, for a long time.

9

"EVERY SCHOOL HAS a kid like Lester Schott," Lundy began. "Someone who's always on the edge of things, never part of the group. When I think about Lester in those days, I think of him grinning. He always grinned, like maybe he thought by grinning he'd lead us to think he was OK. Or maybe he was really that happy all the time, I don't know. We four—your dad and Mike and Buddy and me—we were the big men at school. What these days you'd call the jocks, although in those days it wasn't at all bad. Okay, we were hellions, I suppose. We got into a lot of scrapes, but we never did anything serious. Nothing really wrong. Nothing illegal.

"And Lester, you know, he was always trying to—to be part of it. Like he'd come up with that grin and offer us a pack of gum, like it was some big deal, like if we accepted a damn pack of gum from him we were doing him some big favor. Here we were going out by the lake in Buddy's car and smoking *cigarettes*, for God's sake, and he thought it was such a big deal to have a pack of gum. So we'd humor him along sometimes, you know, let him think he was a big deal because we'd let him ride in Buddy's car. And he'd sit there, grinning from ear to ear—he looked like a pixie or something like that. He had that kind of face. He was skinny, but his face was round and his ears sort of stuck out—just like you think of a pixie. And we'd be laughing at him behind his back.

"I guess that sounds like we were cruel. Well, maybe we were. But in those days, you know, people sometimes did those sorts of things to people who were different. Hell, people used to drive past the county home just to look at the crazy people there; I mean, it was a Sunday afternoon entertainment, driving past there. People would joke about it, about being sent to the county home if they acted too weird. For all I know, they still do. I don't think we were trying to be cruel to him. Maybe, in our own way, we were even being nice to him. Hell, everyone else'd just ignore him completely. We'd at least let him do things with us every once in a while. Maybe we were laughing at him, but we weren't ignoring him like everybody else did. And he never seemed to know, so what was the harm? He thought it was a big deal to get to do things with us.

"We got him drunk once. He'd never had anything in his life before. We got some liquor and went out in the country, and we parked along the road and we were drinking, you know, like boys do—showing off. Like guys do when they're too young to know any better. And somehow his name came up and all of a sudden we decided it'd be a real hoot to get him out there and juice him up. So we went cruising all over town, looking for him. We finally stopped at his house—where else would he have been? Nobody else did stuff with him. And we got him to come out with us, and we went back out and we poured that stuff down him until he was rolling on the floor, until he pissed in his pants and everything. And we were rolling on the floor, too, laughing. And Buddy was swearing because it was his car that was getting puked in and pissed in. That was one hell of a night.

"Afterwards, when I got to thinking about it, I decided that Lester probably wouldn't ever speak to us again. After all, we'd made such a fool of him. But, you know, it wasn't like that at all. It was like he thought he was part of our gang after that, because we'd let him get drunk with us. We'd *let* him! He was so . . . so naive that he thought that was a sign that we'd accepted him. And he was back, hanging around, grinning his grin. Hell, the more we made fun of him, the more he hung around. It was like he was a dog or something. You know how a dog is: The more you throw sticks for him to chase after, or make him jump through the hoop, the more he hangs around, loving it. That was how Lester was, like that kind of attention was better than what he'd get otherwise, which was no attention at all."

All the time he'd been talking, he was facing away, looking out the window. He turned now toward the room again and looked at David, who still stood beside the billiard table. David's gun still lay on it. Lundy stepped toward the table and lay his shotgun on it, across from David's.

"I got me a couple of rooms in the back over there," he said, gesturing toward the doors. "We can sit in there. It's a little more comfortable." He walked forward, moving past David. He opened one of the doors and turned on an overhead light. It was a kitchen, what had obviously once been the lodge's kitchen, now devoid of almost all equipment but an old gas range and a battered refrigerator.

"I been at this place a long time, since before it closed up for good. They're letting me stay until they sell it, which may or may not take a while, seeing as how they're asking an arm and a leg for it. I keep an eye on the place, and in return I get a roof over my head. When the lodge was in business, I used to keep it clean, and cut and split the wood for the fireplace, that kind of stuff. No one bothered me, and I didn't bother anybody. Want a cup of coffee?" He motioned for David to sit down at the tiny table.

"I went to see your ex-wife. She says to say hello."

Lundy didn't say anything; his back was turned. He reached for an enamel mug that was in the sink, poured out some cold black coffee, then rummaged around in a cupboard until he found another mug. He peered into it, rinsed it out, and poured from an enamel coffeepot that had been sitting on the stove. He doesn't have company much, David thought. "I said I went to see your ex-wife," he said as Lundy set a mug down in front of him.

"I heard you." Lundy walked back to the drainboard, got his own mug, and joined David at the table. It was covered with yellow plaid oilcloth, dirt-smudged and greasy to the touch and held down by thumbtacks at the corners. "How is she?"

"She seems good. She was making pies like mad when I was there."

Lundy smiled. "She made a hell of a pie. Melt in your mouth. That woman could really cook. She's married again, isn't she?"

"Yes."

Allen Lundy leaned forward in his chair and took a noisy sip of coffee. "We had a daughter; she was born dead."

"She told me."

He seemed surprised at that, and a little hurt, as if no one had a right to tell that but himself. "It was what I deserved. It was what we all deserved."

"You talk as if you think it was some kind of punishment."

"That's what I think it was."

"What happened to Lester?"

"He died. He was killed. We took him along as a joke, like all the other jokes we'd played on him, like taking his gum as if it were a big deal, like getting him drunk, like making him go with us to steal watermelons out of some farmer's field; and he ended up dead. He was the only innocent and he ended up dead."

"It wasn't your fault. He might have gone anyway, even if you hadn't taken him with you."

90

"No. If we hadn't taken him, he wouldn't have been able to go."

"You can't be sure of that."

"Yes, I can. He was younger than us. We forged his father's name to the papers. If we hadn't done that, he couldn't have gone." Lundy's eyes fell to the surface of the table. With the thumb and forefinger of his right hand he creased the oilcloth along the edge of the table. "You know what we called him?" he said softly. "We called him Shitless. It wasn't just us; everybody called him that, everybody in the army."

"Shitless?"

"It came from his name. At roll call, the sergeant would yell out, 'Schott, Lester!' It only took a couple of roll calls before everybody started calling him Shitless from that, from 'Schott, Lester.' It was bound to happen, his name being what it was and him being like he was. Anyone who knew him would have called him that. Shitless. It was obvious he didn't have the guts for war, that he wasn't going to kill people, that the bombs and the guns would terrify him. It was obvious he was a real innocent."

"I'm surprised you all were able to stay together during the war. I thought the army didn't do that."

"They did in those days. They were pouring guys into Europe as fast as they could get them. Hell, if you enlisted and had two arms and two legs, you'd be on the line somewhere—like as not, next to your buddies. There was no way Shitless should have been out there, but he was. We covered for him in training and we covered for him as best we could on the line. It was the only way. We did it at first for the laughs during training, but later it was because we could see it was the only way he was going to survive. The best thing we could do was keep him behind us, to let him hide behind us and not have to shoot or be shot. But in the end it didn't matter." Al took a long drink of his coffee. "In the end he was dead anyway. A mine got him, or maybe it was a bomb. One minute he was behind me, the next minute he was gone, just like that."

"Even so, his brother—Victor—can't be killing everyone because of that."

"Why not?"

"Because it wasn't your fault! And it sure as hell isn't my fault."

"Let me tell you something. We all went to war thinking it was going to be another lark—just like all the things we'd done in high school, the ultimate lark— thinking we were going to be heroes. And what we ended up was killers. We're the ones who should be dead. Shitless is the one who should have lived. We had no right to take him with us. And we had even less right to come back and take up our lives as if nothing had happened, breeding more children to carry out more wars. We should not have come back; we should not have had children. I had a child and it was born dead. That's what I deserved and that's what your father deserved, too. That's what we all deserved, for our children to be dead, because we killed children. We bombed them, and we threw grenades into towns where women and children lived, and the innocents died. I was being punished for that when my child was born dead, for all the children that had been killed, or that never lived because of the war. Have you ever seen those pictures of the cemeteries over there? Row after row of white crosses. One of those is Shitless, I suppose. He was one of the innocents, and he died. We were the guilty ones, and we survived. There's no sense to it. You aren't going to like this, but in my gut I know that you should not be alive. Shitless never had any children; why should your father have had any? What made your father better than him? Nothing. Your father was worse, because he went to be a hero and he ended up a killer. We all did. Only Shitless kept his innocence. You should not have been born. Neither should any of the others. We—your father and I and the rest—we forfeited your right to live when we became killers."

"We didn't start that war, you know. We weren't the ones who were putting people in gas chambers."

"No. That's right. We didn't put people in gas chambers. We only took people like Shitless into war with us as a joke, and then watched them die."

A fly walked across the yellow tabletop. Elizabeth was dead, and Elizabeth was an innocent, too, as was the child she might have had. And Jenny and the child she might have had. "He can't keep on doing this. He can't go on killing in revenge over and over again. It's not going to bring his brother back."

Lundy stared at him across the table, his pale blue eyes squinting nearsightedly. "No, it's not."

"How long have you known he was doing this?"

"It wasn't like I just knew one moment. It was like it gradually came to me, like it dawned on me over a period of time. He was in Fairfield once, years ago—it was 1964, as a matter of fact. He doesn't live there now, and he didn't live there then. I don't know where he lives. He was in town for our class reunion, that's how I remember the date. I didn't want to go; that kind of thing don't interest me, never did. And things were never the same after the war. I never—never could get my life on track, it seemed. But Evelyn wanted to go. She loved a party! Just loved a party. There was so much in her life that was unhappy, so much that I . . . disappointed her about. I couldn't not go, she wanted to so bad. So we went. And Mike Carpenter and his wife were there. Your father wasn't. Buddy wasn't, either.

"Victor Schott was there, and he cornered me. He had this drink in his hand and he boxed me in against the wall, and he said to me in this sarcastic way—it seemed like he was a little drunk—'You never told me what happened to my brother in the war. You never told me how he died.' He had me against the wall and what could I say? His brother was dead, for God's sake; he'd been dead for almost twenty years. I said that; I said, 'That was twenty years ago.' He looked me in the eyes then— maybe he wasn't drunk after all—and he said, 'For you it's twenty years ago, old history. You've forgotten all about it, haven't you? But it doesn't change things. He's still as dead as he was that day, and it's still just as much your fault. Yours and Mike's and Buddy's and Dave's. You all go on living as if he never existed, and you have no right.' There was such hate in his eyes, such anger. And there was nothing I could say to him, because even then, in my heart, I knew he was right.''

He got up and poured more coffee. "Sometime later Mike was dead. He died in a boating accident. That's all anyone thought it was, even me at first. Except that I felt some kind of relief, as if a little bit of a burden I'd been carrying had passed from me. You can say it was guilt— maybe it was. But I felt somehow that it was justified. It wasn't until your father died and I heard about it that I began to wonder if they might be more than accidents. Maybe it was God, I thought. Or maybe it was Victor, because Victor believed we had no right to live when Lester was dead. For a long time I rolled that around in my head, not knowing what to do with it.''

"Why didn't you go to the police?"

"The police? Would they have believed me? Would it have made sense to them? No, it didn't even make sense to Buddy when I went and told him. He thought I was out of my mind. 'It's over,' he kept saying to me. 'That's more than twenty years ago. No one in their right mind goes around avenging a death after twenty years.' It seemed so logical when he said it, but still I knew, *I knew*, what was happening. I knew it was Victor."

"So you tried to warn Buddy, but he wouldn't believe you."

"I stayed with him for a while. He was a good guy, but he kept telling me I was carrying around a load of guilt, that I ought to get rid of it and make something of myself. Like he had. He kept putting himself up to me as an example of what I could have done with my life. Except that I could tell he felt guilty, too. He never admitted it, but I could tell. It was the first time I ever lived with a family since I was a kid myself. I didn't really live with them, but I stayed over the garage in a room they had there. I was around. Buddy had five kids, all little kids. The oldest, that girl, that curly-headed one, she was a honey. She would have understood, if I had been able to tell her, but I never could. Finally Buddy got mad at me and sent me away. I already knew where I was going; I'd already been up here and I liked it. It's quiet, you can get away from people. You can hide. As guilty as I felt, I didn't want to die. I just wanted to be alone, to forget all those things, not to bother anyone, and not have anyone bother me. I told that little girl where I was going to be. I knew Buddy was going to die, and then she'd be without a father. I guess I imagined I could be a father to her, if she needed me."

"She's grown into a very attractive young woman."

"She's the one who told you where to find me."

"Yes." David nodded.

"And now he's killing the children."

"He must be out of his mind. It doesn't make any sense to kill us. We had nothing to do with it."

"You're your father's son. You're carrying on his name, carrying on his bloodline. You're doing for your father what no one ever had a chance to do for Lester.

What Victor is thinking is that you should not have been born, and he's setting about to take care of that mistake."

"That's crazy! You talk as if you think he has a right."

"He has a right? I don't know about that. But I do understand it. I know why he's doing it."

"He has to be crazy! He has to be out of his mind!"

Allen Lundy looked away, not saying anything.

"Why didn't he kill you?"

"He never found me. Until you showed up, no one ever came here looking for me. There was no way anyone could have found me."

"You told Andrea."

Allen Lundy shrugged. "Maybe I wanted her to know."

"If Victor had asked her the same questions I did, she would have told him. She wouldn't have known not to."

"I guess you can make out of that what you want."

"A person might say that you wanted him to find you, that the guilt you felt made you want him to kill you."

"A person could. I also could have stayed in Fairfield and gotten killed, if I'd wanted to die."

"He might be crazy, but he's very smart. Until Elizabeth, it always looked like an accident. No one ever suspected it was murder."

"Victor Schott was the smartest kid in school, a bookworm. *He* didn't go to the war like the rest of us did; *he* went to officer's training school. When he was done there, the war was over."

"What else do you know about him?"

"Nothing much. He was a loner, but he was one by choice, not like Lester, who really wanted to have friends. Nobody liked Victor; he was one of those kids who knew the answers when no one else did. Mike and your dad were smart enough, maybe smarter than Victor, for all I know, but they didn't trade on their brains like he did. You can tell I didn't like him very much."

"You don't have any idea where he is?"

"Nope."

"For some reason, he's changed his style of killing. After more than ten murders, he's letting them look like murders instead of accidents. If he's so smart, he's doing it for a reason."

"Maybe it's just that he doesn't have much time left. Maybe he's sick or dying and he doesn't have time to set up a so-called accident. Maybe he's got to get the rest over in a hurry."

"Maybe." How long does it take to set up a hit-and-run? How long do you have to follow a man around before you have the opportunity to do something to his car to make it stall on the highway so that he'll have to walk to the nearest service station so that you can hit him as he walks along that highway? How long does it take? How much patience? And then why turn around fifteen years later and simply walk up to a car parked beside a lake and pump a bullet into the forehead of a teenager and another one into his girlfriend when you probably don't even know—how could you?—that she's carrying his baby? And did he know about Elizabeth? Did she die because she, too, was carrying a baby, or because she took the car on a day that her husband ordinarily would have?

Allen Lundy's chair scraped the floor as he stood. "Would you like another cup of coffee?"

"No, thanks." David looked at his watch. "I'm going to have to be leaving."

"Don't go. You can spend the night here. There's all kinds of beds. There's heat; I can turn the heat on."

"No, really, it'd be too much—"

"Please."

"I'm sure I can find a place in town. Didn't I see a motel—"

"Stay here tonight. I've got clean sheets, I can cook supper and breakfast for you."

"I can find a motel. There's no need—"

"Yes, there is." Lundy was standing over him, looking down at him, pain mirrored on his face. "You have to stay."

"I don't understand what you're trying to say."

"Do I have to spell it out? Do I have to spill my guts out in front of you? Do I have to tell you about all the nights I woke up screaming and Evelyn had to . . . Do I have to tell you things I don't want to talk about to make you understand why you have to?"

And I've brought it all back, David thought. The pain and the guilt and the fear. They're all back—in his eyes, in his face, in the way his hands move restlessly. I've made him remember the things he came here to forget. "Yes, OK," he said. "I'll stay."

10

THEY WERE LEANING over the concrete railing of a bridge, watching the water flow by beneath them. She picked up a stick from the walkway and threw it as far upstream as she could, and then they both watched it float toward them. It caught for a moment in a backwater eddy and she cheered it on, grinning when it came back into the mainstream and passed below them, beyond the other side of the bridge and out of sight. "My boat," she said, "taking me downstream on all kinds of adventures. All I have to do is say the magic word and I'll be tiny and can get on my boat and go off wherever I want." She was laughing, but her eyes, dark blue as he had never before imagined eyes could be, were serious.

And then there was a car coming. It came from their right, driving around the bend, obscured by birches and thick pines until it was nearly at the bridge. It came over the bridge with a rush, and just at the middle something was thrown out, something that clattered on the road like a beer can still full of beer and then the car was gone, off down the road, leaving a trail of dust behind it, and something on the bridge that sounded like a beer can but wasn't. Too late, he guessed what it must be and he grabbed her arm to pull her away with him. But she turned toward him in surprise, not understanding, laughing still, and that's the way her face was when the explosion came.

He was running then, clawing his way as the bridge shuddered around him, still hanging onto her arm, still trying to pull her with him. But the bridge crumbled beneath her feet and she went through, screaming, and he was still hanging onto her arm trying to pull her up with him to safety. Cracks skittered across the concrete and the bridge fell away, piece by piece, into the water, and the part around him shuddered and dislodged, and they were both falling toward the water and it seemed as if they would never reach it.

He woke with a start, sitting up in the unfamiliar bed in the unfamiliar room. Where was he? What had happened? Then he remembered Allen Lundy and the lodge and his promise to stay the night. But it was Allen Lundy who was supposed to have the bad dreams, not he.

Why had he dreamed of Andrea? Why hadn't it been Elizabeth? Why hadn't he seen Elizabeth in his dream— the only place he could see her now? *Elizabeth,* he thought, and he ached to see her again. It will never be the same; it will never be the way it was. *You must have loved her very much,* Andrea had said. He thought about being in the canoe with Andrea and thinking about Elizabeth, and he couldn't understand why he was dreaming about Andrea when he wanted to dream about Elizabeth. This is a nightmare I'm living, he thought; is it going to be in my dreams too?

I'm psychic, Evelyn McAndrews had said. *He's alive; I'd know if he were dead. I'm psychic.* Did he believe that? Could a person really be like that, knowing when there was no way to know? Was that what the dream was, not just a dream but a warning? That Andrea was next, and then he himself would die? Andrea, where are you? Are you somewhere safe? Are you with Nickie?

He closed his eyes as a great weariness came over him. What time is it, he wondered, without even the energy to open his eyes and look at the lighted digits of his watch. Sleep, blessed sleep, stole over him, and the last sound he heard was the irregular breathing of Allen

Lundy, lying on a cot only a few feet away. Allen Lundy, who'd been afraid to spend the night alone, was sleeping like a baby. It was David who was having the nightmares.

He awoke again with a start. Something, some noise, had awakened him, but now it was quiet again. He lay in the dark suddenly wide awake, wondering what the noise had been. Silence hung around him like a cloak. Lying in the dark in the unfamiliar room, it seemed almost unbearably quiet. He listened, straining to hear a sound, any sound at all, that would relate to the world of the real, that would let him know that this was not another nightmare, but there was nothing. Nothing. . . . *Why couldn't he hear Allen Lundy breathing?*

He slipped out of bed, bare feet on the cold bare floor, and crept over toward Lundy's cot, only a darker mass in the dark room. He reached out his hand to touch the cot, fearful of what he might find, and there was nothing. A rumpled sheet, covers thrown back, nothing more. Allen Lundy was gone. He stood up in the dark, his mind racing. *Was the noise he heard Allen Lundy? Or had Lundy gotten up to investigate? What was happening? Where was Allen Lundy?* And then he heard it again, almost felt it more than heard it, a soft thud against the side of the building. He was in Allen Lundy's room, right next to the kitchen. Each room has its own entrance from the outside. Whatever was making the noise was just outside the bedroom wall.

Brett slipped back to his own bed, felt for his clothes piled at the end of it, slipped on his pants and shirt, and grabbed his shoes. Almost as an afterthought, he felt around for his jacket until he found it—the gun was in the pocket. He held his shoes and jacket in one hand and moved quietly into the kitchen. He peered out the window, but there was nothing to see in the angle of vision it offered. He felt along the wall for the kitchen door, then realized that whoever was outside would see him coming out. Desperately, he tried to remember the main room of the lodge—the door he'd come in along the front side of the building, the long fireplace on the adjoining wall, a long wall of windows—if he broke a window, it would be heard. *Who was outside? Where was Allen Lundy?* There was no other way out—the front door or the windows. Then he saw again in his mind's eye the fireplace wall, and right in the corner, at the edge of the stone fireplace, a door through which wood could be brought. It was at the opposite end of the building from the kitchen and the bedroom.

He felt in the dark for the door, found it, and moved into the main room. The two long rows of windows afforded little light—there was no moon. Wooden chairs had been scattered across the room randomly; bumping into one would make enough noise to alert whoever was outside. He chose the long route, feeling his way along the wall, one hand holding his shoes and jacket, the other sliding against the wall, across the windows and wall until he came to the corner and the door that was just beyond it. Carefully, he turned the knob to make no sound, but the door held. He pulled hard, thinking it was just stuck, but it wouldn't budge. Perhaps a bolt held it? He felt along the edge of the door, but there was nothing, and then he found the lock beneath the doorknob—and the key was in it. He turned the key, the latch clicked back. He stood for a moment, listening, but he could hear nothing. Then he turned the knob again and slowly pulled the door open. Just outside he could see a tall pile of wood against the side of the building, a narrow step down to the ground, a patch of grass, and then, perhaps twenty yards away, the deep darkness of the woods. He'd run for the woods, lose himself in their darkness, and then slip around to the other side of the building and find out who was there. He took a deep breath and ran toward the woods, seeing nothing but its darkness ahead of him, hearing nothing, feeling the cold damp grass and weeds under his bare feet.

The moment he hit the woods a low-hanging branch knocked him in the face and he stepped on something sharp among the leaves—a stone, a broken bottle? It was too dark to see. He stopped, turned around to see if he could see anything, and just then, with the roar of a thousand storms, the whole end of the lodge burst into flame.

He stepped back in awe, then farther back in fear and horror. Someone had set the building on fire; someone was still trying to kill him, someone who knew he was here! *Where the hell was Allen Lundy?*

Even at this distance, forty yards or more from the opposite end of the building that was on fire, he felt the heat against his face. *And the light!* He moved farther back into the shadows of the woods. He'd forgotten about the branch that had hit him in the face, about the pain in his foot. All he could think of was getting away. Whoever had set the place on fire must not see him, must not know that he had gotten away, must think he was still inside the building.

He slipped his shoes on, pulled on his jacket, and kept moving away from the building, running parallel to the clearing, trying desperately not to get lost in the woods. As he ran farther from the lodge, he moved closer to the edge of the woods, running still in their shelter, but as close as possible to the clearing, in order not to get hopelessly lost. He had to get away. As soon as anyone saw the fire, the alarm would be raised, firemen would be called, onlookers would show up. Standing on a hill as the lodge did, the fire would be seen for miles and would attract the curious, perhaps among them some of Allen Lundy's friends. And at least one of those friends knew that someone had been in Northport looking for Allen Lundy, someone out of Lundy's past, perhaps someone who had enough against Lundy to want to set the place on fire and kill him in the process. He stopped running and looked back at the lodge. The whole place was engulfed in flames, but not a person was in sight. *Where was Allen Lundy?*

He dashed across the clearing, across what had once been the skeet range, and slammed abruptly into a barbed-wire fence. He spread its wires gingerly, crawled through, skittered down the embankment, and plunged into more trees. He turned to his right and ran along the edge of the embankment. There were no sirens yet, no signs of alarm. He had to get away before anyone showed up. He was not yet out of the trees when he saw the ghostly white of the car he had parked close to the locked gate. He ran around its side, fumbled in his pants pocket for the keys, unlocked it and got inside. He started the engine and backed up furiously, just missing a ditch along the side of the drive. Back onto the road—no cars in sight—he gunned the engine and drove away. He was just driving through Northport when the fire sirens began to wail. He would be halfway to Traverse City before they would even think to put out an alarm for him, and once beyond Traverse City, there would be no way for them to find him.

Only Allen Lundy knew his name and where he had come from, and Allen Lundy had undoubtedly died in the fire. Or else he had started it.

He drove on, trying not to think, but the thoughts kept coming. What had happened to Allen Lundy? If he'd awakened at the sounds outside, why hadn't he wakened David? And if he'd started the fire himself, why? Had that whole story about Lester and Victor Schott been made up just to throw him off guard? But why? Allen Lundy had held a gun on him, had been in a position to shoot him if he'd wanted to. And if Allen Lundy hadn't set the lodge on fire, who had? Who else knew he was there? Only one person—Trim. But there was no reason for Trim to kill him. Whoever had set fire to the lodge had meant to kill the person (or persons) inside—it had gone up in flames right at the bedroom corner of the building. *Who? Why?*

11

"MORE COFFEE?"

David Brett nodded absently, and the waitress refilled his cup. "Is there a telephone?"

"Sure. Back there." She pointed vaguely with her left hand.

At the telephone he dialed a number, taking it from a torn piece of paper in his hand. The phone rang several times and he glanced at his watch. When the receiver was finally lifted, there was a pause, then a tentative voice. "Hello?" It didn't sound like Andrea.

"Mrs. Jacobs?"

"Who is this?" The voice was shrill, almost out of control.

"This is David Brett. I came to see you a few days ago—" The rest of what he would have said was lost in a scream, and then the receiver was slammed down and there was silence. David stared at the receiver in his hand and all he could think of was Andrea.

He paid the bill and left the restaurant, got into the car and began driving. Andrea's dead, he kept thinking. He's gotten to Andrea and killed her.

But she couldn't be dead. He'd told her to go someplace safe; surely she would have done that, wouldn't she? *Wouldn't she?*

He was on the freeway again, driving, just driving. He didn't even know what direction he was taking. Eliza-

106

beth was dead. His father was dead. Mike was dead. Mike Carpenter and Buddy Kramer were dead. Lane and Jenny were dead. All those other people he'd never seen or heard of before this started happening were dead. And now Andrea . . .

With a sudden swerve he pulled off the highway, and the car behind him let out a blast from its horn as it passed, the sound of the horn fading off down the road. He slammed his fist against the steering wheel in anger, and then did it again and again. When he stopped, he stared coldly ahead, down the length of the highway, seeing and yet not seeing the cars that sped by in both directions. No one else knew what he knew. No one would believe it if he told them. If it was ever going to stop, he was the only person who would do it. He heard the rush of cars going by, but he felt very much alone, and he spoke aloud into the emptiness of the car. "For Elizabeth." And his breath caught, because he still couldn't really think of Elizabeth dead. "For Elizabeth and all the others. Whoever you are, you're going to die."

But first he had to find out about Andrea.

He waited until late in the evening, when someone else ought to be home, and then he called again. This time the phone rang only once, and it was a man who answered.

"Mr. Jacobs?" David guessed.

"Who is this?" the voice demanded.

"My name is David Brett, and I—"

"Stop calling this number."

"Wait! Don't hang up! Listen to me; I have to know. Is Andrea all right?"

"I'm not going to discuss that matter on the phone."

"Look, I know your wife is upset, but you must have talked with Andrea. She must have told you that whoever killed her father is after me too. He's tried twice. I'm not trying to hurt her; I just want to know if she's all right."

"Yes, she is." The voice was curt.

"Is she someplace safe?"

"I'm not going to tell you where she is."

"All right, all right. Just make sure she's safe, someplace he can't possibly know. Believe me, don't take any chances. He knows everything."

"That's obvious."

Almost as an afterthought, it occurred to him to ask, "How about Nickie?"

There was no response.

"Oh, good Lord, don't tell me something's happened to Nickie?"

"Do you know who is doing this?"

"Is she . . . *dead?*"

There was a long moment of silence. Then, "Yes."

"Oh, God."

"Hadn't you better go to the police?"

He thought of Decker in Fairfield and his anger became almost uncontrollable. "No! No, I can't! I've been to the police and they won't . . . they don't believe any of this. No, this is something I'm going to have to do myself."

"They have facilities at their disposal that you couldn't possibly—"

"No! I'm going to take care of this myself."

"And in the meantime? Aren't you being selfish? What happens while you're trying? How many more will die before you find him?"

"There are only three of us left—Andrea, another young woman, and myself. Andrea's safe, you say. So is Joan. As long as they stay in hiding—"

"And meanwhile . . .?"

108

"Meanwhile I find him. It's not going to be done any other way."

"Don't be stupid. Call the police."

"Keep Andrea safe." David hung up. There was no way he was going to call in the police. This was *his* battle. They'd lost their chance when Decker had accused him of his own wife's murder.

He dialed another number, taken from another scrap of paper he'd had in his wallet. A woman answered.

"This is David Brett. Is Shirley Carpenter there?"

"No, she isn't." The voice was cold.

"Is she OK? Is Joan OK?"

"Yes, as far as I know."

"What do you mean, as far as you know?"

"I mean, as far as I know. That's what I said, isn't it?" the voice responded testily. "What business is it of yours?"

"Can you get a message to them? I have to talk with Shirley."

"Maybe."

"Can you or can't you?"

"I might be able to."

"How long will it take?"

"I don't know. A day, maybe less."

"Oh, for God's sake! *I'm on her side!*"

"I don't know you from a hole in the wall."

"Just get the message to her. Have her call me, David Brett." He looked down at the motel telephone and read off the number. "As soon as possible."

"I'll do what I can."

"I'll be here. Try not to make it too long."

"I said I'd do what I could." She hung up.

He stared out the window, wondering how long he was going to have to wait.

*   *   *

Phillip Decker leaned back and gazed at the man seated across the desk from him. "How do you know he got away?"

"Because his car was gone. He was driving a white station wagon—one of them little cars."

"Someone else might have taken it."

The older man shook his head. "No. He would have locked it. He would have had the keys. It happened too fast. No one else would have been able to."

"It takes about six seconds to break into a locked car. It sat there all night, didn't it?"

The man's watery eyes stared at Decker, and Decker wondered absently if he needed glasses. "I'm telling you he didn't die in the fire. He got away."

Decker leaned forward and put his elbows on the desk. "He's blown your cover, you know. Now this Victor Schott knows where you've been hiding. He'll be coming after you again."

"No, he won't. He thinks I'm dead."

"He followed Brett there. He must know Brett was looking for you."

"Oh, he knows that, all right; but he thinks I died in the fire."

Decker raised his eyebrows, but didn't say anything.

"You know small towns, Decker. You've lived here practically all your life, haven't you?" Without waiting for a response, Lundy went on. "Around Northport, the place people hang out is the Happy Hour. It's kind of a bar. I talked to a friend of mine, someone who's a fireman, and he did it for me. They're all volunteer firemen around there, you know. He went to the Happy Hour and let it drop that they'd found a body in the wreckage. He did a real good job of it, too. Said that the sheriff was keeping it quiet until they did an arson investigation, that it wasn't supposed to get out that they'd found a body. You know how things like that get around in a small town. It won't matter what the sheriff says now, nobody's going to believe it, not when one of the firemen says something like that. Victor Schott may have guts, but no stranger is going to walk up to the burning building and make sure there aren't any dead bodies there. No, he'll have waited around to hear the gossip, and he'll have heard about the body."

"You must have some pretty good friends up there."

Lundy nodded. "I ain't got a lot, but what I have take care of me pretty good."

"What if Schott thinks it was Brett's body?"

"He won't think that; Brett's car left. He'll know it had to have been Brett getting away."

"You could have been nice to Brett. You could have let Schott think they found two bodies."

"I could have. But, be realistic, one body the sheriff might keep secret; two bodies would be a different story."

"So where do you think Brett went?"

"He'll have gone looking for Victor Schott."

"And where does Victor live?"

"Beats me."

"Does Brett know you're still alive?"

"If he got out of there—and he must have—then he probably knew I wasn't in there, either."

"And when we find Victor, we'll find him. Is that what you think?"

"No doubt about it. He'll go looking for Victor."

"What do you think he'll do when he finds him?"

"He's going to kill him."

"Did he tell you that?"

"No. I don't even think he knows it himself, but that's what's in the back of his mind. When he finds Victor, he'll realize that's why he came after him."

"Will he shoot first, or will he give Victor a chance to talk?"

"Oh, he's a talker, that one. He wants to know why. He won't kill him until he's had a chance to hear it from Victor himself. What if Brett gets there before you do?"

"He won't." Decker straightened some papers on his desk. "We appreciate it, Mr. Lundy."

Allen Lundy stood uncertainly. "What are you going to do?"

"We're going to wrap everything up. Where will you be if we want to get hold of you?"

"I don't think you're going to need me anymore," Lundy said, going out the door.

I don't think so, either, Decker thought, watching him go. But I wish I could be sure we'd find Victor Schott before Brett does. As soon as Lundy had passed through the outer office, Decker punched the intercom. "It's Decker," he said brusquely. "When Jack checks in, relay the call to me, wherever I am, no matter what time it is."

"Got it."

Decker stood behind his desk. Somewhere out there David Brett was looking for Victor Schott. Phillip Decker was going to have to beat him to it.

The sound of the telephone in the little room was shrill. David Brett reached for it, hesitated a moment, then answered it.

"David? It's Shirley Carpenter. Where are you?"

"You won't believe it. I'm in a motel near Detroit somewhere."

"You found Buddy's widow, then?"

"I found more than that. I've been to see Al Lundy."

"He's alive? How did you find him?"

"It's a long story. Are you okay? Is Joan with you?"

"She is now. I don't know how much longer she'll stay. She wants to get back to work."

"*She has to stay!* Do whatever you have to do, but make her stay with you."

112

"She's a grown woman, David."

"She'll be a dead woman if she goes back home. Look, in the last few days he's killed another one. There's only three of us left. She can't go back."

"Will you talk to her? She thinks I'm a little dotty after Lane. In fact, that's the only reason she's stayed as long as she has. She thinks I've gone off my track."

"If it keeps her there with you, go off it some more. Where are you, anyway?"

"I'm at—"

"Never mind, don't tell me. But who was it I called?"

She laughed. "That's my sister-in-law. Mike's sister. She thinks she's wandered into the middle of a spy novel or something. She's having the time of her life. We've got passwords and codes and everything."

"It's not a bad idea. He's out there and he's killing people. Nickie Kramer must have been seventeen or eighteen. She's the latest." He decided not to tell her about the fire.

"Is it Allen Lundy?"

"No, it's not. Have you ever heard of Victor Schott?"

"Victor?"

Of course. They'd been in school together; he'd forgotten. Everyone in Fairfield knows everyone else.

"David? Victor Schott? *He's* the one? But why? None of those guys had anything to do with Victor."

"How about his younger brother? Lester?"

She didn't say anything for a while. Finally she asked him, "What do you know about Lester?"

"I could ask you the same thing."

"He was a year or two younger. The kind of kid who's always on the outside looking in. He trailed after them a lot, wanted to be a part of things. At the time, I suppose we thought it was funny. Now it seems pathetic."

"Is that all you know?"

"I don't know what you mean. He was always around."

"Shirley, they took him to war with them. He was killed over there."

"Oh, God." She hadn't known.

"They carried around a load of guilt about that, especially Lundy. They signed the papers for Lester—he was too young to go without his parents' permission. They forged his father's name."

"That's why Mike always . . . All of a sudden a lot of things become clear."

"And that's what Victor Schott is doing."

"Revenge? He's doing it for revenge? But that's crazy! How many has he killed? For Lester? What's he killing little children for?"

"Yes, it's crazy, but he's doing it. And what's just as crazy is that it all makes sense to Al Lundy. He doesn't seem to think there's anything wrong with it."

"That can't be. Al was a very gentle person."

"And what happens to a very gentle person when he goes off to war and starts killing people for no other reason than that they happen to wear the wrong uniform, or live in the wrong country? What happens to a person like that when he sees that war can mean killing old people and women and children?"

"Are you telling me that Al is crazy, too?" she asked.

"Not crazy, but some of his ideas are a little far out. They took Lester as a kind of joke. It wasn't the first time they played a joke on him, using him for laughs, as I understand."

"No, it wasn't. . . . Oh, poor Lester . . ."

"The way Al Lundy explains it is this: None of them had the right to come home, not after what they did to Lester. They should not have come home, started their lives back up again, gotten married, had children. So he's just taking things back to where they should have been. All of them dead—casualties of war. No children."

"No grandchildren either."

114

"Right."

"David, he must be out of his mind."

He looked out the window for a long moment. "Shirley," he said finally, "I need you to find out where Victor is."

"What are you going to do?"

"I'm going to go see him."

"You're going to kill him, aren't you." It wasn't even a question.

"I'm going to end it."

"What happens if he kills you instead?"

"He won't. He won't be expecting me to come after him."

"David, don't underestimate him. Victor Schott is very smart."

"So I hear. Are you going to find out where he is?"

"What if I refuse?"

"Joan. Andrea Kramer. And me. That's all that's left. If I don't get him, he's going to get us, one by one. You don't have any choice, unless you want to be responsible for Joan's death."

"One thing I'll say about you, David, you don't pull any punches."

"That's the way it is."

"Go to the police, then."

"No, I'm not going to do that. You know what kind of treatment I got from Decker."

"There must be some other way. He'll kill you."

"There's no other way. Are you going to do it or not?"

"Where can I reach you?"

"How long will it take?"

"I have no idea."

"Call me back here in twenty-four hours and let me know what you've been able to get. I'll stay by the phone."

"I don't know if I can find anything out that soon."

"How much longer will Joan stay with you?"

"If I weren't a lady, I'd call you something for that."

"Go ahead if it will make you feel any better. Just find out as soon as you can."

"I'll try."

"I'll be waiting." He put the receiver back in its cradle. Twenty-four hours. Twenty-four more hours in this blasted room. And in the meantime, where was Victor Schott? If he was out looking for people to kill, there was no point in expecting to find him at home. On the other hand, with the three remaining ones in hiding, there was nothing left for him to do except go home. If Victor Schott was the one. If Allen Lundy hadn't been lying. But why would Allen Lundy lie? *What had happened to Allen Lundy?*

12

FOR CHARLENE MANLEY, the telephone was as necessary as her right hand. She was never far from one, would never go more than half an hour without using one, unless she was asleep—or had died. At sixty-nine, Charlene Manley was far from dead, and she was rarely asleep. Her long white hair pinned back in a careless knot, she was sitting, as usual, amid chaos.

Her desk was covered with press releases, clippings, cryptic notes that only she could decipher, and no one dared touch anything. What looked to the rest of the staff like complete disarray was actually order in Charlene's perverse way of doing business. The desk faced away from the wall. On Charlene's left was the big plate-glass window that looked out onto Washington Street, and on her right was the wide door to the press room, usually left open despite the noise, so that Charlene could keep an eye on things. After more than fifty years at the *Fairfield Sun,* she made sure that nothing happened without her knowledge and at least grudging approval.

She had first come to the paper as a teenager, an unpaid after-school worker fascinated by the world of journalism. Her intent was to finish school, major in journalism at the university, and then go on to some big-city newspaper. But somehow she never made it. She stayed on at the *Sun* after high school—by that time she was getting paid—and she wrote the feature articles, did whatever needed to be done. Ten years later, still at the *Sun,* she married Harold Manley, its unmarried middle-aged editor, and slowly, over the years, the *Fairfield Sun* became a creature of Charlene Manley. Or, more properly, Charlene Manley became the *Fairfield Sun*. Her column in the weekly for the past forty years had been called "Silhouettes," and in it she ranged freely from town gossip to advice-giving to soapbox oratory. If it was true that nothing happened at the *Sun* without her knowledge and approval, it was just as true that nothing happened in Fairfield without her knowledge. Her approval was another thing.

She sat now, gazing absently out the window, her hand drawing boxes within boxes within boxes on the yellow lined legal paper she kept constantly at hand. When her phone rang, she picked it up with her left hand; her right hand was still making boxes. "*Sun.* Charlene," she spoke into the mouthpiece. She'd been saying the same thing for fifty years. No one who knew her called her anything but Charlene.

"Charlene, it's Shirley Carpenter."

She stopped drawing the boxes and her mind flashed to a car by the lake. Two dead bodies. The last murder in Fairfield had been in 1953, when Alice Findlay had shot her husband at point-blank range because she'd gotten tired of being beaten up every Saturday night.

"Yes, Shirley. Sorry to hear about Lane." Her first guess would have been that Shirley was calling to complain about the obit. People did that, as if somehow something of the dead person's life should have been caught up in that last printed paragraph that wasn't. But Shirley wasn't doing that. She was making the sorts of comments that Charlene had long ago learned meant that she was getting the superficial business out of the way before they got down to brass tacks. So what, a week after her son's death, were Shirley Carpenter's brass tacks? "Is there anything I can do for you?" Charlene asked.

"As a matter of fact, there is."

Charlene smiled slowly and drew another box.

"You know everybody in town, it seems," Shirley went on, "and half the people who've moved away."

"Anybody been doing this as long as I have, they'd have to, or else they wouldn't be doing the job."

"Is there any chance you might know where Victor Schott is now?"

Charlene's hand stopped in midbox. She glanced down at the yellow paper and her hand moved swiftly to the name that was written there. Slowly, she drew a box around the name. Victor Schott. "I believe he's out east somewhere."

"Could you get an address for me?"

"Might possibly. Hang on." Charlene Manley laid the receiver on the cluttered desk, pushed back her chair, and thought of all the reasons why she should give Victor Schott's address to Shirley Carpenter. Then she thought of all the reasons why she shouldn't. Then she got up and walked to a file drawer.

"Shirley," she came back on the line, "all I can give you is his business address."

"That's fine."

"The only reason we've got it is he's a subscriber." She paused. "Of course, you realize our subscriber lists are usually confidential."

"I appreciate it, Charlene."

"I wouldn't do it for everybody." She meant it. She liked Shirley Carpenter, always had.

"I really appreciate it."

"Sort of a strange request, though."

"You know he was a classmate of Mike's."

"Yes, I guess I'd forgotten that."

"You have it? The address?"

"Got a pencil? It's a company address—the name of the company is Tech-Optics. One-five-three Burton Road. Framingham, Mass."

"Thanks very much."

"I don't have a home address for him. I suppose you can contact him there. It's where we send the paper."

"Charlene, I appreciate it."

"Think nothing of it." Charlene hung up the phone and looked for a long time at Victor's name with the box drawn around it. Then, quite deliberately, she drew two more boxes around it. She leaned back in her chair. Victor Schott. She stood and walked into the press room. Ralph Gunderson was cleaning his press. Jerry was printing up an order of letterheads for the local Ford dealer. Then she went back into the office, sat down at her desk, and dialed Information, and then the number she'd been given.

"Good afternoon. Tech-Optics. May I help you?" The voice was as personal as an ice cube.

"Mr. Schott, please."

"I'm sorry, Mr. Schott isn't in. Who's calling, please?"

"Charlene Manley. *Fairfield Sun.* That's a newspaper. He'll know it. When do you expect him in?"

"I'm not sure. Could I have him return your call?"

"Will he be back today?"

"I'm not sure. Could I tell him in reference to what matter you're calling?"

"Have him call me when he comes in." She gave the phone number. "That's Indiana," she added.

"Could I tell him in reference to what matter you're calling?" the voice asked again.

Charlene Manley grinned into the phone. She hadn't worked for a newspaper most of her life for nothing. "I'm calling in reference to my curiosity." Then she hung up. All she knew of Victor was from his childhood—and from the occasional calls over the years; always due, he'd say, to his curiosity about someone in town; usually prompted, he'd say, by something he'd read in the paper. Why Victor, who had rarely shown any interest in the town when he lived there, should even be curious enough about it to subscribe to the paper, had always been a mystery to her. If anything would move Victor to call her, this surely would.

David Brett was standing with his hands in his pockets watching through the window as a man on the other side of the parking lot walked his dog in a vain attempt to get it to do something. The dog seemed more interested in sniffing the tires of every car than anything else, and David smiled wryly to himself. Behind him the phone rang. He looked at his watch, as if he didn't already know the time, as if he hadn't been looking at it constantly for the last two hours. Twenty-four hours almost exactly. He lifted the receiver. "Hello."

"David? It's Shirley."

"How'd it go?"

"Easier than I thought. I have an address. It's not his home, though; it's his office."

"That's fine. What is it?"

"Tech-Optics. That's the name of the company." She gave him the address. "Are you going there?"

"What do you think?"

"David, you don't know anything about Victor."

"I know enough."

"You only have one man's word for it. What if he was lying to you?"

"What do you think I'm going to do? Blow the guy's head off without giving him a chance to talk? I know what I'm doing."

"He could kill you."

"He's been trying damn hard."

"I talked on the phone this morning to Andrea Kramer—Buddy's daughter."

"You did? How did you manage that?"

"She called. She was wondering about you, but of

course she didn't know where you were. I gather you left her in the lurch somewhere. She wasn't too happy about that. She should have been mad as hell, but she sounded more worried."

"How did she get in touch with you?"

"It took some doing on her part, but she's persistent, I'll say that for her. You know how it is in a town like Fairfield—you call enough people and someone finally knows something. Even not knowing anybody here, she eventually managed to get in touch."

"I thought you were so well insulated—passwords and codes and all that stuff."

"Small town is small town, David, you should know that. What do you think we talk about all the time we're cooped up here? My sister-in-law knows who Andrea is by now. I told her—Andrea—that I'd just talked with you, but I didn't say I had your number there. I hope that was all right, but I figured if you ran out on her it must have been for a reason and maybe you wouldn't want her coming to find you. I took her phone number; I told her I'd give it to you if you called again. I must say she seems nice enough."

"She is, which is one reason she should stay where she is."

"I told her about Victor. I thought she should know."

"Good. What's her number?"

She gave it to him. "You said you'd talk to Joan. She says she's going home tomorrow. Talk her out of it."

"How am I going to do that?"

"I don't know, but she won't listen to me."

"Is she with you now?"

"I'll get her."

"Shirley—" But it was too late; she'd already gone away from the phone. What the hell do I tell her, he wondered, that she doesn't already know? *They aren't going to cloister themselves for the rest of their lives—*

Andrea's mother had said that, and Andrea had said nearly the same thing. Except that they had to. Until he found Victor Schott, until he was certain that the killing was finished and would never start again, they would have to.

"Hello?" Even the one word was antagonistic.

"My name is David Brett; I'm sure you know that. You're Joan?"

"Yes."

"I don't know what your mother has told you. I don't know how much you want to know."

"Frankly speaking, the only reason I'm talking with you is because my mother wants it."

"Fair enough. At least I know where we stand. Just listen, then: What looks like a series of unrelated deaths—mostly accidental—are neither unrelated nor accidental. You could be next."

"She's told me all that."

"And you don't believe it."

"Not really. People don't go around doing things like that. People don't carry grudges this long."

"I would have said that, too, but it's happening. Both your brothers—"

"I just don't believe it," she interrupted. "It isn't logical."

"This is not my interpretation. This is the understanding of a man who was there—the only surviving one who was there. Why would he lie?"

"I don't know anything about you, David Brett, except your name. Why should I believe you?"

"Forget about me. How about your mother? She's frantic. If you won't do it for yourself, how about doing it for her?"

"My mother's a tough lady. She'll handle it."

"I'm not asking for your life. One day. Two days. Three. What can it hurt?"

"I appreciate your concern. I'll tell my mother you did your best. And I promise to be careful. Good-bye."

The receiver clicked in his ear. He stared at it for a moment. Shirley Carpenter, for a nice lady, you've sure raised some headstrong kids, he thought. He put the phone down and looked out the window again. The man with the dog was gone. He would not call Andrea now. She was safe, and she knew he was; there was no point in calling her until he had something worth telling.

Charlene Manley stood, hands on hips, watching Jerry clean his press. There was a vague look of distrust in her eyes; these young kids, you couldn't trust them—they'd as soon wreck a machine as give you the time of day. What had happened to taking care of things, making things last? She made a mental note: a good subject for her column—the throw-away society.

"Charlene!" Maryanne's voice called from the doorway. "Charlene, telephone!" Maryanne Forester, secretary, bookkeeper, girl Friday; her best attribute was a voice like a foghorn.

Charlene stopped by the coffee machine and poured herself a cup, sipping at it as she walked back into the office. She sat back behind her desk, set the coffee down, and picked up a pencil with one hand and the receiver with the other. "Charlene," she said.

"Hello, Charlene. This is Victor Schott, returning your call. How are you?"

"You know Fairfield. Things go on pretty much as usual. It's been a while since you've been in to see me."

"Yes, it has. You know how things go. I don't get out there too often."

"No, you don't, I suppose." She was making boxes again.

"Your call took me a little by surprise, Charlene. I'm wondering how I can help you."

"You know me, Victor. Always nosy."

"I wouldn't have used that adjective."

"We'll call a spade a spade. Nosy is the word. Best way of learning, I've always thought."

"I can't argue with that, except that now you're making me curious. What makes you call somebody like me our of a clear blue sky?"

"Because, Victor, the other day someone came by and asked if I might know where you were. Have an address for you. I guess I must have a reputation around town."

"You know perfectly well you do. Nobody knows more about anybody who ever lived in Fairfield than you do. Ah, is that the sort of information Charlene Manley gives out? The whereabouts of her subscribers?"

"It is when the person who's asking happens to be Phillip Decker."

"The name sounds familiar. Should I know Phillip Decker?"

"I don't know. He's the chief of police."

"Oh. . . . Did he say why he was asking?"

"No. Just asked about you, that's all."

"Got any ideas?"

"If I had, I probably wouldn't be calling you."

"Do you call everybody whose name comes up in your office?"

"No, as a matter of fact, I don't."

"So now I'm the curious one. Why call me?"

"Because I'm nosy. I already told you that. And besides, I got another call, from someone else, also asking about you. Twice in two days, Victor. It's enough to make a person wonder. So I'm wondering out loud. Why are people all of a sudden looking for Victor Schott?"

"Who was the other one?"

"Phil Decker, I was presuming, was asking on a matter of public interest. As a police officer. I figure what's

125

public is public. I'll tell you about him. The other one wasn't a public request; it was a private party."

"And did you tell the private party my address?"

"A private party is a private party, Victor. It's not the same thing as a police officer."

"Does that mean you didn't give them my address, or does that mean you're not going to tell me if you gave them my address?"

She cleared her throat. "So I'm wondering why people are all of a sudden so interested in Victor Schott. Is there something new about you I should be aware of?"

"Not that I know of. Same old person. Sorry."

"People don't ask for nothing, Victor."

"Why don't you ask Decker, then? Or the other person. Who did you say it was?"

"I didn't."

"I can't help you, Charlene."

"Too bad. I was hoping you could."

"You know what you've done to me now, Charlene? You're going to ruin my sleep for the next few nights. Who the hell is trying to locate me? An old girlfriend, perhaps? Somebody wanting to name me in his will, leave me a couple million dollars? You sure you want to do that? Why don't you just tell me who was asking? I'll give him a call and find out why he wants to know."

"I may be a nosy old bag, Victor, but sometimes a latent sense of privacy rises up in me. I told you before, private's private. Why is Decker looking for you?"

"We're going round and round, aren't we?"

"I think the word is *devious.*"

"Are we going to help each other?"

"I guess we aren't."

"Then there's no point, is there, Charlene?"

"Call me if you change your mind."

"You do the same. I'll count on it."

"Good-bye, Victor." She put the receiver down. The

fact was, Victor Schott didn't have any old girlfriends in Fairfield. Nobody had liked Victor Schott that well. Or at least, nobody had ever gotten that close to him. And nobody would be leaving him a couple million dollars, either. Whatever it was that Shirley Carpenter wanted of Victor was none of his business until Shirley contacted him. She'd had enough grief in her life already. But the question still lay there like an undigested lump in the throat—what was going on with Victor Schott?

Victor Schott's hand still held the receiver, even though he'd placed it back in its cradle. A man can handle anything, he'd always thought, just as long as he foresaw all the possibilities. The chief of police in a town like Fairfield was one thing; you could figure out how to handle that one. But the other one—who was that? Who else? *Who the hell else?*

13

IT WAS A one-story brick building set back from the road, a twin to another building close-by, except for the neat lettering across the front: Tech-Optics. On the other side spread the vast parking lot of a trucking firm. The lawn and hedges in front had been recently trimmed. Everything was neat, in place. Victor Schott, or whoever ran Tech-Optics, ran a tight ship.

He had driven by twice, slowly. It was not the best of options. To walk in the front door of Tech-Optics was to put himself on Victor Schott's turf. On the other hand, a phone call would be worse, because it would be a warning to Schott. Surprise had a value. And so did people. There would be people in the office—it would not be a place where Schott could do anything dangerous or even suspicious. His own office. His own turf. It might, after all, be the best place to corner him.

The girl looked up from her typing. Too much make-up, especially around the eyes; hair pulled back severely in a twist at the side of her head. He'd been around kids long enough to know what she was trying to do. Putting a few years on, trying to look older than she was. He wondered wryly how long it would be before she'd be doing the opposite. "Can I help you?"

"I'd like to see Victor Schott."

"Beg your pardon?"

"Mr. Schott? Victor Schott?"

She frowned slightly and shook her head. "He's not here."

"When do you expect him?"

"I don't. He's never been here. At least, not that I know of."

"This is Tech-Optics, isn't it? I was told I could reach him here."

"We take calls for him sometimes. And he gets mail here. That's all."

"He takes calls and mail here but doesn't come in?" It didn't make sense.

She shrugged. "I don't know anything more about it than that."

"What happens to his calls and his mail?"

"Ginny takes his calls. The mail goes on Mr. T's desk. I don't know what he does with it."

"Who are Ginny and Mr. T?"

She tilted her head and narrowed her eyes. "Who're you?"

"An old friend. Who's Ginny?"

"Mr. T's secretary. Through that door if you want to talk with her." She pointed vaguely to her left.

"And who is Mr. T?"

She sighed impatiently. "Mr. Timmerman *owns* this place. The least you could do is know that."

"And is he in?"

"As a matter of fact, he's not. He took a couple of days off."

"We should all be so lucky," he said, heading toward the open doorway.

She flashed a grin. "You'd better believe it," she said, turning back to the typewriter.

The nameplate on the desk said Virginia Meagher. The woman behind it was a cool blond—late twenties, dressed impeccably in the requisite skirted suit. The girl out front was not going to get anywhere until she learned the difference between a secretary and an executive assistant.

"May I help you?" It was a professional smile, its warmth a professional warmth. We do business in this place, it said, and I'd be happy to do business with you, but that's as far as it'll go. Self-protection, he supposed, because she was very good-looking.

"I hope so." He suddenly wished he had an attaché case in his hand. Anything to make him look more believable. "I'm in the Boston area on business and thought I'd look up an old friend. I was told he worked here, but the girl out front doesn't seem to think so. Victor Schott? This is his office isn't it?"

Virginia Meagher sat down behind the desk and moved some papers around as if trying to clear the desk. She's stalling, he thought.

"She's right. He doesn't work here."

"He used to, maybe?"

"No, not as far as I know."

"But he takes his calls here."

"I wouldn't put it that way, exactly. An occasional call."

"And how do you relay them?"

She looked him straight in the eye, and the smile was no longer there. "I don't really think that's any of your business."

"Then how am I going to get in touch with him?"

"I don't know."

"It seems a little strange. If I called here, you'd put me in touch, but if I come here . . ."

"That's the way he wants it."

"Let's pretend I called. What happens? Do you give me a phone number where I can reach him?"

"No. If you leave your number, he'll call you. Do you want to leave your number?"

"I don't know how long I'm going to be in the area. How long would it take for him to get in touch with me?"

"I don't know."

"What do you do with the names and numbers?"

"I'm really very busy. I haven't the time to be playing question-and-answer."

"Look, it's quite important that I reach him. How the hell am I going to do it?"

She picked up a pencil. "What did you say your name was?"

He paused a half-second and she looked up at him. "Allen Lundy."

"And your phone number?"

"I'm not sure where I'll be staying. I don't have a motel yet."

She crossed out the name she'd just written, and wrote something else on the paper. "I'll give you our phone number. If you want him to call you, call back with a number where you can be reached."

"Look, he's an old friend. I'd stay around the area for a while if I thought he'd get back to me soon. How long does it usually take? How does he get his messages? What if I wrote him a letter?"

"I don't know what happens to the letters. They go on Mr. Timmerman's desk and he takes care of them."

"Just give me an idea of the time involved. Will he get back to me today?"

"I doubt it, but it's possible. Anytime in the next week, I'd say."

"You can't hurry it up?"

"Look, he gets the messages when he calls. If he doesn't call, he doesn't get them. That's all I can tell you. Now, if you'll excuse me—"

"He calls here for them."

"That's what I said," she said evenly.

"And you talk to him and give the messages to him."

"Good-bye, Mr. Lundy."

"Excuse me. I hedged a bit with you. My name isn't Lundy, it's Brett. David Brett. Next time he calls, tell him I was here. Tell him I'll call back for a message, but I won't leave a phone number. Tell him . . . just tell him those things. But be sure you get the name right: David Brett." He walked into the outer office and the girl looked up from her typing. His mind was racing now, and he was trying to make things fit together. He ran his fingers along the edge of her desk as he passed it. "Thanks for your help," he said as he walked by. "Something of a bitch, isn't she?" he whispered. The girl grinned. He paused, then thought better of it and walked on toward the door. He didn't look back, but he felt the girl's eyes on him as he went. At least that was what he was hoping. And he was wondering: Timmerman and Schott. But nobody ever saw Schott. Were they really two different people?

David Brett followed the green Vega into a discount store parking lot. At last, she was going somewhere besides work. He drove on beyond where she parked and eased into a parking spot. He'd been following the girl, waiting for this, but for four days it had been the same thing: leaving work at precisely three minutes after five, driving home to a small yellow house set close among other houses just like it, and then nothing for the rest of the evening. She didn't go out at night, she didn't go out at lunch. He watched across the cars now as she scurried through the light rain into the store. He left his car and followed her. He was too close, probably, but it was a big store, and it would be easy enough to lose her.

He found her in the cosmetics department, hesitating between shades of nail polish. Her hair had been worn long today, the curl limp now after a day's work, her pale face showing through the blusher that had been put on too many hours ago. He'd seen so many girls like this—mascara worn too thick, eyeshadow worn too boldly, blush a shade too dark—what were they hiding behind it, or looking for with it? Perhaps only themselves. He was one aisle over and she hadn't seen him yet. He picked up a tube of toothpaste and turned the corner, heading down the aisle toward her, his head down, ostensibly reading the label on the box.

When he bumped into her, he said, "Excuse me."

She looked up in surprise. He stepped back, looked away, then looked at her again.

"Aren't you . . . ?" He stopped, narrowing his eyes, frowning. "I've seen you—I know! Tech-Optics, isn't that it?"

She smiled, flattered he'd remembered her. She was too young, too vulnerable. What he had in mind was not fair. And then he thought of Jenny Wilson and Nickie Kramer. They'd been too young, too, and what had happened to them was much worse than not fair. And he thought of Elizabeth. "That's where I've seen you, isn't it?"

"You're the one who was looking for that man, Victor Schott. Did you find him?"

"Not yet. I left my name, but he hasn't called back. That's how it works, isn't it?"

"I don't know. Ginny takes care of those calls."

That was how he was going to do it. He'd known, almost instinctively, that Virginia Meagher was the key that was going to unlock this girl. "She's not the friendliest person I've ever met."

The girl looked away, taking up another bottle of nail polish. She was not going to be easy.

"What is she, private secretary to the boss? Are you two the only women in the office?"

"No, there's another one. Marge. She does the books."

"I guess I didn't see her."

"She might have been out. She goes to the bank a lot. And to the post office."

"Just you three? The receptionist—is that what you're called?—the bookkeeper, and the secretary."

The girl looked back at him. "You'd better not let Ginny hear you call her that. *She's* no secretary. She's too good for that."

"Do I detect that you're not too fond of Ginny?"

She put the bottle back and turned away from him.

"Well, now I know Ginny's name and the bookkeeper's name, but what do I call you the next time I come into the office?" he asked as she walked away.

She turned, tilting her head as she had done in the office. "What are you coming back for? I thought you were only looking for Mr. Schott. You're not going to find him at the office."

"I know that . . . it's just that I . . ." He looked away from her. She couldn't be more than nineteen, an insecure nineteen. "I'm just in town on business. I'm a salesman, a schoolbook salesman, and I've been visiting some of the schools here." A gamble. Maybe something she could relate to. "And, as I said, Victor's an old friend—he's from my hometown. I really thought he worked at Tech-Optics. And . . . to tell you the truth . . . I was hoping he might be able to get me a job there. I don't exactly want to be a book salesman all my life—too much traveling. I'm ready to settle down and find a solid job. What I'm doing now is really a dead-end kind of thing."

"I know what you mean."

"Do you? Most of the girls I meet think I must have the greatest kind of life, traveling all over the country, but living out of suitcases can be a drag, a real drag. I guess I'm probably boring you."

"No, you're not."

"Maybe it's the kind of people I meet. I mean, what chance do I have to meet the kind of people I'd relate to? Motels and restaurants. I can tell you about motels and restaurants, but you don't meet many nice girls that way,

I can tell you that. I'm sorry. I kind of run off at the mouth. You certainly don't care about my problems. I guess seeing you made me think about that Ginny. Most of the people you meet these days are kind of like her— cold. I hope you don't mind my saying that about her. Maybe she's a good friend of yours or something. Is she?"

The girl shook her head. "Not really."

"That's a relief! I wouldn't want you to think I was putting down one of your friends."

"You said she's cold . . . Did you ask her out or something?"

"Her? No way! You can tell the minute you walk into the room with someone like her. She'd think she was too good for me."

"Yeah. She thinks she's too good for anybody."

"Let's not talk about her. I meet too many people like her anyway; I'm certainly not interested in talking about one of them when they're not around. People like that, you can't even talk to them, you ever notice that? They just tune you out. Here I go again, running off at the mouth. I'm sorry."

"No, it's perfectly all right. I understand what you're saying. I feel that way too."

"Do you? Do you really? Sometimes I think I'm the only one. Sometimes I . . . never mind."

"What were you going to say?"

"Never mind. You don't want to hear everything I might want to say."

"Why don't you try me?"

He looked at her for a long moment. The frightening thing is, he thought, it's so very easy. "Here I stand, with toothpaste in my hand! You must have been buying something, too? What do you say we buy what we each came in here for, and then I take you someplace for a cup of coffee?"

"What is it you do at that office, anyway?"

She shrugged and shook her head. "It's just junk work. It's nothing."

He leaned forward, his face the picture of earnest interest. "Really, I want to know." The tabletop beneath his hands was grainy with age. It was a place she knew about, near her own neighborhood. She felt comfortable there, safe. He'd ordered coffee. She'd hesitated; he'd felt the confusion and suggested maybe she didn't like coffee. She ordered a cherry shake. She's very young, he thought. For all her attempts to look older, she's not the kind of girl who would ordinarily dream of going out with a strange man. Elizabeth, he thought, does any of this make sense?

"You could say I was a receptionist. I do that, answer the phone, do some typing and filing. Do all of the filing, as a matter of fact. She doesn't file if she can help it, and she doesn't type either. She's too good for that; it might ruin her manicure or something."

"So what does she do?"

Patti leaned over her shake and giggled. It was Patti with an *i;* she'd made a point of that. "You don't really want to know, I don't think."

"Yes, I do."

"Why?" She looked back at him, challenging, and he backed off.

"Just curious. It seems to me that you don't like her much, and I was wondering why. If I had to guess, I'd imagine that she didn't pull her weight. That she makes you do most of the dirty work. I've seen it before. Some people don't do their share. The rest of us get stuck with theirs and ours."

"You too?"

"Oh, sure. I've got this supervisor you wouldn't believe. He doesn't do a damn thing. I make out his reports

136

and everything. I'm tired of the crap he pulls. That's one of the reasons I want out."

She nodded agreement.

"So what about your boss—Mr. T, you called him. What kind of person is he?"

"He's nice. Sometimes I wish I could tell him how things really are in the office, but he's so busy. He hardly notices. And she's always there, always buttering him up. You know what I was going to say about her before? Maybe you won't like this, but it's true. She kisses his ass. Always. *Yes, Mr. Timmerman; no, Mr. Timmerman; of course, Mr. Timmerman.*" She tilted her head back and forth, mockery in her voice. "And then she shoves the work at me and makes me do it."

"She's been there longer than you have."

"Oh, sure, everybody has. I don't think anybody stays in my job very long. I'm sure as hell not going to. I'm leaving as soon as I can find another one."

"Where does my friend Victor Schott fit into the picture? How does he happen to get messages there?"

"I told you, I don't know anything about it."

He leaned on the table toward her. "Don't you see, Patti, he must be a good friend, or maybe he really is the owner. Are you so sure Timmerman owns the place? Listen, if Victor has some influence, and if I can contact him, then maybe we can work it that you wouldn't have to look for another job. Maybe, in fact, we could work it that it would be Ginny that would be looking for another job."

"What do you mean by that?"

"Come on. You're a smart girl. You can figure it out."

"Would you really do that?"

"Sure. Why not? Patti, I'm serious. I want out of my company. I'm looking for something else. I want to settle down. You . . . haven't got a boyfriend or anything, do you?"

She looked out the window.

"I'm sorry. I shouldn't have said that. You probably think it's none of my business."

"No, I don't have one. I used to, but I don't anymore."

"I didn't mean to embarrass you."

She shrugged. "You didn't."

His eyes caught hers and held them. All the lonely girls he'd ever known were in those eyes, in her face. "How old are you, Patti?"

"Twenty-two. How old are you?"

"Twenty-six." She would believe it because it would not occur to her not to.

"I think I'd better get going."

"Sure. Am I going to be able to see you again?"

"How long will you be around?"

"It depends. When is Timmerman coming back?"

"Next week."

"What are the chances he might be hiring somebody in the near future?"

"I don't know. What can you do?"

"I'm not a bad salesman."

"We already have a salesman."

"Just one? Surely he might be interested in another?"

"No, most of the people come to him. He has connections. He knows a lot of people in the government. We sell a lot of things to the government—the army and the air force."

"What exactly, does Tech-Optics make?"

"Lenses. Like for space things, high-powered telescopes, surveillance, that kind of thing. It's not the sort of thing you go out and sell; it's the kind of thing that if someone wants it, they come to you. We do mostly special-order stuff. Big-deal stuff, some of it's secret. I don't know much about it. I suppose that's why they let me work there. I only do the things that anyone can do.

138

Mr. T's got all sorts of security clearances; he's always going to Washington."

"You're talking about the FBI?"

"Maybe. Nobody ever mentions anything like that. But I always thought it was mostly CIA. Mr. T used to be in it, you know. It always kills me when people go into his office for the first time, they see that plaque on the wall. They can't believe it. I was the same way, the first time I went in there."

"Wait a minute, back up. He was in the CIA? How do you know that?"

"Because he's got this plaque. It says something like 'In recognition of Joseph Timmerman, for meritorious service,' something like that, and it's from the CIA."

"A plaque? On his wall?"

"Sure. It says that, just what I told you."

"CIA men don't have plaques on their walls."

"Yes, they do. They can, anyway, if they're retired. I've heard him tell it a dozen times. Everyone who comes in asks about it. No, not everyone. I guess some already know. In fact, I suppose that's how he has his connections with the government. He must already know a lot of guys who need the kind of things we make. But to the others, he always tells them because they always ask. It's like this: When you retire from the CIA, you can keep your cover or you don't have to. If you keep it, it might be an advantage to you, if you were doing certain things for them when you worked there, but there can be some disadvantages too. So if you don't need to keep your cover, it's better if you don't. That's the way he always explains it. I don't know what it was he did for them. It always seems that people, when they find out, always try to get him to tell what he did, but he never does. The other ones, the ones who already know because that's how they knew him—they know better than to ask. He never tells, anyway. He's very . . .

elusive, I guess you'd say. So I think that's how he has his government connections. And that's why he really doesn't need salesmen all that bad. The business usually comes to him."

"How hard is it to see him when he's in the office?"

"Not hard at all. You just come in and ask."

Not hard to see Timmerman; hard as hell to see Schott. "Is it possible that they are the same person—Timmerman and Schott?"

She frowned, thinking. "Why? Why would he do that?"

"Maybe he's not as much out of the CIA as he says."

"I suppose . . . No, they can't be. I've answered the phone when Mr. Schott called, and it was not Mr. T's voice. No, it can't be him. Listen, I've really got to go. I hope you don't mind."

"Patti, I'm really grateful that you've been willing to spend some time with me. It's been the nicest thing that's happened to me in quite a while."

"It was nice for me too."

"Will I see you again? Can I call you at work?"

"Sure, but I'll give you my home phone, if you want it. The only thing is, if I'm not home and you leave a message and I don't call back, don't think anything about it. I don't always get those messages about who calls me."

"Don't worry. I'll keep calling until I reach you."

"Dave. There's something I ought to tell you. I didn't tell you the truth before."

"About what?"

"I'm not twenty-two. I thought you would think I was too young. But now, if I see you again, you might find out and then you'd be mad. I thought you wouldn't be interested if you thought I was . . . only . . . eighteen."

"Is that what you are? Eighteen?" And a very young eighteen in too many ways.

"Are you mad?"

"No." He smiled. "I guess I'm flattered."

"Will you still call?"

"Yes." And what would he tell her when he called? Look, I'm sorry, but I was just using you?

"You could always call me at work if you can't get me at home. At least you can call me there as long as Ginny doesn't get me fired."

"We'll form a club—the Ginny Meagher anti-fan club."

She giggled. "Good-bye, Dave. I really enjoyed it."

His eyes followed her car out the drive and into the busy intersection, but he was thinking of something else entirely. Timmerman, the CIA, and Victor Schott. Suddenly the lack of information about Schott, the relayed phone calls and letters all made sense. And the sense it made scared the hell out of him. He started his engine, then eased the Pinto into the oncoming traffic. A moment later a tan Volare pulled into the traffic behind him.

14

DECKER SAT FACING the window, his back to the door. On the street outside, Willard Bean drove by slowly, his left arm hanging out the window. Decker craned his neck to watch as the car neared the corner. Yes, Will's hand stiffened to signal a stop, then turned up to signal the right turn he was about to make. Decker grinned to himself. Will had taught Decker's father how to drive, back in the days, as Will liked to say, when cars were made for people with brains instead of the way they're made now—for dimwits and kids.

In the outer office the phone rang, and Decker closed his eyes, waiting. Maybe it was Turner; he needed to hear from that guy. His own phone rang and Decker lifted the receiver. "Yes?"

"Sir, phone for you. It's Charlene Manley."

"Charlene? OK, put her on." The connection clicked and he said, "This is Decker."

"Phil, this is Charlene Manley."

"Hi, Charlene. What can I do for you?"

"The other day you called asking about Victor Schott."

"Yes." He'd been wondering when she'd get back on that one, but he wasn't going to give her any help. She was quick enough by herself.

"I didn't ask you then, but I'm asking you now—why? What's the interest in him?"

Decker leaned back in his chair. "Charlene, you know better than to ask those things."

"I'm the press, remember? I have a right to ask."

"That sounds more like big-city talk than something someone in Fairfield would say."

"You can cut the crap, Phil. Is Victor involved with any of these killings?"

"Not unless you know something more than I do."

"Then why were you looking for him?"

"I told you the other day. I was doing it for a friend. Someone who lives out of town and thought I might be able to find out."

"Want to tell me the name of your friend?"

"Sure. . . . It was . . . it was Dick Bean." In his mind's eye he saw Willard's car turn the corner again. And good luck at finding Dick Bean, he thought.

"Where is Dick these days?"

"California, or at least that's what he said."

"You must be the only person in town who's talked with Dick in the past ten years. I don't think even his father knows where he is."

"Well, Charlene, one thing about being a police officer; when people need help, they come to you. But you've got a point; I guess I'll have to tell old Will that I was talking with his son. He'd probably like to hear it. Will's still around, isn't he?"

"He's not dead yet, if that's what you mean."

"Dick didn't even ask about him. Seems mighty strange, don't you think?"

"That's not all that seems strange. How come Dick's calling after all this time? What does he want Victor for?"

"Damned if I know. Next time he calls—if he does— I'll send him your way. You can ask him."

"You're not the only one who asked about Victor, you know. Two of you in the same day. That seems a little strange, too."

"Lots of strange things going on, I'd say, Charlene. Who was the other?"

"Shirley Carpenter. That's why I thought it might have something to do with those killings."

"Just coincidence, I guess."

"I'm not a strong believer in coincidences, Phil."

"Neither am I. I guess this must be the exception that proves the rule."

"So you're not going to help me."

"I would if I could, Charlene." He sat upright in his chair. "You know me, Charlene, always willing to help out. Tell you what: If I get any leads, you'll be the first to know."

"Have you ever handled a murder case before, Phil?"

"You know as well as anybody the answer to that."

"Seems like you might need all the help you can get."

"You telling me you've got some ideas?"

"I'm telling you you don't want to alienate the press. How long has it been—a week? People are going to begin to wonder if you're good enough to do the job."

"Good point, Charlene. I'll keep it in mind. I'll bet people would also like the cops not to spend so much time on the phone. Sorry, Charlene, but somebody's just walked in with a bunch of papers for me to look at. I'll get back to you."

"How soon?"

"Soon as I can. As you say, we need all the help we can get."

"Good-bye, Phil."

He hung up. Some tough cookie, he thought.

The drizzle had turned to a steady hard rain. David Brett was on the turnpike, driving west. He'd gone back to the motel, gathered up his things, and checked out. He was running scared now, and he knew it. Suddenly so many things were explained. How Victor Schott had managed it. If he was in the CIA, he would know how to find people; he would know how to make a murder look like an accident. And that brought to mind another thing: Why did the killings no longer look like accidents? What was he trying to do?

He passed an exit sign: Marlborough. Worcester was up ahead, a good-size town, a good place to lose himself. Worcester would be close enough to Framingham if he wanted to go back, far enough away that Schott would not think of looking for him there. But he couldn't think of any reason why he would go back. He was going to have to think the whole thing out again. If Victor Schott belonged to the CIA, there was more available to him that Brett could imagine. There was no way he could hide. On the other hand, Lundy had managed it. A loner, divorced, no ties, no one to keep in touch with, doing odd jobs—no records kept of his existence, no IRS forms, no social security. The only way to hide from Victor Schott? David wondered if Lundy had known what he was hiding from, if he had known it would take an existence for which no records were kept, no ties made, no government agencies involved in his life, to keep him safe. And was that the way it was going to have to be for him, and for Andrea and Joan? But they would never live that way, and neither would he. He would not become an Allen Lundy in order to keep safe. He was going to have to handle it some other way. He was going to have to end it, and that could mean only one thing: He was going to have to bring Victor Schott out in the open and get rid of him. He almost smiled to himself. Four simple words: *get rid of him.* The idea went against all that he knew. There were better ways; one did not solve problems with killing. *Get rid of him.*

Let's say what you mean, he said to himself. Let's say it in words that no one can misunderstand. We're talking about killing him. Killing Victor Schott. Taking the gun you've been carrying and really using it. It was not something he'd ever thought he would do, and even now he wondered if he could. Elizabeth, lovely Elizabeth. Going to the garage and getting into the car and turning on the ignition. When he forced himself to think of that, he knew he could kill. Jenny Wilson, too pretty for her own good, locked in a relationship with Lane Carpenter that would mean her death. Jenny Wilson, dead at the age of seventeen. Lane Carpenter. Nickie Kramer. Dead. All dead. And the next one, the last one, would be Victor Schott. Whatever it took to do it, he would do. However long it took. And he would have to take care, because he was moving now in Victor Schott's world, where Victor had all the advantages and David Brett had none—no, correction, had one: the need to do it.

He flicked on his turn signal for the exit, and automatically his eyes went to the rear-view mirror. He saw the signal begin to flash on the car behind him, and sudden fear gripped him. That's ridiculous, he told himself; stop looking for bogeymen. People turn off at exits. It doesn't mean anything. Stay calm. I'm going to have to stay calm. I'm not going to beat Victor Schott at his own game if I get jumpy, if every car on the road terrifies me so that I think someone is following me. But his eyes stayed on the car behind him.

He turned toward town, and saw in the mirror that the car behind him did the same. It's nothing, he told himself. But still I'll keep my eye on him. He pulled into the first motel he came to and watched in the mirror as the car drove on by. A tan Volare. See, it's nothing. A car behind me, that's all. It doesn't mean he's following me. After all, how on earth could he have found me?

He took a room, cleaned up quickly and got back into his car, driving toward downtown. He'd asked the desk clerk for directions to a good restaurant, but he only half-heard the directions (third stoplight, turn left . . .). Would Victor Schott have access to telephone-company records? Was it safe to telephone, or would the call be

146

traced? Surely one phone call from somewhere in Worcester would mean nothing among all the other calls. But would he be able to pinpoint the call from the time of day it was made? No, that's stupid, he thought. Schott doesn't know I'm here. That car meant nothing. For all Schott knows, I'm still in Framingham. If he even knows that. There's no way he'd know where I am now. He saw a gas station with a telephone-company insignia, and pulled into the drive.

He dialed a number and waited while it rang. He glanced at his watch: She ought to be there. Wherever "there" was. He didn't know; Shirley evidently hadn't known. Better that way. No one could reach her, even if . . . but Victor Schott was not going to kill anyone else. He'd already done all the killing he was going to do.

"Hello?"

"Is Andrea there?"

"Andrea? Andrea who?" The voice was guarded. Good. It would not be easy to reach her.

"Tell her it's David."

"David who?"

"David Brett. She'll know." He almost laughed, except that it wasn't funny. He heard the receiver set down, and he waited.

"David?"

"Glad I found you. You're still there, then?"

"Where are you?"

"I'm in Massachusetts. Not having too much luck, I'm afraid." No, he would not tell her. There was no reason to make her any more scared than she already was.

"Did you go to his place?"

"Yes, but it's not exactly his place. He takes messages there, evidently, but he's not part of the business. I'm not sure what his connection is. My best guess is just that he's a good friend of the owner."

"Can't you find out from the owner?"

"He's out of town, I'm afraid." He hadn't even thought to ask Patti where Timmerman was. Get with it, Brett; you're no match for the CIA the way you're going. How the hell could anyone be a match for the CIA? First lesson: Ask everything. No unturned stones. Nothing left to chance.

"David? Are you all right? What's the matter?"

"Nothing. It's been a discouraging kind of day." He'd allow that.

"There's no way to reach him, then?"

"He calls for messages. That's the only way I know of. I've left one for him. Just that I called, no address or phone number where I can be reached. How's everything out there?"

"Okay. . . . I'm worried about you."

"Don't be. But, Andrea . . . stay where you are. Don't go back home yet."

"Something's wrong. What is it?"

"Nothing. I just don't like the fact that he's got himself so well protected."

"Doesn't anyone know where he can be reached?"

"No."

"It seems a little strange, doesn't it? David, maybe you shouldn't be doing this alone."

"Stay where you are. He's a dangerous man, Andrea. I've found that much out."

"There's something you're not telling me."

"Just stay where you are. That's all."

"Go to the police. Tell them everything you know. Get some help, David."

"I can't do that." He shifted his weight, leaning against the other side of the glass enclosure, and his eyes caught something familiar. Parked down the street, the spill of light from the gas station barely lighting it, was a tan Volare. He caught his breath, then deliberately breathed out deeply. It's nothing, he told himself. There must be a million of those cars. But his eyes held it. "I'm going to have to go, Andrea," he said. "Stay where you are. Don't go back home until I tell you. I'll keep in touch."

"Be careful."

"Don't worry. I intend to." He hung up the phone. Slow down, he told himself. Don't look alarmed. You haven't seen anything, because the reality is that you probably haven't. He got in the car and drove off in the opposite direction. Behind, in the rear-view mirror, he could see the Volare making a U-turn in the street.

Don't panic. Don't let him know you've seen him. Maybe it's a coincidence. Maybe it's nothing but a car turning around. It could be. OK, even granted he's following me, he doesn't know what I know. He doesn't know I know he's there, doesn't know I've connected him with the CIA. Can't let him know how much I've learned. Let him think I know nothing, and I can get away that much faster. And how do I manage that? Lesson two: Don't panic. Drive at a normal speed, keep driving, get into traffic, find the main streets. He won't do anything with an audience; your safest place is where there are other people. Traffic? Can I lose him in traffic? Keep thinking. Lesson three: Keep thinking.

Got to stay with the car. Strange town, don't know my way around. I can't afford to get separated from the car. On the other hand, he'd watch it. I could park the car someplace, like at a restaurant, he'd stay outside and keep an eye on the car, and I could leave another way, steal another car. . . . Sure, Brett, have you ever stolen a car before? How long's it going to be before the police get on your tail? Just what I need—to be in police custody. He'd come in with his CIA stuff, pull rank, and I'd be out of the frying pan and into the fire. Literally. No, stealing a car is not an option. Lesson four: Stay out of trouble with the police. How do the CIA and the local

149

police relate? Maybe not at all, for all I know. Leave it. Stay away from them. This is no time to find out. Assume the worst.

The car was still following him, there was no doubt now. Am I driving aimlessly? Is that the way it looks? It's no good. It'll make him suspicious. So what do I do? I was coming to town for dinner, so I eat dinner. And stay with the car, good trick. A drive-in. There's always a solution. Keep going, there's bound to be a drive-in.

He saw it up ahead, the familiar sign lighted, a beacon for hungry America. Behind him, the tan car had dropped back; two cars were between them. An expected tack; don't stay too close, don't be too obvious. And David smiled. It's your mistake, he thought. You don't stay with me, you're going to be suckered.

He slowed and signaled for a right turn. Let's take it easy. Let's lull him into this one. He pulled into the takeout drive. In the mirror he saw the two cars behind him drive on down the street; the tan car followed him into the drive. Brett pressed the button and gave his order, then drove to the pick-up window. He watched the tan car behind him curiously. Will he play the game, he wondered. The man in the car behind him reached out and pressed the button. He's going to give his order, Brett thought, then thought better of it. No, don't assume that. The most important lesson, maybe: Don't assume anything.

What if the man in that car *was* Victor? David tried to see the man's face in his mirror, but it was impossible. The man was sitting back, deep in the shadows, out of the bright fluorescence cast by the drive-in window.

David's order came to him in a white bag. Now, he thought, reaching for it. Now we see what kind of stuff we're both made of. He pulled the car to the end of the drive and looked down the street. To his left, a block or two away, the light was green, and this time of night the

150

traffic was heavy. To his right, the traffic came steadily, with few breaks. He waited for the traffic to clear. The light down the block turned yellow, then red, and the street cleared. He put on his left turn signal, an afterthought. In the rear-view mirror, the turn signal of the car behind him began to blink. He took a drink from the paper cup, holding it up so the man behind him could surely see, then suddenly dropped it, spilling the drink on the seat beside him. Sandy, he thought, I'll get it cleaned. He bent over, moving his arms, wiping the seat off. From the corner of his eye he could still see the street to the left. The light turned green again and the cars started toward him. Just exactly right. Don't panic, stay calm. He kept watching as the cars came toward him. At the last possible moment, he straightened up, the cleaning task finished, looked to his left, saw the cars coming toward him, and slammed his foot down on the accelerator. The car shot forward.

A Trans-Am in the far lane screeched to a stop as the Pinto pulled out and cut in front of it. He stepped on the brake to miss a pickup, then slid behind it and gathered speed again, pulling around the pickup and back into the same lane, ahead of the pickup now. At the first side street he turned off his lights and made a sharp turn. Only now did he have an unobstructed view of the main street; the Volare was nowhere to be seen. No. There it was, coming up on the corner. He was halfway down the block before he saw a house with no lights. He pulled into the driveway and drove back to the garage, his lights still out. He couldn't see the main street from there, couldn't see if the Volare had caught his turn, but he sat there in the dark, waiting for a car to come slowly down the street. None came, and it was long enough; the Volare had missed the turn. But he didn't dare wait too long, or the Volare would catch on and be back. He backed out of the drive, lights still out, and paused. No car sat in the street, no one was waiting for him. He backed the rest of the way out and drove on down the street. It wasn't until he stopped at the first stoplight that he realized how much his hands were shaking.

He unfolded the map and examined it as he drove. He would not go back toward Framingham, and not on west. For sure he would not stay in Worcester. He thought of the motel, where his clothes were, and made a mental note. Take care of that, he thought, but first get out of here. Where would he not expect me to go? A city, where I can hide. He looked at the map again. Providence.

He headed west out of Worcester, stopping at the first gas station, and made a call. "This is David Brett, room thirty-seven. I've been in an accident, and won't be able to get back for a few days. I'm calling from the hospital; they say I've got a couple of busted ribs and maybe something else internal. Could you clear out my room for me and hang onto my things? I'll get back as fast as I can."

The desk clerk's voice sounded doubtful. "We have a policy—"

"Listen. There's nothing I can do. What's your name? Find a place to store my things and I'll make it worth your while. Fifty dollars? That sould OK?"

"What hospital are you in?"

"Are you kidding? They bring you in the ambulance, you don't stop them and ask the name of the hospital. It's not in Worcester; it's . . . ah, the accident was near Marlborough. I don't know the name of the place. What's your name?"

"Michael Phillips."

"OK. Michael Phillips. You work nights all the time?"

"Yeah."

"All right. Fine. A few days, a week at the most, and I'll get back to you. That all right?"

"That's fine."

David hung up the phone and went back to the car. He turned around and headed back toward Worcester. Following the signs, he found the freeway and turned south, toward Providence. Let him trace the call, he thought. Let him do what ever the hell he wants.

The next night he rented a red Mustang in Providence and drove back to Worcester to pick up his things. "There was someone here asking about you," Michael Phillips told him laconically.

David tensed; then, by an act of will, relaxed. "Did he say what he wanted?"

"No, just asked if you'd checked out."

"When was that?"

"Late last night. No, early this morning, just before I went off. Maybe four or five in the morning."

"Did he give his name?"

"No."

"What did he look like?"

"Not too old. Late twenties, early thirties, I'd say. Dark brown hair." He shrugged. "I don't know. Nothing out of the ordinary."

"What did you tell him?"

"That you were in an accident somewhere near Marlborough. Maybe you were in the Marlborough hospital, I wasn't sure. That you said you'd be back for your things in a week or so. You know this guy?"

"I think he was someone I was supposed to meet."

"He didn't come to the hospital?"

"No, he didn't." Late twenties or early thirties? Then it wasn't Victor Schott in the Volare. But if it wasn't Victor Schott, who in the world was it? Who else was looking for him?

"Tech-Optics. Can I help you?"

"Patti? It's me, David."

"How are you?" Her voice was noncommittal.

"Not too bad now. Listen, I'm sorry I didn't get in touch with you sooner. I was called out to Marlborough. My boss, you know the one I was telling you about? He got himself in some kind of jam, and I had to come and bail him out. I got so frustrated that I finally quit."

"You quit your job?"

"I told you I was going to."

"But what will you do now?"

"I'm hoping to get in touch with Victor Schott. You don't happen to know if he's called yet, do you?"

"Ginny would have to tell you that. Someone was in here looking for you, though. Yesterday or the day before, I forgot. I don't think it was him, though."

"Late twenties, early thirties? Drives a tan Volare?"

"I didn't see the car, but it was probably him. Who is he? Why did he come here?"

"I don't know why he came there. Did he say anything?"

"No, just asked for you. Oh yes, then he asked for Victor Schott. I couldn't help him with that either."

"Did you send him to Ginny?"

"Uh-huh."

"Did they talk a long time?"

"No. Who is he?"

"A guy I know. He's looking for a job, too. I told him I thought maybe I had connections there. I guess he thought he'd beat me to it. Wait till I get my hands on him." Who the hell was it and what was his connection with Victor Schott? "Maybe I should ask Ginny if she's heard from our friend yet. Can you switch me?"

"Sure. . . . Am I going to see you again?"

"You sure are. It would have been sooner, honestly, but—"

"Never mind. I don't have any business asking, anyway."

"Hey, Patti, I promised, didn't I?" And now he was going to have to see her again.

"Just a minute, I'll switch you. . . ."

The phone went on hold, then was picked up again. "This is David Brett, calling back for Victor Schott. Did he call yet?"

"Oh, yes, Mr. Brett. There was someone looking for you here. Do you have any idea who that might have been?"

"Sorry. I haven't the foggiest. What did he want?"

"I'm sure Mr. Timmerman would not appreciate your using this office as your answering service. I can't imagine why people would think they should be looking here for you."

"I can't imagine why, either. What about Victor Schott?"

"Mr. Schott left a message for you, as you asked. He wants you to meet him this coming Friday at Macy's department store, the Herald Square store, in New York City. In the ladies' lingerie department. Eleven o'clock in the morning. Do you want me to repeat that?"

"Macy's?"

"Ladies' lingerie. Eleven A.M. This Friday."

"Is that all he said?"

"Yes, it is."

"Does he . . . usually make such odd arrangements?"

"Mr. Schott's business is not mine to discuss."

"Thank you very much."

"Good-bye, Mr. Brett."

He hung up, hardly knowing what to think. Macy's. It was totally unexpected, and that was what worried him. If he wanted to see Victor Schott, he was going to have his chance. Macy's. A crowd of people. Neutral territory? It ought to be safe, but he'd have until Friday to decide if he could risk it.

15

THE MOMENT JOAN Carpenter reached for the leash, Baron began barking. Running back and forth between the kitchen and the front door, he could hardly contain himself. It was the luxury—the highlight—of his apartment-bound day, a brisk walk around the corner and down the street, across bustling Fifth Avenue, and then a jog through the park. He was a chaser at heart, and if it weren't for the leash, he would have made the circuit in a fraction of the time that his mistress did. In fact, she had let him loose once or twice and that was exactly what he had done. But she was frankly afraid of losing him, so the leash was nearly always a part of their daily routine. Baron was a companion, but much more than that. A mongrel of indeterminate origin, his size and deep suspicious growl was what kept her feeling safe on the city streets and in her anonymous apartment building. The moment anyone paused in front of the apartment door, he would set up a fury of barking that would make even the closest friend think twice. Or would have, if Baron's characteristics had been less well known to Joan's close friends. For although he was a ferocious barker and a threatening growler, in actual confrontation he would not hurt a flea. And that was not all bad either, Joan had reflected more than once. One does not need to be sued for dog bites. Better a dog that puts up a big show and does nothing than one who attacks without warning.

On the street, as at home, Baron growled menacingly at every stranger. And his size was intimidating. Size, however, was not everything, as Joan had learned. She herself was close to six feet tall, what the stores politely referred to as queen-size. In truth, she was built like her father and brothers, who had all been football players. She had learned early on that her size could be an intimidating factor, and here in New York, where women hesitated to live alone, it was a distinct advantage. Accompanied by Baron, she could feel free to go wherever she wanted at any time of the day or night. However much her mother worried about her, she was secure in the knowledge that nothing could possibly happen to her. Even David Brett's warnings had failed to concern her. He would not, she suspected, have been so solicitous if he had ever seen her in the flesh. He would not have been the least bit worried if he had ever seen Baron.

She snapped the leash to Baron's collar and took the light gloves from the pocket of her jogging suit. It had been a clear bright day and, even now with evening approaching, the air held a clarity that one rarely sees in Manhattan. Nevertheless, it was cold, and she knew from experience how the wind could blow across the reservoir and whip through even the most sheltered paths. Down the hall, in the elevator, across the empty lobby, and out into the street, Baron tugged at the leash. This was what he'd been waiting for.

They entered the park at Eighty-first Street, nodding at the little man who stood warming his hands over his own roasted peanuts. That would come after—Baron's daily treat, a sackful of peanuts to munch on the way home. A dog who ate peanuts? Joan's friends never believed it until they saw it with their own eyes. Baron's two luxuries—a run through the park and a peanut orgy. It was not, Joan sometimes reflected, a very compatible pair of habits, but Baron, good friend that he was, deserved some recompense for spending his days cooped up in the apartment.

There were not many joggers on the path. Too cold for any but the most determined, she supposed, and it was fine with her. Baron rarely made a fuss over other joggers, but on the rare occasions when he did, sometimes the ruckus he made was almost more than even she could overcome. Joggers did not take well to strange dogs who acted as if a jogger's leg was what they most enjoyed for dinner. Besides, with few people on the paths, Joan could concentrate on other things. Sometimes it was, she ruefully admitted, her most productive time of day.

She crested a little rise and entered a bower of trees hanging down over the path. It was getting noticeably colder. She made a mental note: Cut the run short or it would be fully dark before they even left the park.

She turned a corner in the path and saw ahead of her a splash of color on the ground. Someone in an electric-blue running suit was sprawled at the side of the path, and now, closer to him, she could tell it was an older man, his face twisted in pain. Baron was already straining at the leash.

"Can I help you?" She came to a stop, bent down to the man. Baron growled a throaty warning.

"I think I've sprained my ankle. I can't seem to put any weight on it."

Joan looked around; there was no one else to be seen. Baron had begun to show his teeth, the growls more ominous. "Quiet, Baron." She turned back to the man. "He won't hurt you. He likes to put up a show, but it doesn't mean anything."

"I've been told that plenty of times before. I've noticed that owners of dogs aren't always terribly realistic when it comes to their pets."

"Really, in this case it's true. He wouldn't touch you. Do you think you could walk with help?"

"Probably. If you wouldn't mind, we could try it."

158

"Put your arm across my shoulder, that's it. Baron, get out of there!" Wagging his tail, the dog had maneuvered himself between them, the leash cutting across the man's face as he tried to shift his weight to Joan's shoulder. "Just a minute," she said, leaning forward, allowing the man to rest on the ground once again. "This isn't going to work. Baron"—she turned to the dog, snapping off the leash—"now stay here with me. Don't go running off someplace and get lost." As if she hadn't said a word, Baron took off the moment he was freed, his shaggy tail a waving flag of farewell as he disappeared up the path.

"Will he come back? You haven't lost him?"

"No. He'll make a quick circuit of the path we usually take and then he'll be back."

"But you won't be here if you're helping me."

"He knows where to find me. We always stop for peanuts on the way out."

The man smiled gamely through his pain. "I appreciate your help."

"Nothing to it." She bent again and felt his arm across her, an almost dead weight leaning on her. She turned to see how well he could manage walking, and suddenly his hand was clamping her shoulder. She looked at him in surprise; the pain was gone from his face. Something tense and angry had replaced it, and immediately she felt the shock of fear. It all happened so fast—the hard dull metal pressed against her stomach, the mouth open for a scream that never came, the terror, the soundless explosion, the nothingness. . . .

"For Lester," the man said, letting the limp body fall to the ground. He wiped his blood-and-flesh-spattered hands on the front of his running suit. Then he unzipped the jacket and pulled it off, drew down the pants, wiped his hands once again on the bunched-up suit, and carefully wiped the gun and its silencer. Then he picked up an attaché case from behind some shrubbery, and started off in the direction from which Joan had come. As he walked, he opened the attaché case, took out a navy blazer, put the running suit into the case, and pulled on the jacket over the gray flannel slacks and white shirt he'd been wearing under the jogging clothes. He could have been a businessman, caught unprepared for the sudden chill of evening and taking a shortcut through the park, hurrying home to the warmth of his apartment.

David Brett drove slowly, partly because of the rush-hour traffic and partly because he was looking for a place to park. He looked at his watch, but there was no need for impatience. Macy's didn't open until ten. He had plenty of time. Up ahead now, finally a parking garage that displayed no FULL sign. He pulled into the drive and a bored attendant handed him a time-punched card. A bored attendant at the parking garage, a bored attendant on the tollway, the bored faces of those who'd crossed the streets in front of his car, a whole city of bored people. Damned depressing, he thought.

He walked the three blocks to Macy's and still got there before the doors opened. He was an hour early. Would Schott have thought of coming early, too? Of course he would. He was a professional; he thought of everything. Then what the hell am I doing here, David asked himself. Do I have a choice? Not unless I want to go underground for the rest of my life. And unless Andrea does, and Joan. Joan's in New York; I suppose I ought to look her up. She hadn't seemed likely to change her mind, though. Maybe I could convince her face to face? A woman with a mind of her own, that's how she'd come across. There's no convincing me, she'd seemed to be saying. So maybe he should try anyway? Maybe. He'd see. After he met with Victor Schott. If there was an after. Self-consciously, he put his hand to his coat pocket. The .38 was there, hard against his hip. For the first time, he'd come to terms with really having to use it. In Northport he hadn't actually thought he'd have to. In spite of what he'd said to Andrea, he hadn't thought he would. It had seemed then as if he could change things some other way, as if the gun was only a kind of insurance in case everything went out of control.

He knew now that everything had already gone out of control. There was no way to track down Victor Schott, no way to catch him by surprise. Whatever Victor Schott was, he'd covered his tracks beautifully.

A woman inside came to the doors and unlocked them, one by one. The crowd around Brett moved forward as one body and he was taken with it. Too late to turn back now. He was inside the store, one hour early, but here, waiting. He would never have a better chance at finding Victor Schott. He had never been so vulnerable.

The only person in the women's lingerie department was a bored clerk leaning against the counter by the cash register, staring off into space. It was not an orderly department. Circular stands of underpants blocked the aisles, display cases stood at random with no apparent design. Wide aisles ended abruptly at display counters. In a triumph of modern merchandising, Macy's had made it virtually impossible to walk a direct route through the department. A trap? It would be difficult to make a fast escape. It would be, he considered, just as difficult for Victor Schott as it would be for him. He circled the area slowly, casually, looking for a place to wait, a place where he could see anyone who came into the department, and yet a place from which he could run, if need be. If need be. I'm a fool, he thought. He's a professional. What the hell do I know? How do I trap someone like him, how on earth do I even things up?

He found the spot he was looking for, an angle of wall that was out of the way, yet next to a main aisle down which he could run if he had to. From there he could see everyone who came by. He had never even seen a picture of Victor Schott, had no idea what he looked like. In no way could he even things up. Victor Schott had all the advantage, even down to knowing what he looked like. He'd had his chance, too. The same yearbook that had contained his father's and all the other pictures had also contained Victor Schott's. If after all these years he was still recognizable. Damn; if he'd known then, he could have turned a few pages and looked. When he'd been at Shirley Carpenter's house he hadn't even known about Victor Schott. Less than two weeks ago he'd been in Shirley Carpenter's little sitting room, looking at an old yearbook, looking at those graudation pictures. Less than two weeks ago. It seemed like forever. It seemed like a lifetime that Elizabeth had been gone.

"May I help you?" It was the clerk. He'd noticed her eyeing him curiously. A man, alone, standing around the lingerie department. Hardly the usual, he supposed. That was how Schott figured to know him, just in case he had any doubts; that was how he figured to know Schott. And in the meantime, he looked mighty out of place. "Sorry, no. I'm just waiting for someone." She gazed at him doubtfully and turned away. OK, he thought, so it looks strange.

A couple of women walked by, looked askance at him as they passed, but kept on going.

He looked at his watch—ten-fifteen. Schott ought to be coming early to check things out, just as he had. He ought to be here anytime. A man older than he, close to sixty. How many such men would there be on an ordinary morning in the lingerie department?

"Can you tell me where the girdles are?" An elderly woman peered up at him through thick glasses.

"Sorry, I have no idea."

"You don't work here, then?"

"No, I'm just waiting for someone."

"I'm sorry, I thought you might be a clerk. Do you see any clerks around?"

His glance swept the place. Two clerks now talked desultorily on the opposite side of the department. "See those two over there, the one in the green sweater and the other one in white? They're clerks, I believe."

"Thank you very much. Sorry to have bothered you." He watched as she ambled away, barely using her cane. Her cane—white with a red tip. She was blind? He watched as she made her way toward the clerks, as she asked her question of them and as the one in the green sweater took her over to the girdles. He saw the old lady lift up a package and hold it to her face, barely an inch away from the glasses. He hadn't even noticed the white cane until she had walked away. Back there, somewhere in Massachusetts as he recalled, it had been one of the things he'd promised himself he'd do. Notice everything. *Notice everything.* Not an elderly lady, a *blind* elderly lady. What else had he missed? God knew. God help him; one mistake like that with Victor Schott and it would be all over.

It was nearly eleven and he was becoming more and more concerned. It was crazy, he with no experience at all, thinking he could outwit Victor Schott. For more than fifteen years Schott had been killing people off, never making a mistake, and suddenly he was going to make one? Not likely, not bloody likely.

He had one eye on his watch now and one on the people who casually shopped through the department. No men came alone, and only one came through with his wife, an apparently reluctant shopper. More than once he caught the clerks eyeing him suspiciously. What did he expect; surely it did look suspicious. What was he doing there? *What the hell was he doing there?* Letting

Victor Schott set him up, that's what. He looked at his watch again—eleven-seventeen. Something was wrong. Something was very wrong.

It was worse now that Schott was late—or wasn't coming. What in the world was happening? What was Schott trying to pull? He was not the kind of man who made mistakes. Whatever it was was purposeful, but what was it? What on earth was it?

If he left now, what would he do? How could he ever locate Victor Schott? How could he get in touch with him again? There was always Tech-Optics. Another call to Ginny? Another relayed message? This time, *he'd* set it up. This time it would be on his terms. Except, of course, that Schott wouldn't show up for that one either. It was not Victor Schott who was having a hard time finding the man he was looking for. It was not Schott who didn't know how to get in touch. It was not Schott who was looking for anybody. Schott had always known where to find him, and that's what made this all so crazy. Why here? Of all places, why here?

It was after twelve. The clerk in the white blouse was leaving. She walked his way, a middle-aged woman with thin pale hair, frizzed up to appear thicker than it was. She stared at him over the tops of her glasses. "Is there anything I can do for you?" she asked as she came even with him.

"No, I think not," he said. She walked on by, hadn't even slowed down for his answer. He glanced back at the clerk who was left, and she was gazing at him. Don't try anything, her expression said, and suddenly he knew it was useless. Victor Schott was not coming. If he had been late, it would have been nothing to call the department and give David a message. He was not coming, maybe never had planned on coming in the first place. And that gave David pause. *What the hell was going on?*

What if he's following me, he thought; what if he plans

on getting me when I leave? Was that the plan? Why had he been sent here? Why, if not for Schott to tail him? What now?

He left Macy's and crossed to the other side of Thirty-fourth Street, realizing as soon as he had done it that he'd already made a mistake. Trap him, he thought. Notice everything. Let him make the mistake.

He walked down Thirty-fourth until he came to Sixth Avenue. This time, he thought, I do it right. He came to the intersection just as the light was turning green; he paused and looked around as the other pedestrians surged on into the street. He turned and walked several yards to his right along Sixth Avenue, then, as if changing his mind, turned back toward the corner. He came to it just as the light was changing. The last of the pedestrians darted across as the light changed. He looked about quickly and stepped into the street. Already the traffic had started up. Thank God it was one-way; he had only to look to his right. Horns honked angrily at him as he wove through the oncoming traffic. He looked back once—no one was following, but a horn blared almost in his ear and a taxi driver rolled down his window and shouted, "You crazy asshole!" David dodged around the back of the taxi, then, struck with the idea, ran back and banged on the taxi's fender. The driver slammed on his brakes and started out the door.

"Can you get me to Times Square?" David asked while the driver still had one foot in the cab.

"What the hell—?"

"You're empty, aren't you?"

"Get in," the driver snarled.

David grinned and opened the door. All around, horns were blaring, but as he looked back, there was no one else in the street, no frustrated-looking man standing on the curb. He got in and slammed the door behind him. "Times Square," he repeated.

"I'd believe it," the taxi driver grumbled. "I'd believe it even more if it was about two o'clock in the morning. Your kind don't come out in broad daylight."

"Just the ride; no sermon to go with it, if you don't mind," David replied. He looked back as the taxi gathered speed. No other car was stopping to pick up a passenger. He'd made it. Maybe.

At Times Square he paid his fare and left the taxi, backtracking only as far as the Criterion Theater. He'd seen it when they came into the area, and it had given him an idea. He was feeling better now—he was thinking, making things fall into place. He was beginning to feel that he could handle Victor Schott after all.

He bought his ticket and went up the broad staircase, hardly taking time to notice the ornate lobby. Another time he would have done so, but this was now, and there were more pressing matters. He came into the theater from the loge, and paused to let his eyes adjust. The theater was mostly empty; he hadn't even noticed what was playing. He sat down; he was on the left-hand side. From where he sat he could turn halfway around and see if anyone else entered the theater. He watched for a good three minutes, but no one else came in. Now he looked around him and saw what he was hoping to see—an exit sign at the front, on the left side. He judged the distance and then turned to look back at an attendant who was lounging at the back.

A pair of women came in—no good; they, too, sat on the left. He'd try one or two more. A couple of teenagers came in and went down the right-hand aisle. He watched them decide on seats, and he was up and moving down the aisle and at the exit door. The attendant hadn't seen him. He slammed his hands against the panic bar and the door flew open. Only then did the man see and call out, but he was already gone, running down the outside metal stairway that led to the street. It was a good gamble—in the theater and out the exit. Good and clean—the exit leading to the outside. There was no one loitering around the bottom of the stairway; he was home free. He hit the sidewalk running, looking up to catch the street name as he came to the corner. He paused at the corner long enough to orient himself. The light was green and he ran across. He'd done it; he'd lost Victor Schott!

He stared at the painting on the wall. After a while motel rooms all began to look alike. This one, outside Elizabeth, New Jersey, was no different. Why had he stopped here? Because of the name? Because he didn't know what else to do, where else to go? The thought flashed through his mind: It had begun with Elizabeth, let it end with Elizabeth. Morbid thought. I'm not ready to die yet, but how the hell do I end it? How do I find him and stop it? What can I do to trap him? What would bring him out into the open? Go home and let him come after me. But what if he goes after one of the others instead? He can't, not if they're in hiding. If Andrea still is. And of course Joan isn't. Should have contacted Joan while I was there. Would she have listened? No. Should have done it anyway. It wouldn't do any good.

She has to go into hiding. I can't draw him out unless she does; he could just as easily go after her. And how would I draw him out? How would I know how he's going to do it? Check my car every morning for bombs? Stay up all night to keep him from burning the house down? He deals in accidents—how the hell do you protect yourself from an accident? He doesn't always deal with accidents. A bomb in the car, a bullet in the head—those aren't accidents. What's he doing? Why can't I figure it out? Call Joan. I'll start with Joan.

"What city?" the operator asked.

"New York."

"What borough?"

"Ah . . . I don't know. Try Manhattan."

"What's the name?"

"Carpenter. Joan. I don't have the address."

The operator came back on the line. "I have no Joan Carpenters listed. There are several J. Carpenters. You want to try one?"

"Several? How many?"

"Oh . . . ten, twelve, it looks like."

"Never mind." He'd call Shirley and get the number. He ought to be checking back with her anyway, see how she was doing, see what was happening in Fairfield, if anything.

He dialed the number, and it rang several times before someone lifted the receiver. "Hello?" The voice sounded uncertain. He couldn't tell who it was.

"Shirley?"

"Yes?"

"It's David Brett. How are you?"

"Where are you, David?"

"I'm in New Jersey. I thought I was going to meet Victor Schott, but he threw me a high one and didn't show up. I've been thinking about getting in touch with Joan. Can you give me her address?"

"Don't go there! Come back here, David."

"Why?"

"I can't tell you over the phone. Trust me. Come back."

"What is it?"

"Have you ever been to Angola, to the park there?"

"I've heard of it; never been there."

"How long would it take you? A couple of days?"

"Shirley, what is it? What's wrong?"

"David, I have to talk to you, but it's not safe here. Meet me in Angola in two days. I'll try to get you a reservation at the inn there. If I can't, ask for me in the dining room. I can't talk any longer. Be there, David, please."

"What—" The phone clicked in his ear. He stared straight ahead, listening to the silence on the other end. Panic rose in his throat. Something had to be very wrong.

Shirley Carpenter wiped the tears away with her fingertips and clenched her jaw. She was not going to cry anymore. She had cried all she could; now there had to be something more effective to do. She dialed the number but the tears still kept coming. The phone rang twice and then it was answered. "He called," she said.

"Did you tell him?"

"Yes."

"Is he going to do it?"

"I think so."

"It had better be more than thinking so. He's got to do it."

"He will. I told him two days."

"At the inn?"

"Yes."

"Good. There will be a reservation in his name. I'll take care of it now."

"What happens if he doesn't show up?"

There was a long silence before he spoke. "You'd better start praying that he does."

16

"ANOTHER CUP OF coffee?" He leaned back as the waitress poured. For the first time in . . . how many days? . . . he was relaxed. There had been a room reserved in his name, just as she'd said, although there was no sign of her. He wouldn't worry about it now. He wouldn't worry about anything now. He hadn't been followed, he knew that. Across Pennsylvania and Ohio he'd kept his eyes on the rear-view mirror. There was no sign of a tail. Whatever Victor Schott had had in mind by sending him to Macy's, it wasn't to pick up a tail. And he was safe here now. Only Shirley knew he was here, and it was her idea to come here so that he wouldn't be seen in Fairfield. That meant she wouldn't tell anyone she was meeting him here, and that meant safety. He couldn't remember when he had last felt safe. Before Elizabeth had been killed, he supposed. A lifetime ago. They'd always talked about coming here, about coming in the fall to see the colors, or in the winter for the skiing, but they never had. Suddenly he wanted to be alone, to go into the room and close the door and be alone. He signaled for the check.

The room was like all the motel rooms he'd been staying in, except that instead of the ubiquitous expressway, there was only rolling lawn and woods outside. Instead of the hum of truck tires, there was silence. Silence and a chill November rain. He closed the door behind him, sliding the latch into place. He didn't even turn on the light. He wanted it dark, even welcomed the dark, because he wouldn't have to see that the room was empty, that he was the only one here. He no longer even hoped that Shirley would show up; in fact, he hoped that she would not, at least not until morning. He wanted to be alone, and to wallow in the pain that being alone brought. He felt his way to the bed and lay down on it, on his back, one arm flung across his eyes. Darkness, complete darkness. He tried imagining that Elizabeth was lying on the bed beside him, but he could not. He rolled over on his side and let the tears come.

He was walking down the expressway in the dark, going for help; something was wrong with the car. As he walked, the cars tore by him in the opposite direction, their lights catching him for an instant, then flying by as if he weren't even there. It seemed as if he'd been walking forever, one foot in front of the other, no longer even aware of where he was or why he was there or where he would go when the car was fixed. Just walking. And behind him came a noise, a noise like a truck that had thrown a rod, and it kept coming and coming, and then it wasn't behind him but in front of him, and all around him, and his head was pounding with the noise, and he sat up in bed in the dark. He blinked his eyes. Dark. A room. Dark. Where is this? And then he remembered. He was awake now; why didn't the pounding go away? He felt his hands gripping the bedspread, and with an effort of will he made them relax. Someone was pounding on the door. It must be Shirley. Why hadn't she waited until morning?

He felt for the bedside table, snapped on the lamp, looked at his watch—one-fifteen? He snapped back the latch and opened the door. "You could have—"

It wasn't Shirley Carpenter standing in the doorway; it was two police officers, and one had his hand on the butt of his gun with the holster unsnapped. "David Brett?"

"Yes. What is it?"

"May I see some identification?"

He reached for his wallet, then, suspicious, pulled his hand back. "What is this? You don't have any right to come here and wake me up in the middle of the night. I haven't done anything."

"Are you David Lane Brett, of Fairfield, Indiana?"

"Yes."

"You're under arrest. Spread your legs. Put both hands up against the wall."

"Arrest? What for?"

"Hands against the wall."

"You have to tell me what the charges are."

"Keep your pants on; I'll get to that. Hands against the wall or I'll do it for you."

He leaned against the wall and felt the officer frisk him. The wallet was taken from his back pocket; he heard it slapped open. "Yeah, it's him," one of them said. "Put your hands behind your back."

"You can't arrest me without telling me the charges."

"Resisting arrest. Attempted assault on an officer of the law. Theft of police property. Disorderly conduct. That enough for you? You must be some tough guy."

"I don't know what you're talking about."

"Yeah, I've heard that one before."

His mind was racing. Victor Schott? CIA? Could he have been followed after all? But why this way? Why hadn't he just come in and killed him? Or was the scenario going to be that he would be shot as he tried to escape? That sounded like something Victor Schott would think of.

"Who made the charges? I have a right to know."

"He's a regular jailhouse lawyer, isn't he? The warrant is signed by Police Lieutenant Phillip Decker, the complainant himself. From down by Parke County. Town of Fairfield. I don't think I'd want to be in your shoes. You pull something like that against a police officer, they might just lock you up and forget where the key was."

Decker? *Decker?* How did he know? Where did he fit in, and what was this supposed to mean? There hadn't been any arrest.

"Hands behind your back, fella." They pulled his hands down and snapped the handcuffs together.

"Where are you taking me?"

"To the station. We'll give you a nice cell and call your friend Decker in the morning and let him send someone up for you."

"I get a phone call."

"Smart guy. He must watch how they do it on TV."

Who was he going to call? Who could he trust?

He was alone in the cell, an eight-by-eight-foot square, green paint peeling from the walls. At least it was clean. If not dark. If not quiet. He'd lain on the single cot, unable to sleep, staring up at the damned light that was on all night, wondering why it was so necessary to keep the light on. Sometime around five the drunk in the next cell had awakened and demanded to be let out. An officer had come from somewhere, talked to the drunk—evidently a regular customer—decided he was sober enough to find his own way home, and let him out. The radio from the squad room went on all night, no attempt to turn it down, no recognition that someone might be trying to sleep. He probably wouldn't have been able to sleep anyway. Victor Schott's first step: getting him arrested. Then what? Shot while trying to escape? That sounded logical. One more down, two to go.

Phillip Decker, the complainant, that took a little more thinking. How had Schott gotten to him? And why? The CIA agent—if that's what Schott was—and the stupid small-town cop. What was in it for the two of them to be working together? Unless one of them wasn't. . . . But it had to be. What else? It was Schott who was trying to kill him, yet Decker had gotten him arrested. He hated Decker's guts, thought he was a complete incompetent—but crooked? He wouldn't have guessed that. But he must be, trumped-up charges and all. So it would be Decker who would do the killing. He'd come alone, no witnesses that way. Somewhere between Angola and Fairfield there'd be an escape attempt and Decker would have to shoot. He'd mean to shoot at the legs, of course, but somehow the bullet would go higher than he intended and David Brett would be shot in the back and killed. It would have to be just one shot; Decker wouldn't be able to explain more. Which meant that Decker would have to be a good shot. And he would not arrive until morning. Because it would have to be light when the escape took place, light enough to be sure of the target. And how was Decker going to get him out of the car? What was the pretext going to be? Not breakfast or lunch, because that would have to be at a restaurant, and Decker wouldn't want witnesses. It would have to be out in the open, no witnesses, the word of a cop and no one to question it. He would not leave the car. No matter what, he would not leave it. And even if he died, if Decker had thought of some other way, at least there would be someone who would know, someone who would question. The only person he trusted now would know, and would have to know, because if Phillip Decker killed David Brett, then Andrea would have to know that it wasn't only Victor Schott she was running from. His one phone call. Andrea.

It was past noon when the officers came for him. One stood outside the cell and held a gun while the other unlocked the door, let himself in, handcuffed David's hands, and led him out of the cell. They were not taking

174

any chances. The warrant was for resisting arrest and assaulting an officer, among other things. Already he had a reputation. When Decker gunned him down, who would argue?

Decker was standing in the squad room, talking with another officer. He looked up at Brett casually, then looked away and returned to the conversation. You bastard, Brett thought, you're not going to kill me.

The officer handed Decker some papers to sign. "You didn't come by yourself?" he asked.

"Sure did." Decker snapped the ballpoint pen closed and replaced it in his shirt pocket.

"You can handle him?"

Decker looked back at Brett. "He's not such a tough customer. We're going to get along just fine, aren't we, Brett?"

David stared at him wordlessly, then turned to the officer behind the counter. "There was no arrest I resisted. There was no attempted assault, or any of the other things in the warrant. It's all trumped up—"

"I've heard that before."

"It's true, and I'll tell you something else. I'm not going to get as far as Fairfield. He's going to shoot me down on the way; that's why he hasn't got anybody with him. He doesn't want any witnesses. Well, I'll tell you right now, when he gives his story that I was trying to escape, you can be sure he's lying. I'm not going to try. I'm not getting out of that car until we get to Fairfield, no matter what. Whatever he says after he does it is going to be a lie."

"Are you finished?" Decker asked him.

"You're going to have to find some other way to do it, Decker, because I'm not going to give you the chance."

"Never mind him, guys. He hallucinates."

"You know damned well what I'm talking about."

"I know damned well we'd better get going."

"You need any help getting him into the car?" the officer beside Brett asked.

"You heard the guy; he's going to be a model citizen. But just in case I should get tempted to shoot him down on the way to the car, maybe you'd better come along. He seems to want a witness."

They put him into the backseat and slammed the door behind him. Brett noticed there were no handles on the insides of the doors. Heavy wire mesh separated him from the driver's seat. He was locked into another cage. At least he'd had the presence of mind to talk in the squad room. There was no way Decker would dare kill him now.

From the driver's seat, Decker caught his eye in the rear-view mirror and for a moment they stared at each other. Brett's look was defiant. You're not going to kill me that easily, he thought. He couldn't read the look in Decker's eyes.

Neither spoke as they drove through town. Last night's rain had stopped, but it was still cloudy. Puddles lay on the shoulders of the road. At the edge of town they slowed behind a farm truck; then Decker, impatient, sounded the siren one time. The truck pulled over, and Decker drove on by. His eyes flicked up to the rear-view mirror and found Brett staring back at him.

"What makes you think I'm going to try to kill you?"

"Because I've got it figured out."

"Why don't you tell me what you've got figured out?"

"Why don't you tell me how you're going to do it, you bastard."

"So now I'm a bastard in addition to an SOB. Well, the fact is, I probably am. Maybe a hell of a lot more, but I'm keeping you alive. Incidentally"—Brett could see Decker's right arm moving, as if he were working something out of a pants pocket—"you could be a little more comfortable if you wanted to uncuff yourself." He held his hand to the mesh and maneuvered a small key through.

"What the hell are you trying to do?"

"You can see well enough. Take it and unlock the cuffs."

The first step: his hands freed, the illusion of freedom, of the possibility of escape. "I'm not going to fall for that. I'm not getting out of this car until we get to Fairfield."

"What happens in Fairfield?"

"I don't know, but at least there'll be witnesses."

"You really think I'm trying to kill you?"

"You and Victor Schott."

"Anybody else?"

"Maybe." Was there somebody else? Who?

"Take the key."

"Keep it."

"Take the damned key. Don't use it if you like those cuffs so much. But take it."

"I wouldn't give you the satisfaction."

Decker let go of the key and it fell to the floor at Brett's feet. "You've got it now," Decker said. "You can use it if you decide to."

David stared down at the key and back at Decker. "You're a son of a bitch."

"You've said that to me before, remember? We're not going to get anywhere on this, Brett, unless you calm down. I admit I strung you on a little, and I admit it wasn't fair. Wasn't right, even. I'll admit it. But you've done exactly what I sent you out to do, and now that I've reeled you back in, we're going to have to talk. We can do it with your hands cuffed, or we can do it with them loose. But we're going to have to talk, and you're going to have to get that chip off your shoulder, because the only way for us to get your wife's killer is for you to tell me what you know. And the only way for you to stop the next killing from happening is to listen to what I know. And then, Brett, whether you like it or not, you're going to have to become a partner with this son of a bitch for as long as it takes to get the job done."

"I don't know what you're talking about."

"One more murder, Brett. One more: Andrea Kramer. And once that's accomplished, it's all over except to wrap it up with a multiple murder charge against David Brett. This guy—Victor Schott—is one hell of a man, and to tell you the truth, I'm scared pea green that he's got even more up his sleeve than I've figured. The plain and simple fact is: We haven't got time to play games. You can uncuff yourself or not, it doesn't matter in the least to me, but you've got to give me some information and give it fast or Andrea is going to die and then it'll be all over."

"Haven't you forgotten about Joan Carpenter?"

"Joan Carpenter is dead."

He stared into the rear-view mirror at Decker. Decker's eyes flicked up, caught his, then looked back at the road. Joan dead? "When?" Why hadn't Shirley told him?

"Last Thursday night. I'll bet you were in the New York area Thursday night, weren't you?"

"I was in a motel in . . . I don't remember the name of the town."

"But near New York?"

"Yes." *What was it? What was happening?*

"How did you happen to be there? I thought you were in the Boston area."

"How did you know that?"

Decker sighed. "That's a whole other thing. We'll get to it. First let's take care of New York. What were you doing there?"

"I was supposed to meet Victor Schott."

"Thursday night?"

178

"Friday morning. I came down on Thursday so I could get into the city early."

"Anybody see you there?"

"I spent the whole morning in the lingerie department of Macy's."

Decker looked at him wordlessly through the mirror.

"I got a message from Schott. That was where I was supposed to meet him."

"He didn't show up, of course."

"Why do you say 'of course'?"

"You're no dummy, Brett. You tell me why he wanted you in New York."

David shook his head in disbelief. "It doesn't make any sense. Why would I want to kill her?"

"Who knows? But there's a pattern that's as plain as the nose on your face. Everybody looks for a pattern, and there it is. It might be enough to convict you. The first murder," Decker went on, staring at the road straight ahead, "Elizabeth Brett. No obvious motive—"

"That was not the first murder. It started a long time before that."

"I know. But this is the first obvious one. And so we have to ask ourselves why they've become obvious."

"How do you know about the others?"

"Just listen for a minute. Elizabeth Brett, no obvious motive. When there's no motive, you always look to the spouse. Even I did, let's face it. Next murder, Lane Carpenter and Jenny Wilson. I should have said *murders*. Plural. Three murders in Fairfield in less than a week. They have to be connected, don't they?"

"Your story's a lot of crap—"

"Shut up and listen; I know that was a lot of crap, knew it when I told it to you. But it got you going, didn't it?"

"You did that on purpose? You accused me when you knew all along—*what the hell were you doing?*"

"Using you, pure and simple. Those murders had to be

179

connected, but the trouble was, I couldn't figure out how. There was nothing. *Nothing.* And yet it had to be. I couldn't figure it—why anyone would kill Elizabeth—until someone mentioned it: how everyone in Lane's family had died in accidents, how Lane was named after your father and your father had died and now Elizabeth. In accidents. And I thought, no, those weren't accidents, they were executions. But I didn't know where to start looking. Neither did you, I guess, but you had the reason—your wife dead. And the idea in the back of your mind: Should it have been you? It had to be in the back of your mind, because it was in the back of mine. In the front, to tell you the truth. So I figured if I could plant the connection in your mind, you could do it. You: the aggrieved husband. You: the potential victim. Doors would open for you that wouldn't open for me. People would talk to you."

"You accused me of having an affair with Jenny when I was still in a daze from Elizabeth? You let me go out there *knowing* someone was trying to kill me?"

"Yeah."

"Decker, you *are* a son of a bitch."

"Yeah, I know."

"What was going to be your excuse if I'd been killed?"

"You had a backup man."

"What is that supposed to mean?"

"I had someone following you. He was supposed to keep an eye on you, keep anything from happening to you."

"He didn't do too good a job. I almost got burned up in Michigan."

"I know. He lost you in Michigan."

"Wonderful. Wonderful backup man you've got there."

"Shut up."

"I thought you wanted me to talk."

"So talk. What do you know about Victor Schott?"

Brett looked down at the key lying on the floor. "You tell me first. How do you know so much? How did you know I was in Massachusetts if he lost me in Michigan?"

"Because that's where Victor Schott was. Have you seen him?"

"How do you know about Victor Schott?"

"Same way you do."

"Allen Lundy?"

Decker glanced into the mirror and nodded.

"How the hell did you find him?"

"We're going to get pretty mixed up on this at the rate we're going. How about we start from the beginning?"

"Which beginning are you talking about? Are we going all the way back to the war and beyond?"

"You know that story and I know that story; we both got it from the same person. We don't need to go over that. Let's begin where it began for us—where we both came into it with both feet—when your wife got blown up in your car."

Brett let out a long breath. Through the window he saw a pasture, black-and-white cows grazing, a white house with a black Amish buggy drawn up beside it.

". . . not a person in Fairfield would have killed her," Decker was saying, "except maybe you, of course, but I couldn't really see it. And then Lane and Jenny got shot, and it made even less sense. It had to be connected somehow, but there was no sense at all in it, until I went to see Shirley Carpenter to tell her about Lane and I began to think about that—about her family all dying in accidents, her husband and her son and his kids. And her son's wife. And when I found out that Jenny had been pregnant, and you'd told me your wife was pregnant, it all seemed too strange. I don't believe in coincidences, not like that. So I brought you in and I pushed you real hard, and you fell for it, just like I'd planned. When you

181

tore out of that parking lot, Jack Turner was right on your tail. He followed you to Shirley's and to Evelyn McAndrews's and finally all the way to Michigan. He lost you there. You want to fill me in?"

"I went to see Buddy Kramer's widow and then Andrea Kramer in Ann Arbor. I spent a day with her." He saw Decker's eyes flick up to the mirror but decided to ignore it. "By then I had the gun, but I don't think I really expected to use it."

"Where is it now?"

"It's in the glove compartment of Sandy Augustina's Pinto, which happens to be in the parking lot at the inn back there in Angola. You mind telling me how Sandy's going to get her car back?"

"We'll work it out. It wasn't too smart leaving the gun in the car. What if someone had cornered you at the inn?"

"Are you trying to say I should have had a shoot-out with the cops when they came for me?"

"I was thinking of Victor Schott."

"He didn't follow me."

"I'm not sure you should be so smug about that."

"What do you mean?"

"We'll get to it later. You got yourself a gun in Detroit, and then you went to Ann Arbor."

"Andrea was the oldest of the Kramer children. She remembered Lundy from when he came to her house years ago. There'd been a big argument and her dad had thrown him out, but he'd said something to her, something that gave her the idea that he might be up north in Michigan."

"That's where the fire was?"

"I found Lundy there; I guess you must know about that."

"Tell me anyway."

"Why?"

"I like good stories. You notice anybody following you up there?"

"No."

" 'Course we know that doesn't mean much. Turner followed you all the way to Michigan."

"Somebody followed me in Massachusetts."

"Let's stay in Michigan for the time being."

"I found Lundy there, but it was a setup; he knew I was coming."

"He told me."

"Did he tell you about the fire?"

"He told me some. Let's hear your version."

"I didn't especially want to stay the night there, but he sort of talked me into it. We were in the same room. Something woke me up in the night, a noise maybe. He wasn't in his bed, so I got suspicious and slipped out a door at the other end of the lodge. Not two minutes later the whole thing was in flames. I couldn't figure out why he was trying to kill me. What did he tell you?"

"He said he was awake, having a hard time sleeping after all the memories you'd brought back. He thought he heard something and got up to investigate. Went out a door on the other side, worked his way around to the back, and saw somebody pouring what he thought was gasoline on a pile of wood that'd been made there. It was too dark; he couldn't see who it was. Naturally he thinks it was Victor Schott. He tried to circle back to go in and warn you, but the thing went up in flames before he got back to the door. He thought at first you'd been killed, but, your car was gone and they didn't find your body. He figured then you must have done the same thing he did—heard a noise and gotten out. Your car was gone; it seemed to make sense."

"How do you know he's telling the truth?"

"You were sleeping in the same room as him; he didn't need to burn the whole place down to get rid of you."

183

"Then how did Schott find us there? If that's who it was."

"You figure it. He killed your wife. Was that intentional, or was he trying to kill you? Either way, you were still alive. Then he killed Lane and Jenny. Then you take off from Fairfield like a big bird. If he's around, he can figure it; you're going after somebody. And who might that be, if not Allen Lundy, the one left of all the men who took his brother to war with them, the one he hadn't been able to find. You think he wouldn't have followed you, wouldn't have been hoping you were going to lead him to Lundy?"

"Now you're telling me I had *two* people following me up there?"

"One, two; what's the difference? You didn't see Turner; why should you have seen Schott?"

"Didn't your man see him?"

"Unfortunately, he didn't. But that doesn't mean he couldn't have been there. Turner was *following*, remember; he wasn't looking for a tail on himself."

"And certainly not someone like Victor Schott."

"What is that supposed to mean?"

"As you would say, Decker, we'll get to that later." He bent down and picked up the key, turning it over and over in his hand. It could get him freedom. It could get him a shot in the back. "So I led Victor Schott to Allen Lundy. Then who was he trying to kill, Allen or me, or both of us?"

"Beats me, but after that, my guess is that he's not all that interested in knocking you off. I think he's got bigger plans for you."

"You think he wants to get me convicted of Andrea's murder. And maybe Joan's?"

"Of a whole lot more than that, my friend. A whole lot more. Three killed in Fairfield. While you're there. Andrea's sister killed in Michigan, again while you're there;

isn't that right?" He didn't wait for an answer. "Allen Lundy—let's call that an attempted killing for now. And while you're there again."

"And Joan in New York. While I'm there. A lone man standing all morning in the lingerie department of Macy's. How much more obvious could I have been?"

"You didn't mention Framingham, of course."

"Framingham? There's nobody there."

"Patti Styles. The name ring a bell?"

"Patti? He . . . he killed her too?"

"You want to tell me about her?"

"If you know he killed her, you must know something about her yourself!"

"I know she worked in the office where Schott takes his calls. Or at least gets his mail. I thought it was his own office at first, but it looks as if it isn't that simple."

"How much do you know about that place?"

"Not very much. I hope you're prepared to tell me more."

"How do you know what you know? How did you trace Victor Schott there?"

"Same way you did, more or less, except that I was ahead of you. You see, Shirley and I have huddled over this in the last few days. I went to the *Sun* and got the address for Victor Schott. I did it because I knew you were after him—I'd talked with Lundy by then—so I went to our town repository of information, Charlene Manley . . . you know her? She told me—not too willingly, but she did. I gave the address to Turner and he flew out there. It was our idea that he tail you until you located Schott. Then he was supposed to reel you in."

"Was he driving a tan Volare? Around thirty, dark hair?"

"That sounds like him."

"He was following me. I lost him again. He's not too hot at the following business. You're going to have to

185

send him back to detective school, or wherever it is you guys learn your tricks."

"That's not funny, Brett. Let's talk about the girl for a minute. Why would she have been killed?"

"I don't know. I took her out for coffee, that's it."

"You're sure that's all?"

"I was using her, is that what you want me to say? Yes, I was using her for information—who Schott is, how he gets his messages. I saw her one time, that's it. She was just a kid, for heaven's sake. She was eighteen. What on earth did he kill her for?"

"He's killed kids a lot younger than that. She must have told you something. Or he must have been afraid that she would."

"She had nothing to do with anything."

"Well, he killed her, or at least somebody did."

David looked out the window. Patti. He'd done it to her as surely as if he'd pulled the trigger. "How was she killed?"

"Knife to the throat. Very neat. He knows what he's doing. He's pretty good at this kind of thing."

The plaque. "He should. He probably does it for a living."

"You want to tell me about that?"

"Does anybody know what Victor Schott really does?"

"No one that I know. Do you?"

"I've got a guess. And I'm not sure I want to tell you, Decker." He looked at the key in his hand.

Decker stared at him for a long moment in the mirror. Then he let up on the accelerator and pulled the car onto the shoulder. Before the car had even stopped rolling, he leaned his arm across the back of the seat and turned toward Brett. When he spoke, his voice was low and unsteady. "There was another one killed out there." He rubbed his forefinger on the seat back. "Jack Turner was found in the tan Volare, knifed in the throat, just like the girl. Jack Turner. Brett, you have to tell me what it is you know."

Brett stared at him and saw the glisten of tears at the rim of Decker's eyes. "What's going on, Decker? Why was he killed? What's happening?"

"You tell me! Turner was just following orders, for Christ's sake! He was following *you*, keeping an eye on *you*. That's all! He wasn't even all that good at it. He lost you in Michigan—that's how good he was. And then I found out about Victor Schott and sent him out there to look for you. He didn't know a damned thing! And that son of a bitch got him! Jack Turner! He wouldn't have hurt a fly! *You tell me!* What's Victor Schott *doing*? What was he after from Jack?"

"Patti told me two things: one, that she'd never seen Victor Schott, that as far as she knew, he never came into the office. It was Timmerman's private secretary who took the messages, and, as far as I could tell, relayed them to Schott through Timmerman. Timmerman wasn't there, and his secretary was about as uncooperative as she could be. I didn't find out a damned thing from her. That's one thing. The other is something about Timmerman, but maybe it's the connection between him and Schott, as well. The company is an optics company, makes lenses and other special optical equipment, and most of the work is government contract work. Special optical—maybe you could read 'surveillance'—contract work for the government, Decker. And it's Timmerman who has the government connections. He's retired from the CIA."

"I think you're getting a little paranoid, Brett. You're obviously in some danger, but I really doubt that the whole CIA is after you."

"Not the whole CIA, just one agent. One man who has the know-how and the wherewithal and the connections—and a very personal grudge to settle."

Decker stared absently out the window. "You believe Allen Lundy's theory, then."

"How can I not believe it? We're all being killed, aren't we?"

"If Schott is a CIA agent—a CIA hit man even, judging from his expertise—we've got a lot bigger problem than I thought we had."

"You're a police officer. Can you find out if he's an agent?"

"Not if he's still with them."

"We'll never stop him if we can't even find him. We have to flush him out. There's got to be a way to do it."

"There is. We just have to figure out what it is—without getting you and Andrea Kramer killed in the process. How about we shut up for a while, Brett, and put our thinking caps on and try to figure out what that way is?" He started the engine again and the car lunged forward.

David looked into the mirror; Decker was staring straight ahead at the road. He knows everything about us, he thought; and we know next to nothing about him. Except that he's CIA. Maybe. Does he know we know that? No, say what you mean: Did Patti tell him? And what else might she have said? What did she know? What had he told her that she might have told Victor Schott before he killed her? How do we flush him out? *Use everything*—the most important lesson now, perhaps. Use everything we have, which is very little. OK, he's CIA. How the hell do we use that? We could make him go after Decker for a change. Wonder how Decker would like that? *Everything means something:* Use what we know to catch him. But we don't know anything about him. Not quite true: We do know a bit. Maybe not much, but a few things. He kills people, he sets up accidents. He knows how to get at you when you least expect it. He has connections; he's smart. Why is he in a hurry lately? Why is he no longer making the killings look like accidents? What does that mean? We've never seen him; we don't know him. How the hell are we going to get into his head and figure out what makes it tick? How do we pull him out? *Use everything.* Allen Lundy. Shirley Carpenter. Andrea. Someone's going to have to draw him out, and it evidently can't be me. He's already had me in his hands and let me go. He's not ready for me yet. *Andrea.* If Decker's right, then she's next. She's going to have to be the bait. No, I'm not leading anyone else into that. One is enough. Two. If Elizabeth hadn't married me, she'd be alive. If I hadn't talked with Patti, she'd be alive. Three, if you count Jack Turner.

"You play bridge, Brett?" Decker said suddenly.

Bridge? "I've played."

"Every Thursday night the wife and I play with the neighbors. You know the Christiansens—Wally and Joyce? Men against the women. We slaughter the women every week. We're up on 'em about six hundred thousand points. That's a lot of bridge games. I got this theory about bridge. You play in a suit, you got to get rid of your losers. But you play no trump, and you have to make your losers into winners. Abraham Lincoln said the same kind of thing once. You got too many enemies, he said, you have to turn some of them into friends. That's pretty damned smart. That's a whole lot easier than trying to overpower too many enemies. That's how it is in no trump; you've got to take your losers and turn them into winners. Right now Victor Schott's got the lead and we've got to figure out how to make our losers into winners, and then trick him into giving us the lead.

We've got two choices, it seems to me. We can try to figure out what's going on in his head, or we can get him to think like we want him to think."

"Who's his connection in Fairfield? How does he know what's going on?"

"That's the easiest. He reads the *Sun*."

"You're kidding."

"No bunk. He's a subscriber. That's how I got the address of Tech-Optics. That's how Shirley got it, too."

"What about Charlene Manley?"

Decker shook his head. "That's the question mark, isn't it? Can we trust her?"

"You know her better than I, Decker."

"You don't count on a trick with the king when you don't know where the ace is. I don't think we dare trust anybody we aren't absolutely sure of."

"We can use her. She doesn't have to be on our side. She doesn't have to be on anybody's side; we can still use her." Use everything. It doesn't necessarily have to be on your side to use it. He slid the key into the hole and the cuff snapped open. Decker heard the click and caught his eye in the mirror. And smiled.

"It's about time," Decker said. "Are you going to tell me how we can use her, or am I going to have to figure it out for myself?"

"Why did you have me arrested? Why the trumped-up charge?"

"You have to know how the law works, Brett. When Shirley called me and told me Joan was killed, I knew I had to get you back. Two ways I could have done it: I could have pretended there'd been an accident or an illness in your family and notified the state police and had them stop you and give you the message. That was pretty shaky. For one thing, I didn't know for sure which state you were in by then—so was I supposed to call a half dozen or more states? And even then it would have been chancy that they might see you. But even if they had, who was I going to say was having the emergency? Your wife was dead. You didn't have any immediate family members. You probably wouldn't have trusted any kind of message at that point. So that was just about out. But I knew you'd called Shirley before, and I thought maybe you'd do it again. *She* could give you a message you'd trust. And why Angola? Why not bring you down to Fairfield in the first place? Because, Brett, I don't know if he has anyone there or not, and I guess I wouldn't have wanted to risk it. Besides, that gives us a nice long time to be alone and work some things out. Which is exactly what we're doing.

"And on top of that," Decker went on, "it looks so good, in case anybody is watching. It looks very good, having you arrested. Why that charge? Because it's something I could personally bring against you. My word against yours. Doesn't require a judge to sign the warrant. Just required me to say that you did those things. So I hope you don't mind, Brett. You treat me good and someday I'll drop the charges. Where are we going with this discussion, anyway?"

"The question is, Decker, how can we use it? OK, you got me arrested and we can let him know anything we want through the *Sun*. Certainly we can let him know you've arrested me, so we might as well use it now that it's done. We've got precious little else we can use."

"I've arrested you for the murder of your wife. And of Jenny and Lane. That's obvious."

"That ought to make him happy."

"Not quite. He's not ready for you to get arrested yet. He wants you loose for now because Andrea hasn't been killed yet."

"He'll let Andrea go this time. You've got enough on me as it is. She can always die in an accident later."

"That works for Victor Schott, but not for us. We

191

don't draw him out that way. You've got to be on the loose, available to kill Andrea. You're going to have to escape, Brett. Now that's something that would hit the *Sun* for sure."

"Except there's one problem. The *Sun* is a weekly. By the time Schott reads it, it's going to be old news."

"Then how do you suggest we let him know?"

"I don't know, Decker. That's going to be your problem. I'm going to have escaped; I won't be around to worry about those details." He looked down at the handcuffs lying on the floor. "If we did it . . . ," he said slowly, very slowly because Decker was a bastard and therefore not to be trusted, ". . . we'd have to have more of a plan than just that."

"You'd better believe it. A whole lot more. And one thing for sure: a relay. Because once you're gone, there's got to be absolutely no contact between us. You're going to be Jean Valjean and I'm going to be Javert, and I am going to leave no stone unturned to find you. And Victor Schott, with all his connections, is not going to be able to find the link between us. That's got to be number one, what makes it believable as far as he's concerned. That we have no communication at all. So there's got to be someone who can relay messages."

"Why do we have to relay messages? Why can't we have it all worked out in the first place?"

"Hopefully we will. But there's always that eight you forgot about that takes a trick. There's always something you didn't count on."

"Who can we trust?" asked David. "It's a mighty short list, isn't it? Shirley and Andrea?"

"Allen Lundy?"

Brett caught Decker looking at him in the rear-view mirror, and nodded slightly. "I suppose so. On the other hand, he half-thinks Victor Schott is right."

"He's got a stake in it, too, remember."

192

"Do you know where to find him?"

"Yes."

"Then all we have to do is figure out how to make it work."

"That's all. And we're going to have to do it before we get to Fairfield."

"Why?"

"Because that's going to be your best chance to escape, just when I'm bringing you in. I can say I unlocked your cuffs because of the long drive, but once I get you in the jail at Fairfield, it'll be a whole lot harder to get away. No, Brett, we're going to have to think fast, because it's all the time we'll have. After that, the only contact will be through the relay. The wife has a sister in Toledo; that might not be all bad. That way you don't call Indiana and I don't call Michigan."

"Michigan?"

"You know damned well it's got to be Michigan. It's Andrea you're supposed to be killing, after all."

"No, we don't drag Andrea into this."

"Andrea is already in this. She was in it from the day she was born and she'll be in it until the day she dies, unless we get Victor Schott first. It has to be her. There's no other person who would draw him out. It's going to be Andrea; it's going to be Ann Arbor. The only question is: How are we going to do it?"

"I'm not doing it that way."

"You haven't any choice and you know it." Decker's voice was suddenly hard.

"What happens if she gets killed?"

"What happens if you get killed? Or me? Why don't you think about Jack Turner for a while? Or Patti Styles? To say nothing about Elizabeth. Are we going to try and stop him or aren't we?"

"And then what?"

"I don't know what you mean."

"Yes, you do, Decker. I mean are we going to kill him?"

"I'm an officer of the law. That's not the way the law works."

"How does the law work for CIA agents?"

"That's what we're going to find out, aren't we?"

"That's not good enough. I have to know that he's going to be put away forever. I'm not putting Andrea's and my lives on the line for anything less."

"We're going to bring the damndest case against him that can be brought. There won't be a judge in the country that would dare let him off."

"That's not good enough. Elizabeth is dead. My father and brother are dead. Andrea's whole family, Lane and Jenny, Lane's family. They're all dead. He's got to die. I've got to know that."

"It's not just self-preservation, is it? There's a little bit of revenge in there, isn't there?"

"Don't be so sanctimonious. What about Jack Turner? Don't tell me that doesn't mean anything to you. Don't tell me you're going to risk Victor Schott getting off."

"Sure it means something. You bet your ass I care that Jack's dead. But it's going to be done right. If we kill him, then we're no better than he is. He's killing for revenge, too, you know."

"But he's the killer! It's not the same thing! We didn't do anything!"

Decker drove on in silence.

"It's not the same thing, Decker. He's the killer. We didn't kill anybody."

"We get him in our sights, then we decide what to do with him."

"We decide now."

"You want his blood on your hands, Brett? You're not going to be so innocent after that, you know."

"He killed Elizabeth."

194

"It all boils down to that, doesn't it? It's not self-preservation at all, is it?"

"We're going to kill him, Decker; there's not going to be any argument."

Decker sighed. "It's all academic anyway, Brett. If he's a pro, there's going to be only one way we can take him, but it would have been nice to think that we wouldn't have chosen it."

"There are a lot of things that would have been nice."

Decker took a long look at him in the mirror. "You OK, Brett? You going to be able to handle this?"

"I've handled it so far, haven't I?"

"Better than you think. It was perfect the way you mentioned to those guys up there in Angola that there might be an escape."

"I didn't say there was going to be an escape. I said you were going to shoot me and try to make it look as if I'd tried to escape."

"Yeah, well, same thing. It put the idea in their minds, anyway. And by the way, I *am* going to have to shoot you."

"That's not funny."

"It wasn't meant to be funny. He's not stupid, Brett. He knows all the tricks we can think of, and then some. He's not going to believe this escape if I just stand there and let you run off."

"I'm not going to believe this escape if you shoot."

"I won't be aiming to kill you; police aren't supposed to do that, didn't you know? I'll be aiming to wound, maybe a superficial wound in the leg. Something that won't slow you down too much. But it's got to look real."

"I don't believe any of this. Jack Turner is probably back in your police station now, healthy as I am. I'm going to pick up the handcuffs right now and put them back on, and that's going to be the end of it."

"And someday Andrea will die, and you can blame yourself for that just like you blame yourself for Elizabeth and for that girl out in Massachusetts. And like you might as well blame yourself for Jack while you're at it, because, unfortunately for him, he is not sitting back at the station, nor will he ever be again. And don't bother calling me a son of a bitch; you've already done that."

"In plain words, Decker, I don't trust you. I don't believe that you're going to let me escape and shoot at me without shooting to kill."

"To tell you the truth, I don't give a damn whether you believe me or not. It's Victor Schott who has to believe it."

17

DECKER DROVE INTO town slowly, stopped meticulously at the stop sign at Third Street, then drove on. There was no one on the streets, but lights were on in the windows of every house. Suppertime. Everyone home. Or almost everyone. He looked at the back of Decker's head, wondering about his wife, what she thought her husband was doing, what kind of woman she was. He supposed he'd seen her, but he didn't remember her. Was she waiting dinner for her husband now, wondering how late he'd be? He leaned over and picked up the handcuffs. They caught the light of a streetlamp and reflected it for a moment, then moved into shadow again. He twisted the chain between the cuffs until it was taut. I'm not even going to say I'm sorry, he thought.

The car turned at Main Street—all the stores closed now—and turned again a block later at Washington. Decker signaled each turn with his flasher just as if there had been other cars on the street, then turned once again into an alley, drove slowly until it broadened out into a small parking lot behind the police station. Another squad car sat carelessly parked in the lot. Decker pulled up beside it and turned off the ignition. "Good luck," he said, not even turning around. "I guess that goes for both of us."

"We'll need it."

"Decker turned around then and grinned. "You'd better believe it."

He opened the car door and stepped out, closing the

door behind him. Then he unlocked and opened the back door and Brett got out.

"Do you mind if I stretch a minute?" Brett asked.

"Go ahead. It was a long ride."

Brett raised his arms. The parking lot light was behind him, his face and the front of his body in shadow. Decker would not see, or would not think anything even if he saw, the handcuffs in Brett's hands, raised now toward the night sky. He yawned, stretched, and brought his hand crashing down on Decker's skull, the handcuff catching the side of Decker's head. Decker reeled back against the other car in surprise and pain, but Brett didn't see him. He was already running. He was almost at the edge of the lot when the first shot came, struggling through the shrubbery of Ray Madden's real-estate office when the second one came, still running when the last one was fired. He would have only minutes to get where he needed to go. Already he was feeling pain in his left leg. After all that, Decker had gotten him anyway.

Harvey Rogers was sitting inside the station, listening to the radio and throwing bank shots at the wastebasket. Twelve or fifteen balls of crumpled paper lay on the floor, perhaps a half dozen inside the basket. At first he thought it was a car backfiring on the street outside, but he had a clear view of the street from where he sat, and there were no cars out there. Then he realized that the noises were coming from behind the building and he thought they must be firecrackers. "Damn kids," he muttered, swinging himself out of the chair and heading back through the hallway. The lights were out in Cummins's and Decker's offices and in the cells as well, because there was no one in the station except Rogers.

He shoved the back door open, prepared to dress down the kids who, he imagined, were setting off firecrackers in the parking area, but he saw no one. No kids scattering off toward home, nothing. Except another squad car parked neatly beside the one Rogers had

198

driven back from supper. And then he saw movement between the cars. Kids hiding there? "Get out of there!" he shouted, but no one ran.

He unsnapped his holster and loosened the gun in it. It was the most threatening move he had ever made. He'd never drawn his gun out of the holster except to clean it.

"Harvey, is that you?" The voice came from between the cars.

"Lieutenant?"

"Get your ass over here!"

Harvey loped toward the voice, then stopped dead in his tracks when he saw the lieutenant. Decker was slumped against the car, his gun drawn, the whole left side of his face scraped raw. Blood glistened thickly in the spill of the overhead light.

"Lieutenant, what in—"

"Help me up, damn it! Get me inside and then go call Thompson and Cummins, and anybody else you can think of. We've got a damned escapee on our hands."

"Brett? You don't mean Brett? Didn't you go up there to get him?"

"I did, damn it! Watch it, that hurts. Rode all the way down here with him sweet-talking just as big as you please. *Who, me, Decker? I don't know what you're talking about, Decker.* All the way down here. One step out of the squad car and he attacks me. Watch that door. Mr. Innocent, that's him. All broke up about his wife's death. Yeah, I'm sure. All broke up, all right. That's why he comes near to killing me. No, not in my office; in the squad room. I want to be where things are going on. I'm going to run this show myself. We're gonna get this guy if we have to call in every police officer in Indiana."

"Dave! Come on in! I heard you'd gone out of town."

"I did. I was gone for a while. But you know how it is, Gale, eventually you've got to face things, to get back."

"Hey, listen, Dave, don't rush it. We've got a halfway

199

decent sub for you—old man Dayton, remember him? He loves being back in the classroom again, and the kids are doing OK and you don't have a thing to worry about. Come in, don't stand out there. Hey, Carol will put on an extra plate; we're just finishing up."

"No, I can't stay. I've just come to ask a little favor."

"Come on, you're probably tired of restaurant food by now—"

"No thanks. I've had supper."

"You don't look too good. Been eating OK?"

"Sure. Fine." He ran a hand through his hair. It probably looked as if he'd been running. "Listen, I'm in sort of a hurry, that's why I ran over here. I've got a friend coming into Indianapolis tonight. I need to pick him up at the airport—hate to borrow Sandy Augustina's car again. You know how it is. . . ."

"Sure, Dave, no problem. Carol and I are going out, but that's the advantage of being a two-car family."

"Well, I wouldn't want to inconvenience you."

"No problem. No problem. Sure you can't stay long enough to grab something to eat?"

"No thanks."

Gale took a ring of keys from his pocket. "Take the Ford; it's in the driveway."

"I appreciate it, Gale."

"No problem. Keep it as long as you like."

"Thanks a lot." He turned to leave.

"Dave?"

He turned back.

"Anything else I can do for you, just give me a call. I mean it."

"I know you do."

He got into the car and sat for a moment, deliberately breathing slowly. Be calm, he thought. you're almost home free, just be calm. The whole thing had taken less than fifteen minutes, from the moment he had stepped out of the squad car. Gale's house was two blocks from

200

the highway; he wouldn't have to go back through town. He started the engine and backed out of the drive.

"Damn it! Get your hands off me, it'll be OK!"

"He hit you one good, Lieutenant. He wasn't kidding around, was he?"

"You better believe it. Is Cummins here?"

"He just drove up."

"OK, listen. He doesn't have a car, not yet anyway. I've already got Rogers out cruising, looking for him—although you know Rogers; he wouldn't be able to find his head if his hat weren't on it. I want you to check out the places he'd go: his home—though that one's doubtful, but you never know. His friends. You got that list? His neighbors—all his neighbors. Who else? I'm going over to Shirley Carpenter's; is she back from New York?"

"I don't know."

"He might be there, whether she's there or not. He might think it's safe."

"You can't go over there by yourself, Lieutenant."

"So get somebody to drive me over! What do you think I am, anyway, a damned cripple?"

"You got a nasty blow to the head—"

"You'll get a nastier one to the butt if you don't get a move on! Cummins, is that you?"

"Yes, it is."

"We got ourselves a bugger, Cummins. A real bugger. What're the chances he's going to get a car and get away from here?"

"Wouldn't be too hard to steal a car. Nobody locks them; a few even leave their keys in. He could also borrow one."

"I've already got Thompson going out to his friends and neighbors. It's the best we can do. If it weren't dark, it'd be a hell of a lot easier."

"We need a roadblock."

"You want to tell me which road? Counting gravel roads, there's eight ways to get out of this town. We haven't even got that many squad cars."

"Get some civilians to help."

"Okay, Cummins, you be in charge of that. But they'd damned well better be ready to defend themselves. There's no telling but what he might be armed by now."

Cummins, already on his way to the door, half-turned. "I thought . . . ," he said, then reconsidered and turned back.

"You thought what?" Decker called after him.

"Nothing."

"Nothing, shit! Say it, Cummins."

"I was just going to say that I thought you didn't think he killed his wife."

Decker looked at him a good long time. "My name is Phillip Decker, not Jesus Christ. It's just possible, Cummins, that I could be wrong once in a while."

"Yeah, but I didn't think this was one of the times."

"Neither did I."

"We've got it, Lieutenant, but you're not going to like it."

"OK, give it to me." Decker held the receiver away from his head. The whole side of his face was aching.

"He's got a car; he's had it for at least half an hour—"

"Damn!"

"Sorry. It was Gale Duffield. He was pretty far down the list."

"You got the make? License?"

"We got it all. The hell of it is, he could be anywhere by now, including out of state if he went west. You going to get a warrant?"

"You'd better believe I am. Get back here and we'll put everything together."

"Do you have any guess where he might be going?"

202

"I've got a guess. When you get back, we'll go to work on it." He hung up the phone and looked at his watch. Half an hour.

"Do you fly to Boston?"

"Yes, we do, with a stopover in Cincinnati."

"Do you have anything going tonight?"

"Not that route. Not until tomorrow to Boston."

"Not until tomorrow?" Now what? Use it. How the hell do I use it? "Do you fly Cincinnati–Detroit?"

The airline clerk looked at him curiously. "You want to go to Detroit now?"

"I just want to know if you fly that route."

"As a matter of fact, we do."

"Thanks. I may need to go there on the way back. For now, you can give me a ticket for tomorrow, to Boston, one-way. I'm going to charge it."

"Can you give me your name and address, please?"

David Brett gave him the information, all the while looking around. There had to be a telephone somewhere.

"And your charge card?"

Absently, David handed him the card. His leg was hurting worse, but it had stopped bleeding. It seemed only a flesh wound. Decker had already told him that getting a car stopped on the highway was not all that hard. If Decker could do it, then so could anyone else. Say it: So could Victor Schott. But a plane? Was that any safer? Only if he could outsmart anyone who was looking for him. Make him think what you want him to think. Take over the lead, Decker had said. OK, he thought, so I'm taking over the lead. How the hell do I know where I'm going with it? One step at a time. He hadn't lost much blood, thank God for that. There was a bloodstain on the carpet in the car. He wondered how much he had left on Gale's porch. Not enough that Gale had noticed it right away. Thank God for small favors.

"Sign here, please. I suggest you be here at least half an hour before flight time."

"Thank you."

"Have a good flight."

"Can you tell me where the telephones are?"

"Straight down there, and then to your right."

"Thanks." Two calls. Two calls and then he'd be on his way.

Phillip Decker leaned back in his chair and looked at his watch. Forty-five minutes. His face hurt like hell. "OK, here's how I figure it. He's got himself a car—that means he's going someplace. He might be going into hiding, but he doesn't strike me as ready for that. He's got something else in mind. He's going someplace, all right, and that someplace has to be Framingham."

"You want to explain that?"

"Thompson, there's something very strange going on. Get me another cup of coffee, will you? Not so full this time, I damn near burned my mouth out on that last cup. Something mighty strange. We get three murders here in Fairfield and Brett takes off like a bat out of hell. Goes running around the country claiming to be looking for some character called Victor Schott. And here's the very peculiar part: Wherever he goes, people die. I mean, they don't just die; somebody's killing them. One in Michigan. Two in Massachusetts. One in New York. I don't know what the hell is going on, but for damned sure, something is."

"So who's Victor Schott?" Thompson asked.

"Beats me. Nobody's ever seen him. Maybe he doesn't even exist. Maybe Brett made him up. No, wait, I guess that can't be true. Charlene Manley seems to know about him. Charlene Manley." He looked at his watch. "You think Charlene would mind a call at this time of night?"

204

"It's only just after seven."

"Yeah, but she didn't seem too crazy about me the last time I talked with her. Wouldn't want to get the old gal too worked up about me. Might lose my job. On the other hand, we need some help right about now to locate that Schott character. We'd better call her just as soon as we get this taken care of. If you were running from the cops, Thompson, and you needed to get to Massachusetts, how would you get there?"

Thompson hunkered into a chair. "By plane?"

"It'd be the fastest, wouldn't it? Call Indianapolis airport. Check for flights going to Boston. Also going to Detroit, just in case."

"Why Detroit?"

"I'm not sure, but I've got a feeling. And then get on it with the warrant. And contact the state police and give them everything about the car. Maybe he's going to fool us. Maybe he won't fly. If he's driving, he's going to head for the expressway. Check the routes to Detroit and to Boston. At least we don't have to worry about trains. Did I forget anything?"

"You've got it, as far as I can see, Lieutenant."

"Where's Cummins?"

"You sent him over to check out Brett's house."

"Oh, yeah. I guess that does it, then. I'm going home and get some dinner. I called my wife, didn't I?"

"You did."

"I thought so. You'll call me as soon as you know anything?"

"Sure thing. Can you get home by yourself?"

"He didn't break my damn leg." He winced as he rose from the chair, but Thompson was watching him, so he didn't touch his hand to his face as he might otherwise have done. He walked out the front door and stood for a moment looking up at the sky. The clouds were clearing away—stars were beginning to show. Better than any goddamn city. It always made him think of Nam—the only decent thing about Nam had been the stars at night. When there weren't other things in the sky. A person could look up at the sky and almost think he was back home. Almost. He pressed the button on his watch and the numbers blinked into red. I'm not forgetting, Brett, he thought. You've got one coming from me.

David Brett drove east under still-cloudy skies. He couldn't remember when he'd felt so alone. Maybe when his father had died? No, because he still had his mother and Mike at that time. But when Mike died—was killed—there was no one left. Their mother had preceded Mike by almost a year. Thank God. That had been a hard year, but at least she hadn't been there to see what happened to Mike. At least she hadn't been called to the morgue. It would have killed her. And now he realized even more how much it would have, now that he knew how much Mike had been the picture of their father when he was that age. It would have killed her to have gone to the morgue a second time, to have to identify a body for the second time, and that second body so much like the first had been. He gritted his teeth and his hands clenched the steering wheel. But she had never had a chance to meet Elizabeth.

He looked at his watch again.

18

PHILLIP DECKER SAT hunched over the edge of the bed, his elbows on his knees, his eyes staring vacantly at the floor. From the kitchen below he could hear Sylvia slamming the dishes into the dishwasher; it was her way of letting him know she was still angry. She wanted him to call the doctor. When he first walked through the door, she'd stepped back in surprise because, even though he'd told her over the phone that Brett had hit him in the face, she hadn't expected it to look that bad. "What did the doctor say?" she'd asked right away, and he hadn't had the presence of mind to lie. Instead, he'd told her the truth, that he couldn't be bothered with doctors right now, that he had more important things on his mind. What he hadn't told her was that he was afraid Doc German, in his own conservative way, would have insisted on a shot, or at least a sedative; and this was no time to be under sedation. There was no way he could afford to be less than absolutely alert. Later, maybe, but not now. The fact that he hadn't had the presence of mind to tell her he'd already seen the doctor scared the hell out of him. What else was he forgetting?

He reached out his hand and laid it tentatively on the telephone receiver. This had to be right. This had to be absolutely right. He was no longer so sure. If he could misread—or forget—how Sylvia would react, what other mistakes would he be likely to make? There was no longer any room for mistakes.

He looked at his watch—eight-thirty—and he lifted the

receiver. He dialed the number, and as it rang, he re-sisted the temptation to lie back on the bed. It would be so soft, so comfortable. So mind-numbing. Instead, he lifted the entire phone off the nightstand and laid it on the bed beside him, rubbing its hard plastic side with his thumb, concentrating on its feel, on its smooth hard surface, gentle slopes, sharp turns, and especially on the thin indentation that ran around its base, forcing himself, by his sense of touch, to keep his mind sharp. It was a trick he'd learned back then. . . .

"Charlene." She answered the phone at home the same way she did in the office.

"Charlene, it's Phillip Decker."

"Yes, Phillip, what can I do for you?" She never called anyone by his title; everybody was on a first-name basis with Charlene. You might as well be; she knew every-thing about everybody anyway. She even called old Doc German by his first name; something even his wife had never been heard doing. Her voice was wary now; he could hear the expectancy, even over the phone, and he wondered how much of this she already knew. It was going to be a trick; she'd never quite trusted Phillip Decker, not since the time he was ten years old and she'd caught him stealing raspberries out of her garden. It wouldn't matter what he might have made of himself, or might make of himself in the future; to Charlene Manley he'd always be ten-year-old Phillip Decker, caught in the act of eating her precious raspberries.

"Charlene," he began cautiously, "I need your help." He paused a moment. It was ridiculous to feel ten years old every time he talked with her. "I don't know if you've heard anything yet, bet we've had an escape. Tonight. David Brett attacked me and got away while I was bringing him into the station."

"I heard something about it. Wouldn't mind getting the story right from the horse's mouth, though. So to speak."

"He's been . . . let's use the word 'implicated' . . . in some deaths, Charlene, and I—"

"Let's talk a little more clearly, Phillip. Are you saying you think he killed his wife? Have you got any kind of motive established for that? Are you connecting Lane Carpenter and Jenny Wilson's deaths with Elizabeth's?"

"You know better than that, Charlene; at least you ought to. I haven't got any proof—not yet, anyway. But there is certainly something strange going on, and while I'm trying to figure it out, I've got to cover all bases, and that's why I'm calling you. Can you get in touch with Victor Schott?"

"I think it's time you tell me about that one, Phil. The truth, this time."

"Yeah, you're right. He is connected with this." He paused. Let her ask the questions.

"How? He didn't even know those people."

"If I knew what he had to do with it, my problems would be half-solved. If I knew how to get in touch with him, I'd really be in good shape. You probably know, Charlene, that shortly after his wife was blown up in the car and *after* Lane and Jenny were shot, David Brett left Fairfield. I had a tail on him, so I know where he went, and I almost wish I didn't, because what I know scares the hell out of me. Wherever Brett has been in the last couple of weeks, people have been ending up dead. You probably heard about Shirley Carpenter's daughter in New York. That's just one of 'em."

There was a split second of silence on the other end of the line. Decker grinned, wishing he could see her face right about now.

"Those are pretty strong accusations," Charlene said.

"Yeah, that's the problem. It's all circumstantial. I'm not sure how well it would hold up in court. And now he seems awfully anxious to get in touch with this Victor Schott, and the thing that I have to keep thinking is, why? And does this mean that if David Brett finds Victor

Schott, there's going to be another killing? I wouldn't feel too good about myself if I didn't at least try to contact Schott and warn him, you see what I mean? You know things, Charlene; you got any idea what is behind all this? I mean, why would David Brett be killing people? Nobody seems to think he's that kind of person, but if you could take a look at me right now, you'd sure as hell think—oh, sorry about the language—you'd sure think that he had some kind of mean streak in him."

"I heard he attacked you."

She heard things mighty fast. He wondered how she knew, and what else she knew. "Slammed a pair of handcuffs down on me, that's what he did. Damn near took the side of my head right off. That's downright vicious. I've put out an APB on Brett, and right now I need to get in touch with Schott. Can you help me with that? My best guess is that's where he's heading."

"There's no way you can get in touch with him tonight. You call that place—that Tech-Optics place—and then he calls you back; at least, that's how it worked for me. But you're going to have to wait until tomorrow, when the place is open. You got the address from me before; didn't you call him?"

"No. I sent Jack Turner out there, and Jack ended up dead. It sounds as if you know how it works. Have you actually talked with him recently?" Interesting.

"As a matter of fact, yes. You came by asking about him. Shirley Carpenter called, asking about him. That's quite a bit of curiosity in a few days' time, it seemed to me. Enough to raise my own, in a manner of speaking. So I gave him a call to see if he could enlighten me."

"He say anything that might help?"

"Not really."

"You wouldn't keep anything like that from the police, would you, Charlene?"

"Of course I wouldn't."

Of course she would. "That's all you can tell me?"

"Sorry. Are you going to be available for an interview in the morning?"

"I've already told you everything I know."

"Maybe in the morning you'll know something else. Maybe in the morning somebody will have David Brett in custody."

Touché, and watch it with her. "I really need this one, Charlene. Since I got back from Vietnam in 'seventy-two, there's never been a murder in Fairfield. In fact, I never remember there being any murders here, but for sure nothing since I got back and came on the force. I don't like this, Charlene. Three murders in as many days is not a good thing, for the town or for my reputation. I want to nail this guy. I want to find this David Brett and nail him to the wall."

"There's nothing wrong with your reputation, Phillip."

"Well, I don't want anything to start now."

"You didn't answer my question. Are you going to be available for an interview in the morning?"

"Yeah, sure. If you think of anything else, I'd appreciate your letting me know."

"I'll do that."

He put the receiver back in its place and allowed himself—finally—to lie back on the bed. He closed his eyes and replayed the conversation in his head. It was OK. It was all OK.

"Shoot!" Curtis Andersen thrust his chair back from the desk and stood. It was the closest he ever came to swearing. A childhood incident—a mouth washed out with soap by a stern and demanding mother—and a subsequent promise made to that same woman six years later as she lay dying had stayed with him. Now, nearly fifty years afterward, at six feet three inches and two hundred and thirty pounds, his worst epithet was an occasional *shoot*. Ordinarily, a frown of that one thick eyebrow that swept across his permanently flushed face was enough to express the greatest displeasure.

He stood at the window, his back to the room, and repeated the word. "Shoot!"

McNulty stayed in the chair on the opposite side of the desk but leaned forward defensively, the thick file folder still on his knees. "He's not stupid, you know. He's very, very smart."

"Of course he is, but you're supposed to be smarter; that's your job," Andersen growled without turning around.

"Look, we do the regular tests and he comes up normal. And why the hell shouldn't he? He's been taking them so long he could write the new ones himself. He knows what the responses should be."

"I thought you used thought-reaction ones. You can't fake those."

"We do, and you can, if you're good enough."

"You're saying he's good enough."

"I'm saying what I said in the first place. He's very smart. He's too smart to let something get through if he doesn't want it to. That's what makes him good—the perfect company man. If the KGB get him, they won't get a thing. He could fool them forever."

"And he can fool us too." Andersen sighed.

"You bet."

"And to top it all off, now he's suspicious. That's just great, McNulty. You did a real good job on him."

"That's not quite fair. You take someone who's been in as long as he has. He knows what's usual and what's not. We can't even use a friend to unlock him; he hasn't got any—nobody's close to him. The fact is, you can't talk at all with a man like that without his getting suspicious. We even had him followed for a month. Nothing."

"Everybody has someone who's close to him."

"Not Victor Schott. If you read the file, you'll see that's what made him so good for it in the first place: no family, no friends, no ties. A loner. Quick in, do the job and get out. You go looking for guys like that. For what he does, you *want* guys like that."

Andersen turned and leveled his eyes on McNulty. "And the bottom line is that you didn't get anything."

"He shut up like a clam."

"That at least ought to tell you one thing. He's hiding something."

"Or he just resents being hit by the shrinks."

"He's too darn good to lose for no reason," Andersen mused.

"For no reason? Talk to some of the others who've worked with him—Lopez in San Pedro, or Jamison and Handley. Something definitely wrong happened when he was in Tarnovo. If nothing else, he's cracking."

"I observed him last week," Andersen said. "He seemed absolutely normal to me—just the same as always."

"How well do you know him?"

Andersen sat back heavily into the leather chair. "Not that well."

"They say it's in his eyes. *And* in his manner. As a matter of fact—have you read this file closely?"

Andersen nodded.

"Then you must have seen that someone named . . . Lyons, I think it was . . . mentioned it in a report years ago."

Anderson nodded again. "I did see that. But there's been a lot of water under the bridge since Lyons wrote that up, and no one else noticed it. He could have been mistaken."

McNulty shrugged. "We could all be mistaken. He could be just as normal as . . ." He smiled wanly. "That's just the point, isn't it; he isn't supposed to be normal, is he?"

"He's supposed to be what's normal for him, McNulty. Very cool. Very unfeeling. Just a job. No anger, no hate . . . no guilt. Just a job."

"Why do you mention guilt?"

Andersen's eyes narrowed with a sly smile. "Are you working on Schott or on me?"

"Fair question. In this business you're not supposed to feel guilt, not anybody. Everything has a purpose. Everything is decided higher up. Even *Permit for Action* is a permit, a permission. No one should feel guilt. So why do you mention it?"

"Because *if* something is bugging Schott, then maybe that's what it is. It happens. Guilt."

"It looks to me as if you've decided, then."

"What on earth do I know? You're the psychiatrist, you're supposed to tell me!"

McNulty shook his head. "We're not going to know unless he chooses to tell us. There's not one of us that will be able to drag it out of him against his will."

"And in the meantime?"

"You make the decision anyway."

"He's the best man I've got!"

"Then use him. He hasn't cracked up yet."

"Yet? *Yet?* I'm supposed to send out a man who hasn't cracked up *yet?*"

McNulty shrugged. "Then retire him. Send him to the farm. Let him teach."

"I need him. If only there was some way of knowing for sure."

"Sorry. In my business you usually don't know for sure."

"You know what I mean," Andersen said impatiently.

"I know you want to use him, but you're afraid."

"I've got good men and he could mess them up royally. Jamison was warning politely. The next time might not be so polite. Or the man might not be in a position to warn. I have to be able to depend on him."

"Then you have your answer," McNulty said, rising, "I'm sorry. I wish I could have given you what you were looking for. It's not going to happen." He stood, waiting to be dismissed. Andersen looked at him for a long moment, then nodded curtly, and McNulty left, closing the door behind him.

Andersen swiveled the chair around to face the window. A man rarely goes sour in a few weeks or months. It generally takes years. Jamison thought he was going— maybe had already gone—sour. There's emotion there, he'd said, and everybody who knew Schott knew that there had never been emotion before. So if Jamison was right, then the question was: Was Schott just starting, or had he been like this for years and nobody noticed before? Nobody noticed? How about Lyons? How likely would it be that anybody would notice anyway? And what difference would it make, as long as he didn't mess things up? No, nothing had been messed up yet. *Yet.* How long would it take before the next warning, if there even was one? A man's in and out in a few days, a week or two, no one knows him, no wife, no friends. All the things that made Schott so good were working now to protect him. And where was this emotion coming from, if it was really there? Anger? Guilt? Weariness? Men got tired of it all; it happened. How long has it been going on? And how bad is he? How on earth do I find out? Or do I need to? Nothing had happened yet, no mistakes, nothing. He was like a time bomb waiting to go off, but maybe he never would. And then having retired him would have been a waste. The best man he had. "Damn," he said out loud, the word hanging in the air, unfamiliar in his own voice. "Damn," he repeated.

*   *   *

"*Sun*. Charlene."

"Charlene, it's Victor Schott."

She sat up straighter. "Yes, Victor. You're probably wondering why I called—"

"I'm wondering more than that. I also got a call from your Phillip Decker this morning. Both of you in the same morning. I thought I'd call you first, Charlene, and ask what's up."

"That's exactly why I was calling you. And, as far as I know, why Decker called you, too. Why would David Brett be looking for you, Victor?"

"I haven't the faintest notion. I didn't even realize that David Brett lived in Fairfield. I thought he lived in Chicago or some such place."

"This is the son—David Brett, junior. He's lived in Fairfield for four or five years now."

"Was he the other one who was asking for me some time back?"

"Might as well have been."

"What do you mean by that?"

"It was for him the information was being asked. What's your connection, Victor? You must have some idea. It hasn't anything to do with the father, has it?"

"I have no idea, Charlene. But this is beginning to make me wonder. What can you tell me about Phillip Decker? What kind of police officer is he? You say he's the chief of police?"

"I might have said that. He's not, actually, but he might as well be. Gerritt Foster's the chief, but he's all but retired. Decker runs the place."

"Is Decker local?"

"Oh, yes, born and bred."

"Pretty sharp guy, is he?"

"How sharp do you need to be, to run the police in a town like Fairfield? I don't think he set any world on fire when he was in school. Good steady man, I'd say."

216

"Went to college?"

"No. No, whatever smarts Decker has are natural smarts; he's not a big one for the books, I'd guess. He was in the army, in Vietnam, then came back and joined the police. Nothing spectacular."

There was a slight pause on Victor Schott's part. Then, "If he was in Vietnam, then he can't have been on the police force for too many years, can he?"

"I'd say ten years or so. I'm not as good at remembering the years as I used to be, but it seems . . . 'seventy-two, I think," she remembered from the conversation. Wasn't that what Decker had said? "That's about right."

"It sounds to me as if you're very good about remembering years."

"Not as good as I used to be." She wouldn't tell him how she knew the year; there was vanity there and she knew it.

"That seems like a pretty fast rise to acting police chief for a town like Fairfield. There can't be much mobility in the force. Surely there's somebody else who's got seniority on him."

"He brought some kind of experience from the army; I'm not sure what it was. The most I can do is keep track of the things that go on around this town, without having to worry about what happens to locals when they're away."

"You called me, didn't you?"

"You watch it, Victor; don't read more into it than there is. Something odd is happening, that's all, and your name keeps coming up in connection with it. As for Phillip Decker, he handles things fine down at the police station. I think maybe he might have done that kind of thing in the army. I seem to remember that sort of thing. My mind isn't quite what it used to be. So Decker called you already?"

"Yes, he did."

"You be sure to call him back, now. You're going to be glad you did."

"Why?"

"He'll tell you. Is that all you wanted to know, Victor?"

"Is that all you're going to tell me?"

"It looks like it is."

"Then I'll be talking with you, Charlene." He hung up the phone. Phillip Decker. An unknown quantity. If there was one thing he was not interested in at this point, it was unknown quantities. Vietnam. Interesting. He dialed another number, and when it was answered, the man who answered spoke only a number.

"Two-ten."

"This is six-seven-four, code three-seven-nine-six. I want you to run a name through for me."

"Yes, OK."

"It's Phillip Decker. I don't know the middle name or initial. Hometown—Fairfield, Indiana. Served in Vietnam, probably in the army. Separated about 'seventy-two. That's all I can give you at this moment."

"It ought to be enough."

"How soon can I call you back?"

"It may take a while. I've got some priority things—"

"This is highest priority."

"I'll do the best I can."

"Good. I'll be calling back." He hung up and looked absently out the window. The grass sloped away from the house toward the river a hundred yards away, but the river was not visible yet. The mist still clung to it, even though it was past ten in the morning. The forecast was for clearing, but the fog still hung low. On the opposite bank of the river above the mist a single rider appeared, cantering slowly along the riverbank. He'd be calling back—if they hadn't pulled his number by then. It was day-to-day now. McNulty had been easy—a pushover.

He had his little tests, his little buzz-words that were supposed to make you fall apart all over him; that part was easy. Andersen was different. Andersen operated on intuition, the way any good intelligence man would. Anderson would not be easy, and he was the one who was important. Give me a few more days, he thought, just a few more days. There was only Andrea and Lundy left, if Lundy really had not died in the fire. Brett was taken care of. Oh yes, was he taken care of. This was not how he would have chosen to do it, but with the roof caving in on him, it was not at all bad.

It was ironic, even. The company had been the cause of it all, and now they were closing in on him. It would never have started if it hadn't been for . . . but there was no use thinking about that now. Jelinek was dead. It was years ago. Nothing would change that. Nothing would bring him back now.

Two riders appeared on the far side of the river. The hunt country. "Ever think about retiring?" Andersen had asked. "I hear you've got a place in the hunt country—that's not too shabby. Maybe teach for us for a while?" The last thing they do with you before you're out—although Andersen hadn't pulled the plug yet, not yet. He was still getting his calls taken at Central. But it would happen, only a matter of time now, Anderson waiting in the wings. Well, Andersen could be stalled. He wasn't quite ready for the farm yet, not ready yet to train the new ones. And for what? *For what?* So that somebody else can die in some other unspectacular way in some other part of the world. As if it made any difference. As if anything made any difference.

He shook his head, annoyed with himself. Stupid. Stupid things to think. Stupid way to react. He thought he'd been so smooth with McNulty and he hadn't been smooth at all. McNulty had sensed something. So he didn't know what it was, so what? He could still tell there was something. If I'd been perfect, McNulty wouldn't even have sensed anything, he thought. Maybe it's time I do get out, if this is the way it's going to be. It wouldn't be too bad. The timetable almost fit, with some adjustments. He could stall Andersen long enough.

Andersen would be looking to keep him from any operation—that was all right. All he needed was to keep his code for a while longer. It was going to work out. It was almost over and then it wouldn't matter anymore whether he was in or out—the rest he could do on his own. Just as he'd done everything else on his own. Always. Except . . . Jelinek. And that had been his mistake. That had been where it went wrong. The end, in a sense, as well as the beginning. There was irony there somewhere. As there was irony in what Andersen had said. Retiring to the hunt country. Where the hell did they think he'd spent the last thirty years, and more?

He turned back away from the window. All right, Phillip Decker, acting police chief and whatever else you are, let's hear your surprising news.

"This is Decker." The voice came through as impatient, quite different from the boyish, almost polite voice that had answered the phone at first. This man was used to having his own way, bullish. He was talking from his own office, evidently—the background sounds were different. Victor Schott could hear a radio playing now, bluegrass music. The acting police chief of Fairfield, Indiana, listened to bluegrass music, even in the office.

"This is Victor Schott, returning your call."

"Oh, yes, Mr. Schott. I'm glad you called back so promptly." The voice was easier now; Schott could almost imagine him leaning back in his chair. "We've got a small problem here in Fairfield, Mr. Schott. Maybe you can help me a little with it, and very possibly I can help you a whole lot."

220

"I can't imagine how I could help you."

"Ever hear of a man named David Brett?"

"Sure. I went to school with him."

"No, I'm afraid he's not the one I'm talking about. It's his son I'm referring to."

He hadn't skipped a beat. That was good. "I'm sorry, I've never heard of the son."

"Well, it seems he's heard of you."

"Are you getting at something?"

He heard a squeak and imagined that Decker was sitting up straight in the chair now. "Two, three weeks ago, David Brett's wife died in a rather unusual way. Her car was blown up when she tried to start it. We don't have murders around Fairfield too much."

"I'm sorry to hear that. About the wife, I mean, not about the murder rate. All towns should be so lucky."

"Yeah. Lucky. A few days later two teenagers were killed. Shot. That don't make the Fairfield police look too good, as you can imagine. Next thing I know, David Brett's skipped town. Fortunately for me, I had a man following him. He followed Brett up to Michigan, where unfortunately he lost him, but not before following him to the house of a family that used to be the family of Richard Kramer—someone else you went to school with, I believe. Anyway, Kramer's dead now and his wife's remarried. What they have to do with this is anybody's guess at this point, but what isn't anybody's guess is what happened next. One of the Kramer children turns up dead. A seventeen-year-old girl. Next place Brett turns up is Northport, Michigan, up north. A place burns up and just about kills the guy who was living there—someone else you were in school with, I believe; Allen Lundy. A few days later, for God knows what reason, Brett is in Framingham, Mass.—where your business is—looking for you, so I hear. And two more people turn up dead—my man Jack Turner, who I sent out there to try to intercept Brett, and some girl who worked at Tech-Optics. You've probably heard about the girl. Maybe you didn't know that Jack Turner was a cop from Fairfield, but he was. Then I got word that a girl—daughter of Mike and Shirley Carpenter—is killed in New York, and the police there get the tip that some guy answering the description of Brett was seen in New York the very next day. Well, on the basis of all that, I managed to intercept Brett and arrest him. Not on those charges, unfortunately; things are a little too circumstantial just now for that, but I did arrest him, and I was bringing him in when he attacked me and escaped. This was last night. I've got an APB out on him—that's an all-points bulletin, in case you aren't too familiar with police talk. But I thought I ought to give you a call. He was in Framingham looking for you, as far as I know, when Jack Turner and that girl got killed, and so I can't help but think he might still be looking for you. I don't know what the hell he's got in his mind, but he does seem to be going after people his dad was in school with, or in some cases, their children. Maybe he's flipped his lid—that might explain how he did his own wife in—but anyway, whatever is behind it, Mr. Schott, it looks as if you might be the next candidate. I'm really just calling to tell you to sit tight until we can find that guy and bring him in."

"You don't have any idea where he might have gone?"

"Yeah, as a matter of fact, we thought we did, but it turned out to be a bum steer. This guy is trickier than you might think."

"What are you talking about?"

"He bought a ticket to Boston at Weir Cook Airport in Indianapolis. But he never took the flight. We got the information before flight time, and the place was crawling with cops, but he never showed up. Maybe he was spooked, I don't know, but he did buy that ticket, so it looks as if he's coming your way. If he drove on to

222

Cincinnati or someplace and took another flight, he could even almost be there by now. I don't know what the hell he has in mind, but, Mr. Schott, he's likely to be gunning for you."

There were interesting possibilities in that. "It doesn't make any sense. Why would he want to kill me?"

"Beats the hell out of me. I was hoping you'd know. I talked a bit with Allen Lundy, but he's not saying nothing to nobody. He's about as much help as King Tut's mummy. He don't know nothing, or at least he ain't saying anything. I was really hoping you'd be able to give me a lead."

"I can't imagine that Allen wouldn't cooperate if he thought his life was in danger."

"To tell you the truth, that's just why I think he's *not* cooperating, and now he's dropped out of sight completely. I think this David Brett has got him scared pea green. And to think this guy was teaching in our school. There's no telling what kind of harm he might have done."

"Maybe it wasn't Brett at all."

"I'll tell you something, Mr. Schott. I've been in the police business for a few years now. I may never have had to deal with any murders before, but I can tell you one thing: I don't believe in coincidences. David Brett keeps going where bodies keep turning up, and that's just too much coincidence for me. Besides, anything else might be explained, but there still isn't anything to explain what I'm looking at every time I look in a mirror these days."

"What's that?"

"He's a vicious man, David Brett is. He attacked me when he escaped, and damned near killed me. The whole left side of my face was torn off. It hurts like hell. It looks like hell. And that man is going to have hell to pay when I catch up with him. In the meantime, though, you just sit tight, and watch out for strangers. You want I should send out a picture, so's you know what he looks like?"

"How do you know he bought a ticket at Weir Cook? Maybe it was someone else."

"The damned fool bought the ticket with his credit card. Might as well have left a calling card. It was mighty nice of him, wasn't it?"

Nice. Too nice. Maybe. "How smart a guy is he?"

"How smart can he be, leaving a calling card like that?"

"Maybe he only meant you to think he was coming this way."

"Where else would he go?"

"I guess that's your job to find out, isn't it, Mr. Decker?"

"Lieutenant Decker."

"Excuse me. Lieutenant Decker. So I ask again, is he smart enough to be trying to fool you?"

"I don't know." He spoke slowly, as if he were thinking. "I suppose that's possible. But if he's not coming your way, then where the hell is he?"

"Are you still going to send me the picture?"

"If you want it."

"Sure, why not? You've got the Tech-Optics address?"

"Yes, I do. Until you hear from me, you'd better lie low. There's no telling where he is, and there's no sure way of knowing he wasn't trying to trick us, so you'd best assume he wasn't."

"I'll do that. Call me if you get any further word."

"Listen, you take care. And you call me if you think of some reason why he might be after you. You hear?"

"I hear." Victor Schott hung up the phone, then immediately inserted another twenty cents and called a number.

"Two-ten."

"This is six-seven-four, code three-seven-nine-six. Have you got the information on Decker yet?"

"Not yet."

"I need it now."

"Everybody needs it now. I'm doing the best I can."

"How soon?"

"Soon as I get it, I'll have it."

Schott hung up. And until then? One thing was sure; he was not going to sit tight.

Phillip Decker looked up as Thompson came into the office and shut the door behind him. "You get it?"

"A phone booth in Washington, D.C. We've got the cross streets, for whatever good it does. Anybody can use a phone booth, and he'll be long gone by now."

"Yeah. Thanks. Remember, this is off the record."

"I remember."

"So far off, it isn't even in the same ball park. Only you and me know about this, Thompson. Keep it that way."

"Got it."

Decker watched Thompson walk out of the room. Washington. It could be. It certainly wasn't Tech-Optics in Framingham. On the other hand, Tech-Optics did business with the government all the time. So Brett said. It made a good cover anyway. He looked at his watch. He'd be willing to bet that Victor Schott was not sitting tight. He punched the intercom and waited until Thompson got back to his desk and answered it.

"Yes?"

"One more thing, Thompson. Get me a University of Michigan football schedule, soon as you can."

"A football schedule? For this year?"

"Yeah. Who knows, maybe I'll want to take in a game one of these days."

19

COLONEL CURTIS ANDERSEN always wore his uniform to work. His friends and family sometimes kidded him about that. "You trying to keep those guys at State on their toes?" his brother-in-law would joke. As far as anyone knew, Andersen was on semipermanent loan from the army to the State Department, and did not officially have to wear the uniform. If anyone had been curious enough to check it out, they would have followed the chauffeur-driven Mercury that arrived at the Andersen home each morning at seven-fifteen to the State Department building and seen Colonel Andersen run up the steps and walk three flights to his office. Andersen never took the elevator. Big, bluff Curt Andersen, who never swore and who was as honest as the day is long. What the curious would not have known was that two or three mornings a week, Andersen told Lieutenant Blaisdell, his secretary, that he'd be in conference the rest of the day, closed the door of his office, hurried down the service stairway with which it connected to the sub-basement, stepped into a waiting automobile, and rode out into the early-morning traffic to Landover.

This morning he had done just that. He had not planned to come out this morning, but something was bothering him, and it was Andersen's experience that when something bothered him, it was best in the long run to follow it up.

Joe Rugger looked up from his desk and smiled as Colonel Andersen approached. He liked the colonel. No monkey business. No fucking up. When Andersen did a job, he did it right. "What can I get for you today, sir?" Rugger asked.

"I think this time I'd rather leaf through the files myself."

It was not unusual for Andersen; it would have been for some of the others. "Can I point you toward anything in particular?"

"I'm interested in Lyons's reports—'sixty-three and 'sixty-four, maybe back a couple of years from that." Andersen was holding out his security pass, and Rugger couldn't help grinning more broadly. Andersen was a stickler, but he kept the rules himself. To the letter. Not like some of the others.

"Aisle J, about halfway down. On the right. Anything else?"

"Not just yet. Thanks." Andersen moved toward the door, and Rugger reached with his foot to press the button that released the lock. Andersen pushed the door open and stepped through.

He was in a vast underground storage room of metal security files. Beige in color, the drawer tops rimmed in chrome, row on row of sameness, the scene always reminded Andersen of a morgue. Drawers full of lives, of operations, of classified documents and reports. The heart of the company. No, the memory of the company, Andersen thought. His eyes scanned the drawer labels. Washington was a center of computerized information, but some men trust only what they are familiar with. There were a dozen reasons why computerizing all this would be preferable, but Andersen was among those who resisted. The security of the file system was known. Who could guarantee that the computers could not be breached? Some things were just too important to trust to computers, Andersen thought.

It took him three drawers and over an hour before he

found what he'd been looking for. 1964. Prague. Lyons's report. He wondered idly if Schott had written one, too, or if it hadn't seemed important enough at the time. Schott had a young one along—Peter Jelinek. It had been an interesting situation, as Andersen remembered. Schott, the old hand, even then. Jelinek, just learning the ropes, but good, very good. Andersen skimmed through the details, and now he remembered more clearly. It was early spring of 1964. Novotný's government had had a number of serious problems: economic near-chaos, increasingly bold criticism of the government by the intellectuals, serious manifestations of Slovak nationalism, and a power struggle between Lenart, the prime minister, and Novotný himself. And Russia had been pressing for de-Stalinization, which meant Novotný would have to mow down his own power base. It was a perfect setup. And to top it all off, Bulgaroff, from Moscow, had been in Prague, ostensibly as an economic adviser, but really to oversee the shake-up in the Central Committee.

When Bulgaroff began making signals, Washington sat up and took notice. Bulgaroff's defection would be a coup; would be enough, everyone hoped, to knock Czechoslovakia out of the Communist orbit. So Schott was sent in—the experienced one. And Jelinek, the inexperienced one—except that he was a native speaker and, having left Prague as a teenager, knew his way around.

The details, or as much as had been known, were there in the report. It was a perfect setup, all right, but it was the company that was being set up. The hints, the signals, everything. It was not that Prague would be blown out, after all. It was to solidify power in the shaky government by creating a common enemy, while leaving the Americans with egg on their faces and a reputation for manipulation. A side benefit, as far as Moscow was concerned, would be the irreparable compromise of one of the company's top men.

But it was Jelinek, eager and wanting to prove himself, who had walked into the trap; Jelinek, the inexperienced one, who panicked; Jelinek who was gunned down on a lonely, rain-splattered Prague street. And Victor Schott—the experienced one, helpless—had watched it happen from a fifth-story hotel window.

At the end was Lyons's summary. This was what Andersen had been looking for: "Of course everyone is sorry when an operant is killed, but for Schott to show any reaction is unusual. I hope it doesn't bode something for the future. He'd be hard to replace, but at this point I think he bears watching. Maybe it was just a fluke. It's true that there seemed to be an unusual relationship developing between those two. A first for Schott? If so, this may cut him off; he may never do such a thing again." The words jumped out at Andersen: *he bears watching*. Twenty years later and something comes up again? Twenty years? At this rate it would take Schott a hundred years to crack. Even Victor Schott had a right to show emotion once in twenty years. But something tugged. Something flickered in the corner of Andersen's mind, something he'd read long ago . . . something about a substitute for suffering . . . probably, almost certainly Jung . . . neurosis, perhaps? It seemed right. "Neurosis is always a substitute for legitimate suffering"? That seemed right. How long had it been since he'd read Jung? Was that Schott's problem—blaming himself for Jelinek's death? And now dealing with the guilt? Was that it? And how was the neurosis to be manifested? Anger? Fear? Self-destruction? Will the next time be in twenty months or twenty days? Do we take the chance? Andersen stared at the report. One short paragraph, and that was all in Schott's whole career. Was it enough?

He closed the file slowly and replaced it. A very good man. The best. Well, talk to him again, at least. Maybe let up a little on the retirement bit. Feel him out. See how he reacts. There ought to be ways to handle it; he was too good a man to lose.

"You seem very different."

"From what?"

She grinned easily, not taking her eyes from the road. "From before."

He turned that over in his mind. "I suppose I am. Last time you saw me, I was less than a week from my wife getting killed. At that time I was . . ."

"Still adjusting?"

"Not even that. Denying. I was going through the motions, thinking that eventually I'd wake up and it would have been just a bad dream. Things like that. . . . You think you've got your life together and something happens and suddenly you . . . you don't know where things are anymore. Nothing makes sense anymore. It's like suddenly losing gravity. Or as if you woke up one morning and found nothing beyond your bed, just nothingness where there used to be a room with walls and a floor and a ceiling and windows and furniture and something outside the windows—a whole world, and suddenly there's nothing. It scares the hell out of you."

She didn't say anything.

"You keep hoping that you'll wake up and everything will be the way it was. I wanted desperately for that to happen, but it didn't."

"She's really gone. And Nickie's gone."

He stole a glance at her. Her mouth was open and she was breathing deeply. He recognized the feeling—she had to do it to hang on.

"Why do we have to go to the cottage?" She stared straight ahead as she spoke.

"Because that's the way it works. That's the way we're going to do it. You and I are going to be the bait."

"*I'm* going to be the bait."

"OK, you're going to be the bait. But in case it makes you feel any better, I've got to be there, too."

"Nickie was killed because she was coming to the cottage, wasn't she? Nobody has said it straight out, but that's why she was killed, wasn't she?"

"It seems to make sense, doesn't it?"

"Instead of going to Sid's sister's, where she was supposed to go, she came to me, to where she knew I would be, and he must have seen her and killed her."

"If he was sitting at the end of the road, he would have seen her. He could have recognized the car from in front of your house, from when he followed me to your house. He could have recognized her from when she came out to my car when I was leaving, when she gave me your address."

"Why would he have killed her?" she asked angrily. "Why didn't he just let her come to the cottage? He didn't kill me; why did he kill her?"

"If he saw her and recognized her, then very likely she might have seen him."

"And recognized him. He couldn't let her live then, could he? Because she saw him. She knew he was there." She pressed her fist against the steering wheel. "Damn him! Damn him!"

"Do you want me to drive?"

She pushed herself back against the car seat. "No. I'm OK." She ran a forefinger under each eye. "I should be used to it by now, shouldn't I?"

"Why?"

"I don't know. If enough people you love die, you'd think you'd get used to it. It ought to be that way, but it isn't. Each time is like the first time." She ran a hand down the back of her head and he watched as the black curls flattened under her fingers and then, released, sprang back into place. "Are you past denying now? Have you gotten to adjusting yet?" she asked.

"Have you? Do you ever adjust? I suppose you do. I still think of Elizabeth. I know she's dead. I know that's not going to change; I've gotten that far. I still think of her a lot, find myself talking to her as if she were there, even though I know she's not. There are good days and bad. I haven't had much time to think yet. When everything's finished, then maybe I will. I suppose that's what the adjusting part is."

She stole a glance at him, and he was gazing out the side window. "When this is all over, will you go back to Fairfield?"

"I don't know. I haven't had time to think that far ahead. Right now all I care about is nailing Victor Schott, bringing him out into the open once and for all."

"What if he doesn't come?"

"He'll come. For whatever crazy reason he's got in his mind, he'll come, because he's trying to set me up for murder and there's one more murder to be done and you're it and I'm here and he may never get a chance like this again. How many guys did you get?"

"Twenty, maybe twenty-two. We've got a telephone chain worked out so that as soon as Shirley Carpenter hears, she makes one phone call, and within a couple of minutes everybody knows."

He looked at her finally. "You've been pretty busy yourself in the last day or so."

"Busy enough. It was a nice ride back from the airport last night with Shirley. I like her a lot."

He nodded. "She's very special."

"It was odd; she knew my father better than I did."

"She's also lost as much to Victor Schott as anyone has."

"I know; she told me. Of all the people—my mother,

even—she understands better than anybody what it's like, how I feel."

"You always had to be strong for your mother, didn't you? Even when your father died."

"Especially when my father died. I was the oldest. I was always the one . . . who had to keep things under control."

"You're tired of that, aren't you? No, not tired, really, but perhaps not able to handle it now that you're the last one. Now that there isn't anyone younger to hang on for. Only your mother, and you can't make things right for her, no matter what."

"You have to have a reason to hang on. Sometimes doing it for yourself isn't quite enough."

He looked at her and saw her almost as if for the first time. The pale November sun glinted off her hair. "You're the best reason you've got, Andy. Hang on for yourself, and if that's not enough, then hang on for me."

"Is that what keeps you going, your own survival?"

"I wish it were that simple. When all is said and done, I'm doing this for one reason: to get him."

"Two-ten."

"This is six-seven-four, code three-seven-nine-six. Have you got it yet?"

"It's a big file. Do you want everything?"

"Start in. I'll let you know when I've heard enough."

"First off, I'll tell you how it ends. There've been three attempts to recruit him—twice from us and once from Consular Operations. And three turn-downs. He's not interested."

"Mighty popular boy we've got."

"You come up with the good ones. He's a gem. Enlisted in 'sixty-six. That would have been before the heavy antiwar business. When it would have seemed very patriotic for a small-town Indiana boy to enlist."

"You can spare me the editorial."

"At that time he was two years out of high school. No college; he'd held a series of three or four nothing-type jobs. No evidence of anything spectacular. Enlisted once, re-upped once, that was the extent of his career with the army as far as time is concerned."

"So when did the fireworks come in?"

"I'm getting to it. He had an average to good beginning, was made platoon leader almost as soon as he got off the boat, so to speak, but there's nothing spectacular in that. It seems as if he were made for the job. He wasn't your ordinary grunt; he fought the war more with his mind than with his gun. He was born for guerrilla warfare, evidently. He'd know where the enemy would be; he'd know what they were up to before our men on the other side did. Eventually he was put into recon, and he was a one-man outfit. I've got a quote here from his captain. It was in conjunction with some kind of commendation—he's got an armload of them, by the way—and it says, 'Decker is a natural-born intelligence officer. He knows what the enemy is going to do next before the enemy himself does. When he doesn't, he works it so that they do what he wants them to. He can feint and jab against a guerrilla outfit better than anyone I've ever seen.' That was less than a month before they sent him up to U Minh."

"He was involved in that?"

"He was the brains behind it. They wouldn't have gotten halfway to that POW camp if it hadn't been for him."

"That's not the way Wallace tells it."

"Oh, sure, Wallace got the credit, but that's what this department is here for, to keep you glory guys honest."

"So it was Decker's mission."

"First to last. The only thing wrong with it was that they'd moved the camp before our guys got there. But it was Decker with the information and Decker who ran it."

"And Decker who got them out when it went sour?"

"Seems to have been."

"And what kind of commendation did he get for that?"

"That's an interesting thing I was going to tell you. Nothing. It's buried here in our files; that's the only record of it, most likely. Wallace got the credit, Decker got a nice little pat on the back and nothing else."

"Have you got an explanation for that?"

"Best guess only. They wanted to use him again. And they did. Similar stuff. Nothing quite as spectacular as U Minh, but some very neat stuff. You want to hear about any more?"

"Not just now. When did we try to recruit him?"

"Before he left the army. He laughed in their faces—I should say in ours. We tried again about a year later and again it was nothing doing. So we turned his name over to Consular Operations and they tried. He likes his Indiana home, it appears."

"So it appears."

"Is he on our side or someone else's?"

"I don't know yet."

"Watch him. He'll fool you. If anybody can, he's the one."

"Decker."

"Phil, it's me, Sylvia."

He leaned back in his chair. "Hi, how's everything?"

"Marge called. She said to tell you everything's OK."

"That's it?"

"That's all she said to tell you. Phil, is it safe for her?"

"I told you before, hon, it's safe as a babe in his mother's arms. Don't worry so hard. What's for supper?"

"Pork chops."

"Sounds good."

"Are you going to be home?"

"Would I miss pork chops?"

"See you later, then."

" 'Bye." Damn. If there was any meal he hated to miss, it was Sylvia's pork chops. He swung around in his chair and called out, "Cummins!"

Cummins looked up and sauntered over from Thompson's desk. "Cummins, I've got an idea I want you to check out for me. If he drove to Weir Cook and then decided not to take a plane from there but still wanted to take a plane, where would he take it from?"

"Sir?"

"Where's the airport closest to Weir Cook?"

"I . . . I'm not sure. Cincinnati, I think."

"Check it out."

He looked at all the faces turned toward him and suddenly felt as if he were in the classroom again. Except that this was no classroom, and these twenty-odd young men and two or three young women were not like any students he had ever stood before. In fact, he wasn't even standing before them now. He was sitting on the couch, with two beside him and the rest crowded into the cottage's small living room as best they could. They wore jeans and down jackets against the night. College kids, nondescript except for the one expression they all held in common, curiosity. They already knew why they were here; they only needed to find out how it would work. Two held shotguns, even though he'd specifically told Andrea no guns.

"I don't know what you've been told, and what you've guessed for yourselves. Frankly, it's better if you don't try to guess anything for yourselves. Frankly, also, this is a more or less clandestine operation. It's better if you don't know too much, and if you don't talk about it at all.

236

Suffice it to say, what you will be doing is not illegal. It is nothing more than this: You will ring this cottage. You will wait. You will watch for the signal, which will come from inside the cottage, and then you will close in. You will let him in—you will let anyone in. But you will let no one, and I repeat that . . . *no one* . . . out after the signal has been given. I said no guns and I mean it. You can leave those guns in here. He will not be expecting you. You are what is known as a safety valve. You're the backup in case what happens in this cottage is not what we are expecting to happen. You catch him however you can, but no guns."

"Who is he?" asked the redhead against the wall, one of the two with shotguns.

"He doesn't need to have a name as far as you're concerned. He's a killer; that's all you need to know. He killed Andy's father and her two brothers and her two sisters. He killed my father and my wife and my brother. There's more, but you don't have any need to know that. He's coming here to kill Andy and he will do it unless he's stopped. It's my job to stop him. It's your job to stop him if I fail."

"Then we ought to have guns."

"Twenty-five people in the dark with guns is suicide. I don't think you're interested in dying. Enough people have already died. Let's not let the tally get any higher."

"Is this involved with the Mafia?"

"No, it isn't."

"Why won't you tell us more?"

David Brett sighed and looked at the floor. "Because, once he gets in here, if he's able to leave, it'll be because he killed Andy and me, and it will all be over and it won't matter anymore." He looked up and caught Andy's eyes across the room.

"Then it's even more important that we know who he is."

"If you know who he is, it'd scare the hell out of you. If it goes down that way, you'll have plenty of time to find out."

"Decker."

"Yes, Lieutenant, this is Victor Schott, returning your call."

"You know, Schott, this is a hell of a way to do business. Aren't you ever in that office of yours?"

"Rarely. I'm on the road most of the time. But I get my messages rather fast, I'd say."

"Not too shabby." Decker turned down the radio so he could hear better. "I've got a little bit of news. You'll find it good news, I think."

"Oh?"

"Our friend, David Brett, of the suspicious habits? He may not be headed your way after all. On a hunch, I checked a couple of other airports, just in case, and guess what I found?"

"Brett, evidently."

"You bet. Took off from Cincinnati airport this morning. Bound for Detroit. I don't know what the hell he's going there for; I thought he'd already done his damage in Michigan. But it looks as if that's the way he went."

"You know this for sure?"

"I can understand you'd be skeptical. He's a tricky bastard, and I wouldn't put anything past him myself. But this looks like the real thing. Bought the ticket in his own name. If he knows we're looking for him, he evidently didn't think we'd check Cincinnati. On the other hand, he bought the ticket with his credit card, so I guess he had to give his name, didn't he? He must be running short of money. Wouldn't surprise me, anyway. I'd still take a little care, Mr. Schott, but it looks as if you could at least come out from under the bed."

"Thanks. I appreciate it."

"Glad to oblige. Hey, you haven't by any chance

figured out what he's coming after you for, have you? Can't recall anything about your high-school days that might set him to killing his father's classmates?"

"Sorry, I can't."

"Damn. I was hoping—"

"If you don't mind, I'm rather busy. . . ."

"Well, I just thought you'd be interested in knowing."

"Thanks. If you've got anything else, you know where to reach me."

"Sure thing."

Victor Schott hung up without saying good-bye. Phillip Decker. *He knows what the enemy is going to do next. When he doesn't, he works it so that they do what he wants them to.* OK, Phillip Decker, what is it that I'm supposed to do next? And tell me while you're at it, is the bluegrass music part of the act?

"I've got it, Lieutenant."

"I stalled him long enough, eh?"

"Just barely. It was a public phone in Romulus, Michigan."

"Romulus, Michigan? Where the hell is that? Where's the map?"

"It's here; I was checking it. Romulus, Michigan, is just outside of Detroit. He must be in Detroit."

Phillip Decker followed Thompson's finger with his eyes. Romulus, Michigan. And a big pink square. Detroit Metropolitan Airport. He looked up at Thompson and Thompson was looking at him. He's ahead of me, goddammit, he thought. He's gotten ahead of me.

"Barney here."

"Hello, Barney, it's Victor."

"Victor! How long's it been? Good to hear from you! What's this I hear? You're hanging up your hat? Going to play gentleman farmer or something?"

"Something like that. I need a favor right now."

"What can I do for you?"

"Check on a couple of numbers for me."

"I thought you were finished with that kind of stuff. I thought you'd hung it up and were taking it easy down at the farm."

"Just finishing up some old business. Tying up some loose ends."

"How soon do you need it?"

"Now."

"I'll do the best I can. We're short-handed here right now."

"I need it now, Barney."

"I'll do 'er. Give me the numbers."

Victor Schott read him two numbers from the slip of paper in his hand. "I need all long-distance calls in the last month or so. How long will it take?"

"Are these home phones or business?"

"One's a home."

"Few hours. I'll do my best."

"Thanks."

Victor Schott hung up the phone and turned away. Outside the smoke-colored window a plane was taking off. How much did Decker know? If he knows nothing, thought Schott, there's no harm. Might even help to have him there. He could even get shot by accident. If he knows something . . . if he knows something, he's a worse threat than Brett. Because he can find me. Because if he's a determined son of a bitch, he can come after me in ways Brett never dreamed of. If he wants me, he knows how to get inside the agency. He can find me. No matter how I hide, once he's on the inside he can find me. He closed his eyes to concentrate. Bring him in. Bring him in and disarm him. If it's a trap, he wants me here. But he never mentioned my coming. He knew I would come without his even mentioning it? What game is he playing with me? He opened his eyes and stared unseeing out the window. A natural-born intelligence man. We'll see, he thought, we'll see how good you are.

He walked back to the phone, rehearsing the lines in his head. I think we'd better work together on this, Decker. It's time I told you something about me that might help. How fast can you meet me at Detroit Metro? He calculated in his mind: forty-five minutes or less to Ann Arbor, another half hour to the cottage—if that's where they were—and another hour and a quarter back. Not under three hours. In three hours it would be dark, and that would be good.

"*Po*-lice."

"Phillip Decker, please."

"Sorry, he just left."

"Can I catch him at home?"

"No, he's on his way out of town. Anyone else you'd like to speak to?"

"No thanks." He hung up. Decker was on his way. There were three choices. He could back off now and take the first flight out. He could go to Ann Arbor and find those two and take them out and then get out before Decker got there. He could take Decker out as soon as he arrived. No, that third was too chancy; too many people at the airport if he was flying. No way to intercept him if he wasn't. How much did Decker know? It didn't matter now; what he didn't know now he'd be able to figure out soon enough. Whatever else, he had to take Decker out as soon as he could. But not here. At the other end, then. Wherever they were. If Decker knew, then he'd also know where they were. He could take Decker from there, and the others with him. You don't have to get caught in the trap if you know it's a trap. There's no such thing as a sure trap. Even with backups, there's always something. . . . He wondered what Decker's backups would be.

*   *   *

David Brett hung up the phone slowly, his mind racing. He would not tell her that. He would get her out while she could still go. There were a million places in Ann Arbor where Victor Schott would never find her.

"What is it?" she asked.

He walked to the window and looked out. The late-afternoon sun threw shadows across the grass. In a few hours it would be dark. "He wants us out. He wants to stall it. Victor Schott is already here." It wasn't what he'd meant to say.

"Is that what you want?"

"It's not going to work the way we planned it."

"How is it going to work, then?"

He turned and faced her. "The smartest thing is to leave before he gets here. I want you to—"

"No! No, you left me out before. It's not going to happen again. Whatever happens to you, I'm going to be there."

"What makes you think I'm going to stay?"

"I don't know you as well as I might, David, but I know you that well. You have no intention of leaving. And neither have I."

"He's a *professional*, Andy."

"All the more reason. We stop it now, or we go on running and hiding. I'm not going to do that. And I'm not going to end up like all the others, either."

"You can die. He can kill you. You're not invulnerable. Joan thought she was, and look where it got her."

She shook her head impatiently. "I don't mean that. I know I can die, but I'm not going to die like they did, on some jogging path, on a boat in the middle of a lake, or burned up in my bed at night, when I least suspect it. I'm not going to live with that terror. We end it now. Tonight. We stop running now."

He should have been angry. He should have insisted. He should have leaned out the door and called a couple of the biggest and strongest to come and drag her out of there and take her to a safe place. But all he did was stand with his back to the window and smile. She was bright, quick, and defiant; she would put up a hell of a fight. And for the first time since that awful morning, he was not alone.

20

SHIRLEY CARPENTER OPENED the door to a tall, painfully thin young man dressed in tattered jeans and a much too large army jacket. Obviously a student. He was startled to see her. "I'm selling Care packages. If you're the one who lives here, I guess you wouldn't be interested."

"Care packages?"

"Yeah, you know, like, when it's exam time we bring around a bag of munchies. Keeps you going for the all-night studies. You contract now for yourself or for a friend, and next month when exams come around we deliver. We got the Economy Pack, the Whole Hog, and the Two's Company, depending on your appetite. You interested? I thought it was a student that lives here."

She laughed. "I'm just staying here for a friend. Sounds good, though. How much are they?"

"The, uh, Economy Pack is . . . five dollars. And the others are ten and fifteen."

"How about if I buy one for my friend. The Whole Hog—that's the ten-dollar one?"

"Yeah. You get plenty for that."

"Do you take the money now?"

"Yeah. Ten dollars. And next month—the first night of study days—we deliver."

She took her purse from the table near the door and handed him a ten. "Do you need her name?"

"Yeah. Sure." He fumbled in his pockets and finally located a stub of pencil and a scrap of paper.

She looked doubtfully at him. "You're not going to forget this, now? I'm not just throwing my ten dollars away?"

"Oh, no, she'll get it. She'll get a mini pizza and two kinds of crackers and chips and—"

"That sounds just great. Do you need my name?"

"If you want her to know who it came from, yeah. In fact, it's a good idea anyway, just in case. For our records, you know."

"Do you get much business?"

"Well, to tell you the truth, we just started up. We used to send to the parents at home and see if they didn't want to buy this stuff for their kids, but then we got the idea that people might want to buy them for themselves or for a friend. We aren't doin' too bad."

"Her name is Andrea Kramer. The apartment number is on the door, isn't it?"

He craned his neck to look. "Yes, it is. Apartment fourteen. And did you want to give me your name so it'd be on the package?"

"Yes," she said. "It's Shirley Carpenter."

"OK, well, thanks a lot. Say, there doesn't happen to be anyone else here, is there?"

"I'm sorry, there's not."

"Too bad, thought I might make another sale. Thank you anyway."

She watched as he walked on down the hall, then closed the door slowly.

The young man hurried down the apartment stairs and out the front door. Keeping the slip of paper in his hand, he slid the pencil into a pocket and jogged to the corner, where he slipped into a grocery store. His eyes ranged through the store until he saw the man he was looking for, standing near the deli counter. "Just one person in the apartment," he said. "Her name's the second one of the paper. The first one's the name of the person who has the apartment. I suppose you know that one already, though, don't you?"

The man took the paper from him. Shirley Carpenter. Interesting. "Did she tell you where the girl was?"

"No. I didn't ask. You never said—"

"Never mind. Are you sure there's no one else in the apartment?"

"Yeah, I'm sure."

"OK, then." He palmed a twenty into the young man's outstretched hand and turned away from him. It was just the way he thought it would be. The cottage by the lake. Remote, controllable. Just what he would have done himself.

Shirley Carpenter dialed a number and waited impatiently for the phone on the other end of the line to be answered. "Hello?" It was David.

"I think we've had a contact," she said.

"At the apartment?"

"Yes. A young man came here ostensibly to sell food packages for exam week, but he didn't seem too prepared to actually take any orders."

"It could be."

"He didn't go to any of the other apartments on this floor."

"You could have been the last."

"In the middle of the hall?"

"Keep your eyes open, just in case that wasn't it."

"Have you heard from Phil?"

"Not yet. You either, I take it."

"What happens if he doesn't get here in time?"

"We go with it, whether he's here or not."

"I'd just feel better if I knew he was there with you."

"Don't worry, Shirley. We've got it all worked out. We can handle it just as well without him as with him."

"Take care."

"You too," he said, and hung up. In some ways, he thought, it will be better without him.

Phillip Decker looked at his watch. It was one of the things he hated, being tied to the clock. He looked out the Plexiglas again; it was nearly dark. Below them, the lights of Ann Arbor were coming on. Victor Schott would wait for dark; he was just the type, Decker was sure of that. But Decker was cutting things too close, and that made him uncomfortable. Next to him in the cabin, Del Walker was talking to the control tower. Thank God for Del Walker—and his plane. Without them, he would not even have been in the ball park. He'd been away from it too long; there were too many mistakes. He wondered what else he wasn't even aware of. It was the things you weren't aware of that killed you. He should have known that Victor Schott would come to Ann Arbor before he even heard. He would have put himself in position to act. He was a pro; he didn't wait to be fed his lines. Damn. It was the kind of mistake that he'd have chewed anyone else out for. It was the kind of mistake that killed you.

David Brett leaned back in the brown leather couch and stretched his legs out.

"Aren't you even nervous?" Andrea asked curiously. She was sitting across the room from him, on the floor, her legs crossed in front of her, and leaning against the front of a monstrous blue corduroy chair.

"Sure I am." He closed his eyes slowly and laced his fingers behind his head.

"You have a marvelous way of hiding it."

"I've been chasing this guy halfway across the country and back. Now I've got him walking right into my hands. Why shouldn't I be nervous?" And calm at the same time. It was all going to be over. One way or another, it was going to be over. Only one thing he'd demanded of Decker: that when it was over, Andy would still be alive. He didn't care that much about himself, but he wanted Andy to live. His mind went blank for a few moments. No, he finally admitted to himself, he did care. He wanted to live, too. There'd been a time when he didn't care, but that time was over now. Elizabeth was gone and he'd learned to live with that, now he was beginning to see that he could indeed live with it, that the pain would not always be fresh. Decker had come down on him about that; you have to want to make it work, and making it work means surviving, he'd said. It won't work at all if you're willing to let him take you out. *Take you out.* They used such lovely words, making it all seem like a kind of game. Take you out. Waste you. Kill you.

"Where are you?"

He opened his eyes and looked at her.

"You leave me. You're a million miles away. It would be all right, except that this isn't exactly the time, is it?"

"No, it's not." And she's had enough of people leaving her. "Sorry."

"Why can't they know out there? Why can't they know what's really going to happen?"

"Because if they knew, they wouldn't act the same, would they?"

"I suppose not."

"You don't trust it."

"You forget, I've never met Decker."

"You've talked to him on the phone."

She shook her head. "It's not the same."

"Don't worry. If you'd met him, you wouldn't have any more confidence."

"Why do you trust him, then?"

"It's not meeting him that makes a person trust him; it's watching him work. He's bull-headed with absolutely

248

no compunctions about doing anything, regardless of whom he hurts. But he gets the job done."

"You make him sound awful. He didn't seem that nasty to me."

"Someday I'll tell you about him."

"You don't like him, do you?"

"I don't have to like him. I trust him and that's enough. He knows what he's doing." He looked at his watch and rose and walked over to the curtained window. He pulled the curtain aside for a moment and looked out. It was almost dark. "Sure, I'm nervous. And it looks as if Decker isn't going to make it, so it'll have to be Plan B."

"What if he doesn't come by boat?"

"He will, because that's the way Decker planned it. And when Decker plans something, that's the way it happens." Except for Decker's getting hit on the head. The one thing that Decker hadn't planned, and he wondered how Decker felt about that. Maybe it served as a warning that even in the best-laid plans something could go awry. And then he had a rueful thought: What if Decker had planned that too? What if Decker had figured out that such a thing would happen even before he had done it? After a while, working with Decker, a person could go crazy wondering how much that man was really controlling.

Victor Schott drove down the country road, the beams of his headlights providing the only light in view. This was the first pass-by, the one in which all his senses had to say *go* before he'd take the next step. The side road was just ahead, beyond the rise. So far he'd seen nothing that alerted him. There's something, though, he thought. There's got to be something. If Decker is half as smart as they say he is, there's got to be something.

The engine of his car pulled as it took the rise, and then his headlights, shining ahead, crested it and he saw the something. A single car parked along the roadside. His lights shone on a couple locked in an embrace. They looked back, startled by the lights on this deserted road, and then embraced once again. He drove on past the car, looking straight ahead, and past the side road that led off to the left. He went straight on another two miles and then turned into another side road, this time going off to the right. He drove slowly a hundred yards or more from the main road and then stopped. He sat in the car for a moment, clearing his mind. Then he reached under the seat and pulled out a .22-caliber semi-automatic pistol with wooden grips. He hefted it once in his hand, as if weighing it, then checked the chamber one more time, and attached the twelve-inch silencer. Carefully, he laid the gun down and reached under the seat again. This time he brought up a 9 mm Browning automatic. He opened the car door with his left hand and got out. Then he leaned over and picked up the other gun with his left hand, straightened, and closed the door with his knee. He slid the Browning into his belt and transferred the other gun to his right hand; then he turned to walk back the way he'd come.

He didn't walk on the road, choosing instead the cover of the patchy shrubbery that grew ten yards or so from the shoulder. He walked a mile, following the road, and then he left it, veering to his right. He thanked Decker for having chosen a moonless night, and his ears strained for the slightest sound. In black pants and sweater, he would not be seen, but then, neither would the others. He was counting on one thing: that they'd be amateurs, student friends of Andrea Kramer's, perhaps, and in any group of amateurs there is bound to be a mistake.

He had entered a thin stand of pines, and the shadows were even deeper than before. There. He thought he heard something and stopped to listen, but there was nothing. He moved on, slipping from tree to tree, his rubber-soled shoes cushioned by the spread of pine needles. There! It was not a sound this time, but the quick spurt of a match. He watched from perhaps thirty yards away as it was cupped against a cigarette, and then quickly blown out. But the glow of the cigarette remained. It moved erratically in the dark like a crazed firefly, then vanished as something came between it and its observer. An erratic movement—someone gesturing? Then there had to be more than one—a conversation. He stood longer in the dark and listened. Nothing. A couple on the road. Two—or more—just beyond the pines. And real amateurs. The trap was set, waiting. He wondered what the signal would be. He turned and silently crept away. He had one more thing to check. It was almost a game now, and he wondered how thorough Decker had been.

He was back at the car an hour and a half after he left it. He unlocked the door and got in, leaning down and putting the guns once more under the seat. He started the car and turned around. Only when he was almost to the other road did he turn on his headlights.

He turned right on the main road and followed it as it wound its way around the lake. At times the road ran just alongside the lake shore; at other times it was a half mile or more, he estimated, from the lake. It would have to be one of the places where the road ran along the lake. He drove for more than fifteen minutes before he saw what he was looking for. In the glow of his lights he could see it as he neared it. Pulled up on the sand beach, looking as if it had been abandoned since last summer, was a rowboat.

He drove by slowly, gazing at the boat as he passed it. Everything in place. Very good, Decker, he thought. He wondered if someone were watching the boat. He stepped down on the gas, an almost automatic reaction, and quickly left the rowboat behind.

"Barney here."

"Barney, it's Victor Schott."

"Oh, yes. You're pushing it a little, aren't you? We've got some of it for you, but there ought to be more. Nighttime makes it twice as hard."

"What have you got?"

"Some activity on both those lines in the last week or so. A couple of calls to Indianapolis on the one—to the airport there. Another two to the state-police headquarters. One to the Cincinnati airport. And one to the University of Michigan athletic director's office. That's about all the calls out of that one. The other one, the private line, has some activity both ways to a number in Toledo, Ohio. It's another private line, but I don't have the name of the subscriber yet. We're working on that. I also have two calls from that line to a hotel or motel in Angola, Indiana, and another one to the police station in the same town. And there's another thing we're working on. I don't know if you wanted this—you didn't ask for it. But there were two calls *to* the first number that were traced. We can't always get that reading; it depends on the equipment. You were lucky. The one incoming that was traced came from a public booth in Washington. The other one came from a public phone at the Detroit airport. This guy does a lot of work with planes?" The question was rhetorical. Barney would not have expected an answer.

Victor Schott looked at his watch: nine-twelve. "Thanks a lot. That's not a bad night's work."

"Are you going to need the rest? You want the subscriber's name in Toledo?"

"No, I've got enough." Enough and more than enough. The Toledo number would be a relay. It didn't matter who it was; he already had what he was looking for. Phillip Decker was working him and had been all along. Just as he had expected, it was Phillip Decker who would have to be taken out first.

The telephone rang once. Twice. Shirley Carpenter looked at it as it rang a third time and finally lifted the receiver after the fourth ring. "Hello?"

"This is Victor Schott."

She caught her breath, even though she had been expecting this. "And this is Shirley Carpenter."

"Do you know how to reach Phillip Decker?" No formalities, nothing. Just the question, straight out.

"By phone only."

"Good. Tell him the cottage is out. Tell him I'm not that stupid."

"Victor, wait—"

"What?"

"Why? *Why?*"

His hand was already moving to hang up the receiver. Her voice echoed around the enclosed telephone booth, and he paused just the briefest of moments, and then he hung up. Because you were a golden girl, he thought. Because you all were golden people.

"He'll call again," Phillip Decker said, swirling the coffee in the mug to cool it. Why the hell did college kids only have mugs? A mug'll keep a cup of coffee hot half the night. How the hell are you supposed to drink coffee when it burns your mouth off?

"How do you know?"

"He just will. That was the preliminary; there'll be another one."

"What happens if he doesn't call?"

He looked at her impatiently. "He'll call. He has to. Brett and Andrea are nothing to him now. He's after me now; he knows what I can do to him. We're doing the dance we have to do, to establish how it'll be and where it'll be. He wants me; I want him. We've established our credentials with each other. Now we do the mating dance."

"Why doesn't he just pack up and leave?"

"He can't. I can, but he can't. He knows that, and he knows that I know it, too. As long as he was going after nameless, faceless people, he was safe, and he could always go running back to the agency. But now he's found that I can get inside the agency if I want, and that means he hasn't got anyplace to hide. He has to eliminate me before I do just that."

"And once he eliminates you—"

"Sure, then he can go back and wrap things up with the other two. But first me."

"Then they weren't the bait at all. You were."

"They were the bait for that trap. They still are. They're the bait for the trap he sees that's going to push him into the trap that has no bait. But I'm no damned fool. I'm not about to make bait of myself."

The telephone rang, shattering the silence that had fallen between them. She looked at him. "Wait," he said.

She let it ring again, her eyes on him, and at the end of the second ring he nodded imperceptibly.

"Hello?"

"This is Victor Schott. Did you tell him?"

"Yes."

"Well?"

"He says meet him tomorrow afternoon at the refreshment stand on the west side of the stadium. Ten minutes after the first four downs or the first score, whichever comes first. He says there'll be students outside before the game selling tickets. You can buy one. You can check it out; both of you can watch for the other, to make sure there isn't a trap—neither of you will know when the time will be, exactly. You can position yourself to see that he comes alone. It's a neutral area; don't bring a gun."

"He's crazy! I'm not going into that."

"He says be there. He says there aren't any options."

"Tell him he can go to hell!"

"He says there aren't any other options. *Be there.*" She took the receiver from her ear before she could hear any more objections, and hung up the phone.

His eyes were on her from across the room.

"He says you're crazy. He says he's not going into that."

He smiled and took another sip of coffee.

"How do you know what you're doing is going to work? How do you know he'll do what you want him to?"

He laid the mug gently on the coffee table and stood and walked over to the wall. He gazed absently at a photograph that was hanging there, a black-and-white of storm clouds blowing across the sun and a tiny sailboat, dwarfed by the size of its lake, leaning far over with the wind. "I'm playing him," he said simply. He looked at her over his shoulder and then looked back at the photograph. "It's like fishing, like catching a monster fish. Which is what he is. A pro. He knows all the tricks; that's how he's survived in that very dangerous profession of his. So how does a man go against a pro like that?" He gazed at the photograph, at the roil of water in the foreground, at the menace of clouds overhead. "Did you ever read *The Old Man and the Sea?* That old man caught a marlin that weighed fifteen hundred pounds. *Fifteen hundred.* I can't imagine a fish that big, except a whale. But Hemingway fished the Caribbean all the time. He must have known whether marlin get that big. Fifteen hundred pounds. And that old man, how much do you suppose he weighed? A hundred pounds? A hundred fifty? Not that much, I'll bet; closer to a hundred. Fifteen times his weight, that fish was. But he caught him. How the hell can a man do that, catch something that much bigger? The way that guy did it is the only way: You play him. You dangle the bait and you let him run with it and eventually, if you're smart enough, and if you endure long enough, eventually you can haul him in. If a man knew enough, he could harpoon and catch a whale singlehandedly. If he knew how to play him."

21

DAVID BRETT SWIRLED the dregs of coffee in his cup and then poured them down the sink. He ran water into the cup, poured it out, and set the cup on the counter. Absently, he began opening drawers, knowing what he was looking for, but not wanting to admit it. He hadn't smoked since he was twenty-two. In the third drawer, amid miscellaneous strands of twine and a half dozen keys, he found a pack. He looked at it for a moment, then closed the drawer. He could wait. Then he opened the drawer again and took out the pack and rummaged until he found a half-used matchbook and lit himself a cigarette. *Something's wrong.* He finally let the words come into his mind. *Something's very wrong.*

"Call him," Andrea said from the doorway.

"What are you talking about?"

"You know what I'm talking about. We sit here all night waiting, and nothing happens. We don't hear anything from Decker. Where is he? What's happened? How long are we supposed to wait here? Call him."

"I don't know where he is."

"You do. You don't even smoke, do you? And yet now you're smoking. Something's gone wrong, hasn't it?"

"Maybe."

She looked at him steadily. "Level with me."

"How the hell do I know what's going on?"

"I'll tell you what's going to go on. Pretty soon our trap is going to disappear, that's what's going to happen. It was for the night. They're not going to stay all day, not unless you give them a whole lot more reason than you've done so far. And then what?"

"They're cold and tired. There's pancake mix and plenty of coffee. We can feed them. They'll stay."

"No, they won't. It's Purdue today, and they're going to want to be at the stadium come one o'clock. Ohio State lost to Purdue; we're undefeated so far and so is Purdue. It's today and next week for the Big Ten championship and the Rose Bowl. Purdue today and Ohio State next week. They're not going to miss that game on what you've told them so far. If you think so, you don't know how football-crazy Michigan is."

"Our lives are at stake; they know that."

"They know you've told them precious little. They know they've been out in the cold all night. They might be thinking, like you and I are, that somebody's goofed. That it isn't going to happen. They're not going to be very crazy about staying out there any longer under those conditions. You're going to have to call him."

"I don't know how to reach him."

"Yes, you do. You can reach him through Shirley."

"I'll call him when I'm good and ready. In the meantime—"

"Face it, David. You're disappointed that Victor Schott didn't come here. That you haven't had a chance to kill him."

"Let it go, Andrea. I don't need you on my back."

"I'm the only one here to do it. Admit it, for heaven's sake. It's not going to work the way you hoped it would."

He slammed his fist down on the counter. "Damn it! Let it go!"

"You let it go, David! You're not going to get the chance to kill him! Whatever Decker has figured out does not include you after all. And I can't say that I blame him."

258

"Don't you want it? What about all your family? Don't you want him to die?"

"I want him to stop. That's all."

"That's very noble, and I don't believe it for a minute."

"You know what Decker would say?"

"You've never met the man and now you're going to tell me what he'd say?"

"He'd say you're too emotionally involved. He wouldn't take that chance with you. Which is probably why—"

"Whose side are you on?"

"Whose do you think?"

He stubbed the cigarette out in the sink. "The hell of it is, you're right. He used us for a diversion, a damned diversion."

"If he catches him, the diversion is still important."

"If he catches him."

"Call him." Her eyes were still on him; she hadn't let go.

He turned and reached for the telephone. "If even Shirley knows where he is." There was no response and he turned back around, but she was gone from the doorway.

The phone rang a few times before she answered it. "Shirley, it's David."

"David? Is something wrong?"

"No, or maybe yes. It's almost light and he hasn't come. Something's not going according to plan."

"Wait. Just a minute." She covered the receiver with her hand; he could hear the muffled sound of it. "Sorry," she said when she came back on the line. "I thought I heard someone at the door. Listen, I think he wants you to get out of there. He left me with a message that if you called and nothing had happened by eight, you should leave. Let the guys go and leave the place. He wants you to lie low, not to come back into Ann Arbor, in case he needs to try it again tonight. He suggests you go to Andy's parents' home. It's only an hour or so away from there, isn't it? Go there for the day. He'll contact you there this afternoon sometime."

"Where is he?"

"I don't know."

"What is he planning?"

"I'm sorry, David, I haven't the faintest idea. But I've got to keep the line open; I've got to hang up. He'll call you at Andy's."

He hung up the phone slowly. He still had the feeling; something was wrong. Something was not—

"She was lying, wasn't she?" It was Andy again, back in the doorway. "I was listening on the extension in the bedroom."

"I think she was."

"Did she talk to someone when she put her hand on the receiver?"

"If she did, it would have been Decker."

"Why didn't he just talk with you? Doesn't he want you to know he's there?"

"If he doesn't want me to know he's there, then . . . it's because he expects Victor Schott."

"What kind of game is he playing? Is he playing both sides against the middle?"

"What are you getting at?"

"How well do you know Decker?"

"Not as well as I might, but well enough to know it's no double cross. Whatever crazy thing he's doing, he thinks it's going to work. I know him well enough to know that."

"And my guess is that you're not going to do what he says. We're not going to my folks'."

"We?"

"We."

260

He looked at her for a long moment. "Do you have a gun?"

"Do you?"

His eyes moved beyond her in the doorway to the living room. The two shotguns he'd confiscated the night before still stood leaning against the wall. Her eyes followed his. "There are *two* guns there."

"Have you ever used a gun before?" said David.

"What's to know with a shotgun? You point the gun and you squeeze the trigger. It's not like a rifle, after all."

"You could die."

"Yes, I could. For that matter, I could have been dead for the last ten years. I could have been the first, instead of one of the last."

"Okay," he said. "Don't say I didn't warn you." It wasn't right. It wasn't the way it should have been. But it was the way she wanted it—no, dammit, he corrected himself—it was the way he wanted it, too. If he could just keep her from dying.

A teenage boy came to the door and diffidently changed the sign from Closed to Open. Victor Schott, parked in a car across the street, looked impatiently at his watch. One minute early. Small favor. He got out of the car and walked across the street and into the hardware store, pausing in the doorway to orient himself. "May I help you?" came a voice just next to him. The man was tall and angular, with small eyes behind enormously thick glasses.

"Maybe you can. Do you carry garage-door openers?"

"Sure do. Aisle three, clear down to the end."

"Thanks." He walked away. Passing a battery display, he picked up two six-volt batteries. So far, so good, though he'd probably end up having to go to an electronics store for the reverse micro-switch and maybe even the portable clock radio. But at least things were falling into place all neat and tidy, just the way he liked them.

Ann Arbor—Decker couldn't have chosen a better place. Universities offered more than their share of opportunities. Buildings stayed open half the night for grad students and professors doing research at odd hours. Chemistry labs kept certain chemicals under lock and key, but for the most part the attempts at restriction were only partly successful. Anyone who knew just what he was looking for and who was determined to get it could do so. Physics labs were a joke. Who cared about empty containers and high-intensity wire? He probably could have found the switches there, but why bother when he knew they could be had so easily from any electronics store? He looked at his watch again. There was plenty of time.

"Do you ever wonder if they knew?" David asked her. "Do you ever wonder if your father knew?" They were coming into the outskirts of Ann Arbor. They'd called in the students who had been surrounding the cottage and thanked them, and David had given a little meaningless speech about how helpful they'd been, and they had all exchanged glances, and David had looked over at Andy and she'd smiled back. It made little sense and the students knew that. Something was going on that they were only partly aware of, and most were not sure they wanted to know more. A few had asked questions, but David had been evasive and they had known he was covering. They were, for the most part, glad to be asked to leave. They were cold and tired, and, as Andy had predicted, they were thinking about the football game. "Do you ever wonder if he told them why he was killing them?"

"My father was warned by Allen Lundy anyway, wasn't he? He wouldn't have needed to be told."

"I still wonder," he said quietly.

"You'd like to ask him that, wouldn't you?"

"I'd like to ask him a whole lot."

"Maybe you'll get a chance."

"Maybe. Decker was doing *something*. He wouldn't appreciate being surprised at this point, risking having the whole thing thrown apart. Find a telephone. As soon as we get into Ann Arbor, we'll find a telephone and I'll call and this time I'll demand to talk with Decker. I know he's there, and I want to know what the hell's going on. That'll shake him up.

"You're not going to barge in on him, I hope."

"Afraid I might screw the whole deal?"

"You could get killed. If he's expecting Schott, he could kill you by mistake."

"I was thinking I'd call."

"She'll stall you again."

"Not this time. She'll have to put him on this time. Let's look for a public phone."

They found one in a Greek restaurant near the campus. He put his coins in and dialed the number. "Hello?" It was Shirley again.

"Let me talk with Decker."

"He's not here."

"He's there. Let me talk with him."

"David—"

"Do you want me to mess this whole thing up, or are you going to let me talk with him?"

There was a pause, and then Decker came on the line. "Where are you?"

"I'm in Ann Arbor. Where would you like me to be?"

"Don't screw this up now, Brett."

"Does that mean stay away? Or in your own inimitable way of arranging things, is that your way of getting me to come right over?"

"I know what you're after. You want him dead and

you want to be the one to do it, but he's not even going to be findable if you mess this up."

"How soon do you expect him?"

"Brett, I owe you one. Don't force me to cash it in, which is what I'm going to have to do if you get into this."

"You need a backup, don't you? I don't need to come in or be seen or anything. Just tell me where and when."

"Stay away!" The receiver slammed in his ear, and David Brett smiled.

"I'm beginning to think like he does," he said to Andrea. He was back on track now and feeling good. *Use everything.* He'd almost forgotten about that. "How many entrances to your building?"

"Two."

"They're both on the same side of the building, aren't they? Not directly on the street?"

"Yes, but it's a clear view across the mud bowl to the other side of Washtenaw. We could park along there somewhere. It's far enough away not to be suspicious, but still close enough to see."

"Good thinking."

She broke the last of the onion bagels and handed him half. "Doesn't it worry you that it's been so long?"

"Decker has patience, why shouldn't I? And God knows Victor Schott has patience." Despite his words, he tapped his fingers nervously on the steering wheel. He had not taken his eyes from the apartment building across the street. "The game is at one?"

She nodded.

He looked at his watch and back out across the now-deserted street and the apartment beyond it. An hour ago the street had been bumper to bumper with traffic; now there was nothing. Football Saturday and the big game. Perfect weather. Andy had been right. Anyone who expected anyone else to stay away from the game today was absolutely crazy. Deserted streets. Deserted dorms. Deserted apartment buildings. Decker could have it either way: with the crowd or alone. But, knowing Decker, he'd guess it would be the latter; he could control the situation better. A deserted apartment building. Two men. They could shoot each other to hell and nobody would even know it until the ball game was over.

She touched his arm, but he had already seen. The man was tall and lean, well dressed, in dark slacks and a tan jacket. He looked fit; David would have guessed his age at much younger if he hadn't known.

"He looks just like anybody," she whispered.

"It's his business to blend in; he can probably do it better than you or I."

"Maybe it's not him."

"It is."

"What's the attaché case for?"

"Guns, maybe?"

"David, maybe we should get the police."

"Decker's the police."

"He doesn't have any authority here."

"Schott is CIA, remember? The case against him has to be iron-clad before any police will touch it. Somehow, that's what Decker's doing, you can bet on that. He's going to make a case against Schott that not even the CIA can argue with."

"Even so—"

"And we're going to need that. Unless we don't have to bring a case."

She looked at him. "Unless you kill him."

He reached for the door. "One thing about it; we don't have to worry about carrying guns out on the street. There isn't anybody within seeing distance to notice anyway."

Once inside the building, he touched her arm briefly. "Are you going to be OK?"

She nodded wordlessly.

"Go ahead, then; I'll give it five seconds after the phone is answered."

He watched her start down the hallway, and then he began climbing cautiously to the second floor.

Andrea shoved the shotgun into the utility closet and closed the door soundlessly. Moving across the hall, she pushed the doorbell of the first apartment and waited. Nothing. She stepped across the hall and pushed the bell there. Again nothing. She moved on down to the next door. Someone had to be home. Even for a big game, someone always had a tough exam coming up. A blond girl answered the fifth doorbell. Andrea had seen her around the building but didn't know her by name. "Can I borrow your phone?" Andrea asked. "I think there's someone in my apartment and I'm scared! I don't have any roommates and I don't know who it would be."

"Who are you going to call, the police?" the girl asked.

"No, my apartment."

"Why don't you call the police?" the girl asked.

"Maybe it's just my boyfriend. I'd feel like a fool if it were. But he's never gone up there before without me, and he ought to be at the game."

"Call the police."

"I'll call my apartment first." She dialed the number and it rang three times. Come on, she thought, answer it. Come on, Schott, let her answer it.

Then the phone clicked in her ear and Shirley Carpenter said, "Hello?"

"Who is this? What's going on?" Andrea screamed into the phone. It would surprise Shirley; it would confuse Victor Schott, who was undoubtedly listening in. It would give David the split second that Victor Schott's attention was focused on the phone to ram his way into the apartment and, if things went right, to take Victor Schott unaware.

266

Over the phone line she heard Shirley gasp in surprise. "Who is this?"

Andrea put the phone down and turned to the wide-eyed girl standing beside her. "Something's wrong," she said. "I'm going for help. You'd better stay in your apartment with the door locked until whoever it is comes out of there."

The girl grabbed her arm. "Don't go out there! Call the police!"

Andrea gently took the girl's hand from her arm. "Don't worry," she said; "it's going to be OK." She slipped out the door, closing it quietly behind her. She wondered how David was managing on the floor above.

Shirley Carpenter held the phone to her ear and wondered what was happening. Wasn't that Andrea's voice? What was it? Where were they? Suddenly she heard a crash at the door and David Brett slammed his way into the apartment, shotgun pointing straight at her. "David, what—"

"Where is he?" he demanded, swinging the gun in wide arcs to cover the whole room.

"Where is *who*?"

"You know who! *Victor Schott!*"

"I don't know."

It took him a second to comprehend what she had said. But he'd come in the building. He was here! He had to be here! But if he wasn't . . . Oh, God. *Andrea.*

Andrea ran to the utility closet, opened the door, and pulled out the shotgun. Then she ran to the stairs and took them two at a time. David would be inside now, but she'd heard no shots. It had worked, then. He was inside and she would be his backup. If anything happened, if anyone came out—she pulled the safety back—it would be up to her. Make sure first, he'd warned her. Pull the safety back because you won't remember to do it if it's

Schott and he's running toward you, but for God's sake, make sure first before you pull the trigger. She hadn't heard any shots yet, just voices coming from the room, and then, without warning, there was something hard in her back and an arm flung across her throat and pulled roughly against her neck, and a voice said close against her ear, "Put the gun down or you're dead. There's a silencer on this gun and he'll never even know what happened until it's too late for him too."

She tried to scream a warning, but the arm clenched against her throat and no sound could escape.

"Drop the gun, I said!"

She thought wildly for a moment and then realized that she would be no good at all to him dead and maybe she could help if she were alive, so she dropped the gun.

"Very good," the voice said from behind her. "Now you're going to walk straight ahead into that room and you're not going to try any tricks. It's not you I want; it's Decker."

But Decker isn't even there, she thought. But, of course, he would be. He would come. It was what Victor Schott had in mind. He would come. And then she saw David in the doorway ahead of her and he saw her at the same time, and he dropped his gun.

"Good for you, Brett," Victor Schott said. "You've gotten the picture, I see."

"Let her go."

"In time. Back into the apartment, please." Schott pushed Andrea ahead of him, his arm still tight around her neck. Together they moved into the apartment, and it was not until they were fully inside that he released his arm and shoved her ahead of him, while he used that hand to close the door behind him. His gun—she could see now that it did indeed have a silencer—was pointed straight at her. "You might as well sit down," Victor Schott said to the three of them. "There's no telling how long we'll have to wait." He motioned his free hand to the wall facing the window. "On the floor; I won't bother tying you up." He took a rectangle of black plastic, about the size of a cigarette pack, from his jacket pocket, and, working with extreme care, he used the fingers of his free hand and his teeth to ease off a strip of black electrical tape that was wound around it. The three watched curiously as he worked the tape off, the gun all the time pointed at Andrea. "You'd all better hope I have a steady hand," he said. Then he pulled off the last of the tape and held the small box in his left hand, his thumb pressed against it. "So that we know where we are," he said, "it's a simple solid-state electronic switch, with a reverse switch mounted inside. For the nonmechanically inclined, what that means is that as long as I keep my thumb on the button and press, everything is OK, but if I release the pressure, the signal goes out and somewhere on this bright sunny afternoon, a hundred thousand people are gathered together in one place—at least that's what the radio said—and they will have the surprise of their lives. Of course you can't expect one bomb to kill a hundred thousand, but it can do some pretty fair damage, and, ah, of course panic can also do some harm—"

"You wouldn't!" Shirley cried.

"Try me."

"You know damned well he would," David said.

"We understand each other, then," Schott said to him.

"No, I don't understand at all," David replied. "Why are you doing this?"

"I think you know why."

"Tell me. Once and for all, tell me."

"Your father took my brother to war and let him die there. Your father and all the others—all those golden ones—all of them came back, but Lester died over there."

"Are you going to shoot us?" Shirley asked.

"Maybe, maybe not. It depends on your friend Decker."

"You were supposed to meet him at the football stadium," Shirley said.

"*He* wanted that. I told you I wouldn't do it."

"He said you'd show up."

"He was mistaken." He sat down on the couch. From there he could see them and the apartment door. He was not going to be surprised.

"Will you tell us why?" Shirley asked.

"I told you already. Anyway, it doesn't matter anymore."

"It does to me," David said.

"You above all should understand. Your wife was killed. My one mistake; I'm sorry about that. It was supposed to have been you. You should have taken the car. Although, unfortunate as it was, it made an opportunity I hadn't planned on. Anyway, you ought to understand where I'm coming from, Brett. You'd kill me now if you had the chance, wouldn't you? And it would be strictly for revenge, wouldn't it? If a person is touched close enough, he'll kill for revenge, won't he? Wouldn't you?"

David glared at him. "My father, perhaps. But why me? Why the second generation? And the third?"

"Why should your father have had the right to have children and grandchildren? My brother never had the chance."

"Victor, are you out of your mind?" Shirley screamed. "Your brother was only one person! How many have you killed?"

She looked at him and tried to remember the Victor Schott she'd known all those years ago. "You owe us that much. Even if you kill us before it's all over, you owe us. You owe *me!* You've destroyed everything I've ever cared about." The tears were coming now and she angrily brushed them away. She would not let him see her crying. "Why? *Why?*"

He looked at her and then looked away. David's eyes went to the black box and to Victor Schott's thumb pressed against it. "There are some people in this world who are what I call golden people," Victor Schott said. "That's what I've always thought of them, and you all were that kind of people—the ones who have everything going for them. Looks, brains, money, whatever. It's what you were, what you all were. What was I? Who cared about me? And about my brother you cared even less. He was the butt of your jokes, that's all. The cheerleaders, the jocks. The ones who go off to college and make something of themselves. David Brett—your father—successful architect. His son, another David Brett and just the same; he could have been anything he chose, and chose to be a teacher. And he chose to come back to his father's hometown. And he chose the town's prettiest girl for a wife. That's what you all were; the ones who have everything and for whom nothing goes wrong. And we were the Schott brothers, from the edge of town, with an alcoholic father and an overworked mother. Too light to play football, too short to play basketball, worthless for anything else as far as you were concerned. So we were nothing. I was nothing and my brother was even less, just because he happened to be a little slow."

"We didn't think that way about you. You were the smartest boy in school," Shirley said.

"Because I worked! Because I worked my ass off while Mike and Dave and all the others cut classes and got their B's and C's and everybody knew they would have gotten their ways paid to college even if there hadn't been a GI Bill. Some of us weren't so lucky. For some of us, things don't always go right."

"I thought it was because of your brother," Andrea

said. "It wasn't that way at all, was it? It was because of your own self."

"It was because of my brother. The rest was . . . just . . . how I happen to feel."

"You killed them because they took your brother to war?" Andrea asked.

"Because it was a joke to them. Because in typical golden-person fashion, they cared about nothing except themselves. He had no business in the war! He wasn't even old enough! Dave Brett signed my father's name, and—"

"How do you know who signed your father's name?" David asked.

"Lester wrote and told me. The letter came after he was dead. He hardly got over there before he died. And all the time, he never thought anything; he was innocent. He had no idea that they were laughing at him. And those sons of bitches took him over there to die!"

"They didn't do it on purpose!" Shirley said.

"They took him on purpose. They had to go out of their way to do it—signing my father's name and all."

"You don't go around killing people for that!" Andrea said.

"Wrong. If there's one thing I know about, it's killing people, and I can tell you, there are a lot of people who are killed for less reason than revenge."

"But their children? And their grandchildren?"

They should have died in the war, like Lester did. There shouldn't have been any children or grandchildren. They should never have existed."

"And what about me?" Shirley cried.

"I'm sorry. Your husband died in the war. What can I say?"

"He did not die in the war! You killed him! You went out there on the lake and you killed him!"

"He died in the war. It just took a little bit longer for him to go than it did my brother, that's all."

She leaned forward, barely controlling her fury. "And my children? My grandchildren?"

"If your husband died in the war before you were even married, you could hardly expect to have any children with him, could you? I wonder if you know—your son Lane was going to be a father. That girlfriend of his was pregnant."

"How did you know that?"

"Probably the nicest thing he ever did in his life. He was another golden one—football star, big jock, going with a cheerleader—just like his father, and he probably didn't give a damn for anybody but himself. But when he saw that gun, he did what might have been the best thing he ever did. He tried to get that girl off. He tried to get me to let her go. 'She's pregnant,' he said. 'You wouldn't kill a pregnant girl, would you?' And she was crying, poor little thing, terrified. But, of course, it was the worst thing he could have done to her, telling me that. I might have let her go otherwise, but after that I couldn't, because that one had to die, too."

"And what are you going to do now?" Shirley asked. "Are you going to kill us?"

"I wouldn't have killed you, Shirley. I don't have anything against you. But now you know and so you're going to have to go right along with the rest of them."

"What makes you think Decker is going to come here?"

"He will. When things don't work out the way he'd hoped at the stadium, he'll come here. He'll have to because he'll know where I am. And then I'll have all of you at once in one place. I'm sorry it has to be you too, Shirley; you should have kept out of it."

"It was my whole family!"

"It was my only brother."

"That's not enough reason! You wipe out a family—whole families—for one person? *For one person?* For Lester? You never cared that much about him when he was alive. You never—"

Victor Schott slammed his foot against the coffee table, turning it over, strewing books and magazines across the floor. "You don't know that! You can't say that!"

"I can remember you, Victor. He embarrassed you. You were ashamed of him, weren't you? *You* never did anything with him. You must have known what they were doing when they took him places. You must have known he was the butt of their jokes—"

"Shut up! What do you know?" He rose and stepped toward her, standing menacingly over her. "He was my brother! I *did* love him!"

"Everybody in the school knew they were going to sign up for the army. I can't believe *you didn't*. I can't believe Lester didn't tell you that he wanted to go along—that they were going to take him. He would have been proud of it. I can't believe you didn't know just as much as the rest of us—" His foot caught her mouth in a vicious upward swing. Blood sprang from her cut lip and her hand came up reactively, her eyes wide with surprise.

"Shut up!" he screamed at her. "Shut up! You don't know what you're talking about. I would never have let him go into that. I loved him! Peter—no, Lester—was like a . . ." He stopped abruptly, his eyes wild.

David spoke, one thought on his mind. *Distract, Defuse.* "You said my wife was your only mistake. You didn't intend to kill her, then?"

"I said that," Victor Schott snapped at him without taking his eyes from Shirley.

Then he didn't know she was pregnant, Brett thought,

and I'm not going to give him the satisfaction of knowing. "Did my father know . . . did he know you were doing this?"

"They all knew. Before they died, they all knew. At the moment of death, they knew. Not the second generation, of course; it wouldn't have meant anything to them, but the first generation did."

"And why did you stop making them look like accidents?" Brett asked.

Victor Schott stepped back away from Shirley, and David sat down again, his eyes on Schott. Schott backed away and sat down, too, leaning into the couch. For the first time, David thought, he looked his age. "Because I was getting tired. Because I could not keep it going much longer and I had to finish it. I no longer had that luxury. And, of course, after your wife, I had another idea entirely. I could let them blame you. I could make it look as if you did it and you would suffer double. It was to punish you for what your father did."

"What my father did?"

"He signed my father's name!"

"Why would you punish me for what he did?"

"Because you were David Brett too, because David Brett is the one who made it possible for my brother to die! He's the one who made it so my brother would never come back! And besides," he said more calmly, "it was the perfect way to end it. I could make it look as if you'd done those last killings and then the law would have punished you for me. It would have been the ultimate twist, getting the law to help me punish you. And, of course, there was that bonus—you led me to Allen Lundy. I hadn't counted on that at all."

"There's something else you hadn't counted on." Phillip Decker spoke from the hallway. He held a revolver pointed at the back of Victor Schott's head.

Victor Schott didn't even turn around. "Phillip

Decker," he said. "So you didn't go to the stadium, either. I'd begun to think that, in the midst of all these questions. It was for a reason, wasn't it? It's all on tape, isn't it? And was even Brett's attempted coup part of the plan?"

Decker looked across the room at Brett. "That was Brett's own idea. Among other things. Not bad, Brett, but under the circumstances, it would have been better if you hadn't."

"You're just about as good as they say, Decker."

"We're both pretty good, Schott. But one of us is better."

Victor Schott smiled slowly and raised the little box in response. "You heard the part about the bomb, then?"

"I heard it."

"In the business, that's known as a backup."

"I know that, too."

"So you have a gun on me, and I have a bomb on all the people in the stadium. That's what they call a Mexican stand-off."

"Not quite. When the game is over, there isn't going to be anyone in the stadium anymore."

"When the game is over, I'm not going to be here anymore. And there's nothing you can do about it, either, Decker, because if you shoot me, the bomb goes now and you couldn't quite bring yourself to do that to a hundred thousand people, could you?"

"They wouldn't all die."

"Enough would."

"Not if you didn't really have that bomb there."

"It's there."

"I'm betting it isn't."

"You're betting with other people's lives."

"Okay, then, get up and walk out now."

"I think maybe I'll do that, but not before I have the tape."

Decker looked at him for a long moment. "You don't miss a trick, do you?"

Schott stood, his eyes on Decker now. "The tape?"

David Brett tensed. This would be the chance, but how would he disarm Schott without releasing the bomb switch?

Decker leaned over, jerked a tape recorder out from under the couch, and withdrew the cassette from it. He threw it at Schott, and spun away, screaming, *"Now! Now!"* Schott leveled his gun, but Decker was already around the corner into the kitchen, and behind Victor Schott there was a crashing of glass and Allen Lundy stood on the balcony firing into Victor Schott's back.

David had rolled over on the floor to protect Andrea with his own body, and at the same time he was screaming, "No! He'll let the bomb go!" But Victor Schott was already on the floor and the black box, released from his hand, was lying on the carpet beside him. Shirley Carpenter, as if it would make the bomb stop, reached for the box and pressed the button again. Decker ran out from the kitchen, yelling, "Get out of here! Clear out!" And Brett, who understood now, picked Andrea up from the floor and ran with her toward the door, pulling Shirley behind him. And Decker ran from the kitchen and snatched up the tape from the floor and ran to the window to help Allen Lundy through the broken glass.

"The girl! The girl!" Andy was screaming as they ran down the hall. She took the stairs two at a time and broke away from David at the landing, running for the middle of the hall. David looked after her and then left Shirley to find her own way out and followed. What was she doing? And then he, too, remembered, but there was no time. "Andy! No!" But she was already at the door, pounding and pounding. "Get out! There's a bomb!" she was screaming. And the girl, frightened, was calling through the door, "Who is it?" And Andy was pounding and screaming and all David could think of was the dream of the bridge and the explosion and he tried to pull Andy away, but she fought against him and the girl inside the room was calling, "Who is it?" And Andy answered back, "It's me—Andy! I used the phone. There's a bomb! Get out!"

And the girl timidly opened the door, and Andy and David grabbed her by the arms and pulled her out of the room, and just then the bomb went off and all three were thrown against the opposite wall and everything went black, and the whole hallway was filled with smoke and crashing plaster.

Epilogue

DECKER WALKED INTO the room and paused. The walls were painted a warm rose color, but it still looked like a hospital room. Brett was sitting up in bed, drinking coffee.

"I got a call from Washington, some guy named Andersen," Decker said. "He didn't say who he was, but it's dollars to doughnuts he's CIA."

Brett raised his eyebrows. Andrea was standing across the room, by the windows. "What did he say?" she asked.

"Not much at first," Decker said, shrugging. "He was searching and I didn't make it easy for him. He finally came out and asked it: What did I know about Victor Schott? I told him I knew more than I'd told the Ann Arbor police. That shut him up for a minute. I also told him that he ought to tell Timmerman at Tech-Optics to watch who he gives cover to after this. That took him by surprise, but he said he'd do it. He said, 'Thanks.' Just that, 'Thanks.' I guess in his business that's how you leave things." Decker shook his head in wonder.

Brett reached over and set his coffee mug down on the tray. He winced as he did so, because the sudden movement was more than his head was ready to take.

"You had one coming." Decker grinned. "I think we can call it even now."

"You took quite a chance."

"No way. I don't believe in chances."

"He might really have had a bomb in that stadium."

"No, he wouldn't have. He was torn up inside by hate and guilt, but he was not going to do that. Andersen or whoever else does those things would have gotten rid of him before this if he'd been that bad. He wouldn't have killed all those people for nothing. Not even he would have done that."

"You didn't know that. He was killing whole families."

"There was a reason. Maybe not one you would recognize, but still a reason. You heard him apologize to Shirley. He didn't want to kill her."

"It wasn't enough to go on. You couldn't have been sure."

"Yes, I could. He needed a backup, all right. But he didn't need it at the stadium. He needed it where we were. He needed to make sure we were going to die, even if it meant going with us. The bomb had to be in the building with us."

"We saw him bring it in, you know. We saw the attaché case, but we thought it was carrying his guns."

"You don't ever assume anything with somebody like Victor Schott."

"You did."

"I did not. *I knew*. That's different from assuming."

Brett smiled thinly. "A might narrow difference."

"A big difference. He needed a backup. He had to have it here. No doubt about it."

"And the delay mechanism? Don't tell me you knew about that."

"I guessed. He would have wanted to give himself a chance to get out. Even him. Even in his state. It was too ingrained—he would have intended to survive—at least consciously. A two-minute delay would have made sense. Long enough to run out of the building if he needed to; short enough that we—who wouldn't have known—would still be in it."

"And you had your own backup."

"Of course."

Of course. As if there wouldn't have been a doubt. And with Decker, there wouldn't, not about anything.

280

And that reminded him. "You didn't level with me, did you, Decker? You told me the kids would be a plant—to make him come by boat—but you lied, didn't you? It was all a plant, wasn't it? You didn't change it because he got ahead of you. You never did intend to do it that way, did you? You let me think we were planning it together, when all along you had something else in mind!"

"You can't complain, Brett. That attack behind the station wasn't part of the plan, either."

"Let's just say it was my improvement. You wanted to make it look good. You wanted Schott to believe it, no matter how much he could find out. You said we had to go through all the motions."

"I said that, and it's true. He would have been expecting a trap. To get him out of cover in the first place, I had to let him find out enough about me—to make sure that he found out enough about me to know I could come in after him if need be. Once he knew that, he would have been expecting a trap. I had to let him see one."

"Sure! But the kids were supposed to tip him off—twenty amateurs—a professional couldn't help but see them. That's what you told me, and I believed it. It's true, he would have seen them. But he was supposed to use the boat. You said—"

"Sure. I lied. Is that what you want me to say—that I lied to you? Of course I did. You wouldn't have gone along with it otherwise. Schott would have known the boat was a plant. You figured it out finally, yourself. I wanted him at the apartment. It was all for that, to get him to the apartment—the kids, the boat, the supposed meeting at the game. And you yourself finally figured it. You're getting very good at this, you know. The only thing you're really mad about is that it wasn't you who killed him."

"You knew I wanted to be the one."

"He's dead, isn't he? In the end, isn't that what counts?"

Brett didn't say anything. He felt her eyes on him across the room, but he didn't look at her. Thank God she was OK. A broken arm—that was all. The bandage felt tight against his chest. Six broken ribs and a broken collarbone. They were both all right, and the blonde girl had no injuries at all, except for a few scrapes. Thank God.

"It was right for Lundy to have done it," Decker said gently.

"It's what kept me going! It's the only thing that kept me going! I would have fallen apart in the first place if I hadn't had that, if I hadn't been going after whoever it was that killed my wife!"

"It can destroy you, Brett. It can wreck your whole life. Be glad you didn't have to be the one."

"I wanted to!"

"Decker sat down beside him. "I know you did, and that's why I couldn't let you. It's not as easy as you might think—killing a man—even if you hate him. You live with that the rest of your life. To have killed him in hate would have made you no better than he was. Whether it's one person or fifteen, it's the same thing. You live with it the rest of your life. Look at Victor Schott. You saw how he reacted to what Shirley said. It wasn't entirely revenge that drove him after all. It was also guilt. Do you want that, too? Do you want it to go on and on, eating you up, like it did for Schott? Your wife is dead, Brett, and the man who killed her is dead. Does it really matter who did it? Make up your mind; do you want it to be over or don't you?"

He looked at her now, at the dark blue eyes, and she smiled at him.

"Yes," he said finally. "I want it to be over. And now I think it is."

Decker grinned and ran his hand across the top of his head. The left side of his face was still scabbed from Brett's blow. "You'd better believe it," Decker said.

282